ONLY THE HOLY REMAIN

A FRANK CALHOUN CRIME NOVEL

ALVERNE BALL

CONTENTS

To my mother, Diane, whose love of the written word somehow found its way into me. I'll never forget the story of Lucifer's fall.

To the real Frank "Preacher" Calhoun whose stories of the Korean War and Dinosaurs sparked my imagination and love for storytelling.

To the late Ric Hess, whose unyielding belief in my writing and encouragement pushed me to finish this novel.

To my first readers, JoLynn and Vanessa for continually asking, "What happens next?"

CHAPTER 1

"The city is dead."

I remember those being the last words that Captain Anton Pantone said to me as the B-52 bombers overhead sliced through the skies raining down MK-77 bombs filled with white phosphorus. The jet stream whistle drowned out the hum of the 32nd Battalion tanks while at the same time muffling the heartbeats of the 1st Marine regiment positioned just beyond the border of Fallujah after the fall of Saddam Hussein's regime.

Now, standing before the door of Father Pantone's personal office in the old Uptown neighborhood on the north side of Chicago, I wonder why my former commanding officer has given me a call. My tour of duty as a chaplain in the Marines is over, and though the war in Iraq still drudges on, I want more than anything to leave my memories of Fallujah in that distant arid region.

Staring down into the rough reflection of my shoes, I adjust my blue-square tie. It's moments like this where I wonder why I even attempted to shave the gruff of a three-week-old beard from my brown face when the end result leaves me with a five o'clock shadow that resembles molasses clinging to a moonshine jug. My dark suit, a three-year-old two piece from a bargain warehouse, is partially wrinkled; and that's when I come to the conclusion that I'm a mess, at least by military standards—hell, probably by anyone's standards. But I have to remind myself that this meeting with Father Pantone is totally unexpected.

I expect that Father Pantone will start in on me as soon as he opens the door. He won't waste any time commenting on the fact that my eyes are now the color of coffee: deep, dark, and hard, instead of brown and full of life as he's always known them. He'll probably pat me on the small bulge in my stomach and tell me I've been hitting the mess hall too much and to lay off the desserts. But those are his ways of encouragement. "Chance favors the prepared mind" is his ideal ideology that a chaplain of the marines should always be prepared. Oddly enough, the quote is attributed to French microbiologist, Louis Pasteur. Whoever said that science and religion don't mix hasn't had the pleasure of meeting Father Pantone who believes whole-heartedly that God provides the science that allows men to learn.

I take a deep breath, straighten up my five-foot-nine-inch frame, exhale and knock on the door. There's no sound. I wait a few more seconds and then knock again, adding a little muscle to the tap. After all, Father Pantone is getting old.

The door cracks open slightly under the rap-rap of my callused knuckles. The scent of vanilla wafts out through the crevice as I push at the door and completely open it.

"Father Pantone?" I call out.

Inside the office, I find papers strewn across a large oak desk with leaflets littered across the room. Dirt from a couple of broken flowerpots covers the beige carpeted floor. My heart thumps twice and skips a beat as I instinctively reach inside my jacket for my .38 special, only to remember that I'm not wearing a holster. Since I'm on psychiatric leave, I'm not authorized to carry a piece. It's standard departmental procedure initiated by the upper brass to keep cops like me from eating our guns.

I move into the room cautiously, as if I'm treading across a live minefield, making sure to walk a straight line to keep from corrupting what I fear to be a crime scene.

The mid-day sun shines into the row of windows that face out towards the east side of Broadway Boulevard. A few blocks away, the snail-like scent of Lake Michigan is beginning to penetrate the neighborhood.

A cool breeze blows into the room from an open window and knocks a few sheets of paper off the oak desk and onto the floor, and that's when I notice the drops of blood on the leaflets. My heart begins to pitter-patter like a rabbit thumping its foot as I force myself to remain calm. I haven't felt this way since the fall of Fallujah.

I move in closer to the desk, and as I do, I see the pale wrinkling tips of Father Pantone's fingers extending past the length of the wooden frame. Rushing behind the desk, I find his body sprawled out like a crooked 'K' with his right arm tucked under his gut while blood soaks into the carpet beneath him.

Dropping down on my haunches, I pick up one of his frail arms and feel for a pulse. He has one, but just barely. I quickly undo my tie and double-fold the neckwear to apply pressure to the wound in his chest, all while trying to dial 911 on my piece-of-shit cell phone.

A thought crosses my mind: what if the murderer is still in the room? My instincts tell me to grab hold of a paperweight or anything that can be used as a weapon, but there's nothing within arm's reach as I scan the room before locking my sights on a closet with Venetian paneled doors. I stare at it for a minute, waiting for the boogeyman that I know exists to pop out, but no one shows.

Damn! I might have even passed the bastard on the elevator while coming up.

I let those thoughts drift away as the emergency operator's voice comes in over the line.

"Do you have an emergency?" the female voice repeats.

"This is Detective Frank Calhoun. Badge number 7318. I have a civilian down at 1078 West Wilson Ave, Suite 309." As a peace officer, there are times when you never think you'll be in a position to make this type of call. You tell yourself that you may get the call, but you'll never be the one making it. And when it does, all you're able to do is spit out words like any normal person, hoping that help arrives in time.

I drop the phone and return to comforting my old friend. In my eyes, Father Pantone is the epitome of what one strives to be as a chaplain in the Marines. He's strong, open-minded and his belief in a higher power makes his convictions of helping others even more poignant. To me, he's larger than life, bigger than any chaplain I've ever knowN—hell, he's bigger than most gym-rat marines. But now, sitting here holding his small frame in my arms, I realize just how much weight he's lost over the past few years. He's no longer the Kings-Point-bred, chain-smoking, 250-pound chaplain of pure muscle and iron determination, whose orders I never second guessed during my tour of duty in Iraq. In truth, he's become a mere shadow of his former self.

"F-Fran..." Father Pantone pants through parted chapped lips.

"No, don't try to speak. Save your energy. Just hold on. You're going to be okay," I say, realizing that I sound more like a shell-shocked corporal than I do a man of war.

"F-Frank," he whispers, grabbing at the white clergy collar

around his own neck. His silver hair is a sweaty tangled mess and his face is flushed white. The wrinkles in his face look like cracks on a fine bowl of China. He blinks and tears begin to form in his eyes and already I can see that the blue in them is beginning to lose color.

I rip the collar from around his neck and toss it to the side. "Just hold on, help's on its way."

Father Pantone rolls his head to the side, his eyes darting around the room like pinballs, searching and bouncing off every wall. He lifts his hand again and reaches for his neck, patting the empty space where the collar once was. His lips are dry as he tries to speak.

"No, just hold tight," I plead.

"Th... the... the Corps," Father Pantone finally sputters, his lips quivering with every letter.

"Yeah, I miss the Corps, too." I wasn't lying. I did miss the Chaplain Corps and all the soldiers that I learned to call brother over the years, but I certainly didn't miss the war. To hear Father Pantone utter the word "Corps" forces me to fight back tears as I realize, in some respects, I love this man more than my own father. The fact that the guilt of such an admission hasn't torn me apart is a testament to the walls I've built up since returning from Iraq.

"You'll be all right," I keep saying, more for myself than for Father Pantone. I hold him tight, attempting to keep him warm as the breeze from the lake tickles at the back of my neck. I can hear the hollowed sirens of the ambulance bustling through traffic trying to make its way here.

The smell of the lake's algae is mixing with the aroma of vanilla incense burning throughout the room, but even that can't overshadow the alarming stench that is beginning to set in. I know the putrid smell of death all too well—it reminds me of rotted meat. It was in Fallujah that I first encountered death, staring into its face through the eyes of the dead women and children scattered across the city, their flesh seemingly melting off their bones from the white phosphorous.

But now, as I look down into Father Pantone's dull eyes, I have a sudden realization that death is not only staring back up at me, he's also smiling.

CHAPTER 2

"Who was the first officer on the scene?" A Hispanic man with dark oily hair and cardboard-colored skin asks as he steps off the elevator and into the hall where Father Pantone's office is located.

"That would be me, sir," I hear a young uniformed officer say. He's in his early twenties with bubble-gum-toned skin and short black hair.

Behind the Hispanic man stands his partner, a white man with brown matted hair, small eyes with crows feet, and a thick mustache, which looks as though it's been pulled out of an old seventies magazine.

I'm sitting in the hall on an old wooden bench a few feet away from the entrance to Father Pantone's office, watching them.

"And you'd be?" the Hispanic man asks, flashing his detective's badge.

"Officer Jeff Miller."

"Well, Officer Miller, I'm Detective Lopez and this is my

partner Detective Kawowski. You're the one who discovered the body and put in the call?"

"Not quite, sir."

I see the older white detective raise an eyebrow and step around his partner. "Not quite?" he questions. "What does that mean exactly, Officer Miller?"

"Well... ummmm... *technically*, I wasn't the first officer on the scene, sir."

"Then who was?"

"That would be him," Officer Miller turns and points up the hall to where I sit.

"And who is that?" I hear Lopez ask.

Officer Miller scans a legal pad, which he's been using as an entry log for every person entering or exiting the crime scene. He looks up from the pad. "That's Detective Frank Calhoun."

"Calhoun. Name sounds familiar. He one of ours?" Lope looks puzzled.

"No, sir, he's from Area Four."

"Westside? What's he doing all the way up here?"

"Don't know, sir."

The two detectives turn and step past Officer Miller. When they finally reach me, I stand up from the bench and offer my hand to each man. We exchange names.

"Area Four, huh?" Lopez huffs. "What brings you to our part of town? By the way, your name sounds familiar. Have we met before?"

"Father Pantone was my friend," I say, looking back over my shoulder to the occupied office. "And no, we've never met, detective."

"Is that the victim's name?" Kawowski asks, writing it down in his notepad. He squints and begins studying me.

I don't like the way he looks at me, as if searching for some hidden truth behind my words.

"So you found the body of this Father—whattya say his name was again?" Lopez asks.

"Pantone." I spell it out for him.

"Okay, so you find your friend Father Pantone here dead in his office?"

"Not dead. Dying. There's a difference."

"Okay dying. Please continue."

"I came to Father Pantone's office because we had spoken earlier in the day and he said he wanted to discuss something of importance with me."

"And that something was?" Kawowski asks with his right eyebrow raised.

"I don't know. He never got around to telling me."

"Is that because he was dead before he could tell you or you just didn't get that far?" Lopez interjects.

"Look, I got here around 4:30 p.m. I knocked on the door and got no answer. So I knocked again a little harder, because Father Pantone's hearing isn't what it used to be. The door opens, I step in, and that's when I find him lying on the floor wounded."

"Question," Kawowski says, looking up from his notepad. He wrinkles his nose as if the flowing brown mustache is tickling it for the very first time. "What state was the body found in? I only ask because you're covered in blood."

I didn't even notice that the front of my shirt was covered in the dried crimson liquid, which looked more like I had been splashed with a bottle of merlot. I nod my head, understanding that they'll need this information to compare notes on the medical examiner's findings.

"When I found him," I say, holding up my hand with two fingers and thumb extended, "he was laying in a K position on his side in a pool of his own blood, which hadn't yet begun to congeal. I moved to help him, trying to administer first aid, but it was too late."

I look down at my hands and notice for the first time the dried blood that covers them. The last time my hands were covered in this much blood was the night I discovered Blue's body. I close my eyes and shake my head, telling myself that I'm not ready to relive the incident.

"Detective," Kawowski calls me back into the moment. "Just a few more questions and then we'll cut you loose. Is there someone we might be able to call on your behalf?"

I shake my head. "No, nobody."

"Okay," Lopez says, taking up the questioning. "So you find the father, you call it in, but by the time medics reach him he's already dead. Am I correct?"

"Yes."

Lopez leans back and looks into the office where the forensics team is already fast at work. "I count a full team," he says. "The person that did this had to be cold-blooded and calculated. You know of anyone that might have wanted your friend dead?"

"No."

"You touch anything?"

"What?"

"You know, other than the body?"

"No."

"You sure?"

"If I said I didn't touch anything, I didn't touch anything." I get up in Lopez's face. "I know how to handle an investigation. Are you insinuating I contaminated the crime scene?"

Kawowski moves in between us. "He's not saying that detective, he's just saying we're going to need your prints."

"They're on file," I say, locking eyes with Lopez.

"Well," Kawowski says closing his notepad. "It would seem

for now we've got enough." He reaches inside his coat and pulls out a black business card holder. He slips a card out and hands it to me. "Thank you, detective. We'll be in touch. If anything comes to mind, please give me a call."

Lopez looks at his partner quizzically and then back to me. I reach for the card, but Kawowski holds on to it with a definite grip.

He looks me square in the eyes and says, "You know, I once had an old academy buddy get assigned to Area Four, he'd tell me some crazy stories about what goes on over there. Then about a year ago, he calls me up to tell me about the death of this cop and how it's going to change the face of the department. I don't believe the guy because he's known for sensationalizing a story, but he tells me it's something out a Jerry Springer episode. Turns out the dead cop was killed by his illegitimate father who was also a cop. Now I don't know if that's an Area Four thing, but it seems to me that some pretty weird stuff occurs on that side of town, don't you think?"

"Or maybe that's just life." I yank the card out of his hand while biting on my bottom lip to keep myself from saying anything else.

Detective Kawowski nods his head in agreement and then he turns and begins making his way under the yellow tape and onto the crime scene while I turn in the opposite direction and walk down the hall, leaving Lopez to contemplate our interaction.

"Calhoun!" Lopez calls down the hall after me. He snaps his fingers twice and begins to point, "You wouldn't happen to be *that* detective, would you? The son of the cop killer?"

I turn with a stiff face and my hands balled into fists. If Lopez was within arm's reach I would've taken a shot at him, but instead, I just stare at him, long, hard, and unblinking, and say, "Yeah... that's me."

CHAPTER 3

opez smiles. "I knew it."

It takes everything in me not to walk back down that hall. A year ago, I would have rushed in head first, throwing punches, but I know Lopez's type—he's itching for an ass-whoopin' and I'm not about to oblige him.

"Good for you, detective. Can I go now?"

"Sure, just know that we'll be in touch."

I ride the elevator down feeling as though whatever little pride I had in knowing that I was a detective had just been snatched away from me. The fact that Kawowski knew my identity wasn't lost on me, but knowing that Lopez hadn't put two-and-two together gave me a faint relief that maybe people in the city and especially those in the department were starting to forget what had occurred to my father and me.

The elevator doors part on the bottom floor and I exit. There are a few officers working crowd control, trying to ensure that the other occupants of the office building are exiting properly. On my way out the building, one of the uniforms throws me a CPD loaner jacket, a cotton/nylon windbreaker that's mainly used to provide warmth to a victim after a violent crime. Truthfully, I've never been a fan of wearing the loaner, but when you're covered in blood, you don't have an option. I trek two blocks south to the Red Line subway train where

I stand before the open tracks wondering how I got here. I love riding the trains because it allows me to think, to put my mind somewhere else, but for now all I can think about is Father Pantone staring up at me with his dull blue eyes. The reflection in them was like that of a polished marble, gleaming and unreal, as if he were trying to play a cruel joke by faking his death, but no matter how much I wanted to believe that I knew the truth.

My first inclination upon meeting Kawowski and Lopez was to convince them to let me in on the investigation, but they're playing it by the book and I understand why. After all, I've heard the whispers from the uniforms about me being that guy.

You know: THAT GUY. The one who arrested his own father for murder.

Wait, you mean he's the son of the cop killer, no shit?

No shit.

I can't help that the sins of my father are now my cross to bear, but I'm working through it—why else would the department have me seeing a shrink?

The Red Line train going southbound pulls into the station. I enter the car and take a seat. Sitting here, rocking back and forth, I play over Father Pantone's last words.

The "Corps" as we all call it, is a reference to the Chaplain Corps of the United States Navy. It's a branch of the military where soldiers choose to serve God and Country as one. To become bearers of men's sins while also encouraging the moral and conscious duty of the fighting soldier. It's also a place where I decided to follow a different path instead of following in my father's belief of the blue religion in becoming a cop. But how could I have known that life would lead from the field of battle and back to the path from which I'd run?

I look down at the lapel of my shirt and see three blood dried fingerprints on the fabric. Just seeing those prints brings tears to my eyes. Why would anyone want to kill Anton Pantone? I do my best to bury my tear-covered face in my hands. I don't care if riders see me crying, but I can't let my emotions get the best of me. I've been warned about that, so I close my eyes and try to fight back a flood of pain even though I know I'm just adding to my emotional dam.

An image of a younger Father Pantone decked out in an all white Chaplain's uniform flashes behind my eyes. It's the first day of Navy Chaplain School in Newport, Rhode Island. The Father, then a lieutenant, holds up his dog tags for all of us new chaplains to see.

"These," he says, his voice exploding throughout the room, "are to be placed behind your shield of God." Then he tucks the dog tags in behind the white collar of his uniform. "You are chaplains first and soldiers second."

I open my eyes and jump up from my seat. The train is pulling into the Belmont station as the doors part and I hurry off. All this time the answer has been right in front of me. Father Pantone even tried showing me, but I didn't see that the solution lay in his collar.

After transferring over to the east side of the platform, I open my cell and begin dialing the number on the card to Detective Kawowski, but then I think better of it and close the phone. *Who am I kidding? They aren't going to let me play in the game.* After all, I'm "*that cop.*" Besides, whoever killed Father Pantone has made it personal and there's no way I'm going to take a backseat in his investigation.

An hour later when I return to Father Pantone's office, it's dark out. The EMT unit and forensics team are gone. I enter the building and make my way up the three flights of stairs just in case someone involved in the investigation is coming down on the elevator. Once on the floor where the office is located, I slip off the CPD loaner and flip on a mini mag-lite that I carry on a keychain with my house keys.

Breaking the red crime scene sticker that covers the jamb of the door, I enter the disheveled office and find that the windows are now closed. The last blast of pent-up heat runs across my face and escapes out the door. The room no longer smells of vanilla or algae, but more like a hospital thanks to the chemicals that forensics used. I sweep the large radius of light around the room as I do my best not to corrupt the crime scene.

The leaflets are still in the same position as when I first found them. I'm hoping that forensics hasn't taken the collar. I can't see Kawowski or Lopez getting to it yet because they're most likely canvassing the neighborhood for witnesses or waiting for the results of the autopsy report.

I move around the side of the desk, allowing the light to fall over the blood stained carpet and passed it until my sights fall upon the collar, which is partially dangling down into a heating duct. I tiptoe around the triangular plastic markers that forensics has placed down on the floor to show blood splatter and bend down to pick it up. Placing the bottom end of the mag-lite in between my teeth I examine the collar, turning it over until I feel a bulge in the fabric. I split the material in two and remove a small golden key from it.

What the hell is Father Pantone hiding?

Still crouched over, I slow my breathing and listen.

Someone else is in the room with me. I can hear him breathing hard.

I look up at the closet across from me, with the mag-lite still in my mouth, staring at its retractable doors.

Everything is quiet.

The breathing that I thought I heard has dissipated.

As I start to stand, I get a feeling that I'm being watched but I tell myself it's all in my head. Suddenly, a figure in all black wearing a ski mask darts from the closet's recesses and rushes at me.

My first reaction is to go for my pistol but then I remember again that I don't have one as the attacker drives his fist deep into my midsection. I cough up bile as the mag-lite falls from my mouth and onto the floor. The two silver house keys on the ring cling against one another upon impact. He's about six feet and two hundred and twenty-five pounds, but I muster up enough strength to grab the attacker's shirt as we tumble back onto the blood-soaked tweed carpet. The semi-dried crimson liquid seeps into my shirt and makes the material stick to my body like a cheap spit-on tattoo as I flip the attacker up over me.

I'm pumping on pure adrenaline as I recover from the floor and find that my attacker has done the same. Our shadows are cast against the wall from the luminescence of the mag-lite. My stomach flops and I take a deep breath to prevent myself from throwing up.

"Who are you? Why'd you kill Father Pantone?" I ask.

The attacker doesn't say a word as his eyes shift to the small golden key in my hand.

"Oh, you want this, huh?" I ask inhaling a large waft of air.

"Well you're not getting it." I wipe my mouth clean, taking with it any notion that I may be out of shape. When adrenaline is rushing, the mechanics of the body can produce overtime results.

We're about ten feet apart when the attacker cracks his neck from side to side and begins dancing from left to right in a circular motion towards me. He puts his hands up like a boxer and advances.

I clench the golden key in my fist. Beads of sweat trickle down my back and over my forehead. I look the attacker square in the eyes. There will be no mercy.

I throw a left jab and the attacker dodges to the right. "What are you running for? You want this key, don't you?" I throw a right jab and again he dodges my punch, then counters with a left that catches me just below the right eye.

"Is that all you got?" I shake it off. "Come on, you piece of shit!"

Our shadows dance on the walls as I swing again and counter, again and counter and again before finally connecting with a right hook that sends him stumbling back, dazed but still able to shake off the blow.

I'm breathing hard. I'm not too sure how long I can last since I'm out of my weight class, but I'm determined to test my limits.

The attacker takes up the boxing stance once again, slowly dancing towards me. He throws a left jab which I block, but then he connects with a hard right body shot to my ribs. Whatever oxygen left in my lungs goes right out of me. The attacker swings a hard left hook and splits open the bottom of my right eyelid, followed by an uppercut that knocks me off my feet.

The room spins clockwise and then counter-clockwise. My head is pounding and my eye twitches with pain as if I've got a Tourette's tic. I do my best to rise from the floor, but my body and mind are miscommunicating.

I feel the muscles in my hand begin to relax, and with the last of my strength, I clutch the key even tighter until I draw blood into my palm with my fingernails. The attacker takes five steps towards me, pries open my hand, and plucks the key from it. I grab at air, trying to stop a phantom, not yet realizing that the real attacker has already left. He's out the door and down the hall, I can hear his fading footsteps.

When the room finally slows to a crawl, I pull myself up to stand. My legs feel like uncooked spaghetti noodles, brittle and ready to break at the slightest shifting of my weight. My head hurts like hell and the palm of my right hand aches. I look down at my injured hand and can barely make out the bloody impression the key left in my skin: ERICA RUST. I mouth the words as I try to balance myself against a wall and gather my bearings, but I feel the weight of the world on my shoulders, pulling me down, so I close my eyes and allow it to take me from this land.

CHAPTER 4

The next morning I awake to find myself lying on my back, staring up at the faces of Detectives Kawowski and Lopez.

"Morning sunshine," Lopez says, the scent of Juicy Fruit bubblegum emanating from his mouth.

"What the hell happened?" I ask as I sit up. The back of my shirt sticks to my skin. My head is ringing and the joints in my legs are stiff and beginning to burn.

"How about you tell us?" Kawowski chimes in, flipping open his notepad with pen at the ready.

I sit there on the floor for a second aching all over. My neck pops twice as I roll it around in a circular motion before hanging it low and massaging it with my hand. I'm trying to remember the name from the key: Erin... No. Erwin... No. Eric... No. Erica, yeah that's it. Erica something. Erica... r... rom... re... ru... Rust. Erica Rust.

I slowly stand up holding my head in the palm of my hand and say to the detectives. "All I remember is coming back here because I left my house keys. While I was searching for them, someone got the jump on me and the next thing I know, I'm waking up on the floor."

"So somebody got the jump on you, huh? Is that what it is?" Lopez asks blowing a yellow bubble of gum from his mouth.

"Yeah, that's what it is." I cut my eyes at Lopez. "Look, I don't mean to interfere with your investigation. All I came for are my keys."

"Sure you did," Lopez retorts.

I look about the room as though I'm searching for my keys and then I move over to the desk and bend down and pick them up. The mag-lite has died, which is good since I don't think either detective is buying my story. "See, keys. I can't get in the house without keys." I twirl the single ring with its two keys around my finger.

"Why didn't forensics bag the keys?" Lopez asks.

I hunch my shoulders. "How should I know? I guess they missed them."

"You should have that cut under your eye checked out," Kawowski advises.

"What? This?" I touch the cut trying to act like it doesn't hurt, even though it stings like a son-of-a-bitch. "It's nothing that a cold compress can't handle. Well, if you'll excuse me, detectives, I'll let you get back to your investigation."

"Not so fast, super cop," says Lopez. "I've got a few more questions. What did your attacker look like?"

"Don't have much of a description other than he was about six feet and covered in black from head to toe."

"You didn't get to see his eyes?"

"Yeah, I saw them, but what can I say—they looked just like yours."

"And what's that supposed to mean?" Lopez takes two steps forward.

"His eyes were brown, probably could have even been dark

brown. At the time, I was more focused on saving my life than trying to get a description. Plus, it was dark so it's kind of hard to say what color his eyes actually were."

"That's understandable, Detective," Kawowski says matter-of-factly. He probably fears that Lopez and I might come to blows if he doesn't interfere. He's right.

"Any more questions?" I look to Lopez.

"Yeah, just one more. How is it that you're still on the force after what your old man did?"

I lunge at Lopez's neck, but Kawowski stands between us restraining me.

"All right," he says. "That's enough. I'm sure Detective Lopez meant nothing by it. Isn't that right, Detective?

"Just curious is all."

Kawowski lets me go. Lopez and I lock eyes and stare at one another.

"Do you need a ride home?" Kawowski asks.

"Nah, I'm good. All I need is the train," I turn and step out the door.

After an hour and a half of taking the Red Line train southbound to Jackson and transferring over to the Blue Line train heading west, I finally find myself at home. I live in a brown-brick, two-story flat in Washington Square, a working class neighborhood named after Harold Washington, the only African-American mayor of Chicago. My building sits amongst 19th century gothic brownstones, one-story bunga-lows and at least three different multi-unit apartment buildings.

I've lived in this building all my life but recently took ownership after my father's incarceration. I rent the top floor to a young woman named Gloria with two children, who I'm incredibly fond of.

I decide to take the back way in, cutting in between a gangway before I ascend up the back porch stairs. I don't want Gloria or her kids to see me in these bloodied clothes. Through the backdoor I enter my kitchen, which smells like cinnamon. I close the door and click the bolt shut. The small space is covered in darkness. I maneuver around the square dining table and down the hall past my bedroom, and then further past the living room and into the basement to find the lockbox that contains my father's old service revolver. The six shot standard issue .38 feels heavier than most side arms I've carried. The black steel is cool to the touch, and for a second, I wonder if I can bring myself to carry my father's old pistol. I decide then and there that despite my medical leave, I can't afford to take another unnecessary beating like the one from last night. I'm convinced that no matter where I go after this, there's bound to be more trouble than my fists can solve.

CHAPTER 5

K-Town is an area located on the West side of the city, its moniker based on the fact that all the streets in this neighborhood begin with the letter K, such as Kostner, Kildare and Kilbourn.

The surrounding neighborhoods of this African-American enclave, once made up a sprawling working class community filled with barbershops, grocery stores, laundromats and a plethora of small business professionals ranging from plumbers to teachers.

But with the influx of illegal narcotics, what was once a thriving community soon became a ghetto filled with working class stiffs living alongside pimps, hustlers, murderers, thieves, and whores, all trying to eke out a living while scratching beneath the surface of Chicago's illustrious skyline.

On any given day, one can find hustlers driving up and down the streets in expensive cars with glistening spinning rims and playing music so loud that the bass from the trunk rattles the windows of the Greystone two-flats whenever they pass. A flurry of women, dressed in skin-tight jeans and crop-top tee shirts, stand on corners gossiping and checking out the hustlers as they stride by with limp-gliding swagger and puffed-out chests, displaying a mating ritual that showcases their ordained toughness. Children play tag, chasing one another up and down and around blocks, while teen lookouts working for the hustlers play keep away from undercover cops. The streets are a wasteland of plastic bottles, discarded wrappers and faded political signs. Beyond the trash-covered curb is a row of two-flat tenement buildings painted in a bygone golden hue, which sits in between the occasional abandoned, weed-infested lot and the poor man's alley mechanic.

The energy that vibrates through this neighborhood can be as volatile and explosive as nitrogen in a Formula 1 engine, but its this very same energy that makes K-Town the mecca of street society.

I make my way up the littered street of Congress Parkway in dark jeans and a red tee shirt that has the image of the late Tupac Shakur adorning the left side of the chest. I know that if I need information that I can't obtain from the department, I'll have to hit the streets and allow the chorus of addicts, snitches and street level Chatty Cathys to give me the real deal or turn to Buddy Heim, the one man who knows more about the streets than a pimp turned preacher.

I scan the vehicles parked along the street searching for his 1971 Oldsmobile with dark tint windows and a caramel paint job. Half a block up, I spot Heim crouched down, shaking what I know to be dice in his rough hands. Four other men surround him as they yell numbers back and forth, while passing money as though they are stockbrokers.

"Come on seven, come on." Buddy's voice rises above the huddle of men. His afro protrudes from the group along with an embedded black pick with an image of a fist pointing up as if to say, power to the people. Heim's white tee shirt clings to his tight packed body like a butcher's wrapped meats while the bottom of his jeans look to be falling apart from walking on them.

I saunter over to the group of men. They know I'm a cop as much as I know they're criminals, so a sense of familiarity—or perhaps, hate— is shared between us.

"What down, Preacher?" Buddy asks, still stooped over. Preacher is a name that I've earned on the streets, first as a reverend doing missionary work trying to save souls and now as a detective trying to save lives.

"We need to talk, Buddy."

Buddy looks up from the human pit and replies, "Be right with you, Preacher." Then he turns back to the game, blowing on the dice as they rattle in his hand before scattering them over the cool cement sidewalk.

"Seven, bitch!" Buddy yells, grabbing the scattered pile of tens and twenty dollar bills up off the ground. He stands and turns to face me. "What can I do for you, Preacher?"

"I need a make on a key," I say.

"Ah, you ain't gone let me make some of that money back?" one of the men from the pit says as he chews on the stem of a marijuana plant.

"Some other day," Buddy replies. "But here's a ten to bless you back into the game." He drops a bill on the ground and we begin walking up the block. The sound of the dice clacking off the concrete can be heard as a new shooter takes up the reins of the game.

A quarter of the way up the street, Buddy stops in front of a brick building with a black iron gate and looks around to see if anyone is in earshot, then he looks at me. "Preacher, you know we cool, right? But I don't know anything about any keys."

"Look, Buddy, this is off the record. I promise I'm not here to bust you. I just need some info."

"You serious, man? I know you preachers aren't supposed to lie."

"Buddy, this is me. You know my word is bond."

Buddy bites down on his lip, contemplating my words. He then turns and opens the black iron gate. "Follow me," he says as he climbs a flight of concrete stairs and enters the building. The apartment smells like cheap ketchup and fabric softener.

I follow Buddy down an all-white hall and into a room covered from wall to wall with keys.

He sits down at a workbench smothered with metal shavings that are produced from the mechanical key cutter erected at the end of the bench.

"Let me see the key." Buddy holds out his hand like a child begging for a piece of candy.

"That's the problem. I don't have the key."

"Okay, what does it look like?"

"It's square shaped with an Eagle on it and the name Erica Rust."

"Never heard of such a key."

"You haven't even checked to see if you have it." I point to the racks of keys on the walls.

"Listen, Preacher, you know detective shit and I know keys and I ain't never seen or even heard of a key like that."

"You sure?"

Buddy crosses his hands over his heart. "Never."

"Damn it!" I slap the wall with the palm of my hand.

"Easy on the drywall. Shit, I gotta live here you know."

"Sorry, Buddy, just a little frustrated is all."

"Tell you what I can do though. I can reach out to some people I know and see if I come up with something. But I'm not making any promises."

I jot down every detail that I can remember about the key. Then I slide Buddy a hundred-dollar bill and go on my way.

CHAPTER 6

Skeet's diner on Western and Madison is a small sandwich shop started by retired officer Robert "Skeet" Hellman, my father's ex-partner and the closest person I have to family except for my father. The ironic thing about Skeet's is that criminals help the business turn a profit more than the cops that frequent the place in between shifts. Back in the day, the diner used to be surrounded by the Rockwell housing projects which became towering fortresses for the opposing Gangster Disciples, Black Disciples and Vice Lord street gangs. This trio of warring factions made living in or near the projects like being in war-torn Baghdad after the bombings. Fast forward a few years through the city's new "re-development" program and now three-story condos surround the diner, but the customer base hasn't changed as it's still filled with the proverbial *cops and robbers* of yesteryear.

I take a seat at the "S" shaped counter. The waitress is tall and dark with a complexion that reminds me of chocolate syrup. She runs her tongue across her glossy lips and then holds out a glass coffee pot while looking down at the cup in front of me. She smacks and pops her gum, waiting to see if I'll flip the cup over or push it to the side.

I flip it over and she tops off my cup. I take a sip of the black coffee. It feels good going down as it helps to calm my nerves. I can't help but think about the key. What did it open? What was it for?

When the waitress returns with pen and pad in hand, still popping her gum, I look her square in the eyes. Over the years, I've learned that the way to a woman's heart is through her eyes.

"Is Skeet in?" I ask.

"Yeah, who wants to know?"

"Can you tell him that his nephew Frank is here to see him?"

The waitress smacks and pops her gum once more, and then she drops the pad into her smock and turns to head into the kitchen. I look around the diner, watching as a few uniforms take up three tables on the far left side of the restaurant joking with a blond-haired officer. I can tell he's a rookie because he hasn't yet caught on to the fact that everyone's cleared their plates except him, which means he'll be stuck with the check.

"Lil' cornbread snatcher!" Uncle Skeet calls out to me as he exits the door to the kitchen. His light skin is glistening under the yellow glow of the fluorescent lights. He's wearing a tee shirt that reads 'IN GOD WE TRUST' written over the chest with a forty-five handgun below the words. The hair on his face and head is black and curly, like he could've been one of the Jacksons.

We shake hands and then lean into one another for a hug before he speaks.

"What brings you by, nephew?"

"Need to talk. To clear my head a little, Unc."

"You had breakfast yet?"

Before I can answer, Uncle Skeet turns and yells to the waitress, "Philicia, set us up with a table, some toast, eggs and bacon."

I look around the full house wondering how Philicia is going to accomplish such a task, but within five minutes, she not only sets us up with a table, but has us sitting at the front of the restaurant near the large bay windows.

Philicia pours my Uncle Skeet a cup of coffee and says, "I know you like it black."

"Just like the pioneers," he says. She turns and trots back to the counter, while Uncle Skeet watches her from behind.

"You know that could be sexual harassment on your part seeing as though you're her employer."

"Sexual harassment, boy please, ain't nothing wrong with a man looking. Besides, we ain't here to talk about my affairs, are we?"

"No, we are not, Unc. Last night Father Pantone was killed. He was my old captain from the Marines."

"Sorry to hear that, kid. They catch who did it?"

"Nah, not yet. But we will."

Uncle Skeet leans in and runs his hand over his beard. "We? Hold up, Frank. I thought you were on leave?"

"I am."

"Then what's this talk of we? Let whoever's working the case work it. You're supposed to be dealing with your own situation anyway. Speaking of which, have you gone to see him yet?"

I fall silent. I should have known that the subject of my father was bound to surface when dealing with my Uncle Skeet.

"Oh, so now you've got nothing to say, huh?" Uncle Skeet asks, leaning back in his chair.

"I-I just can't see him now, Unc. I still need time."

"That's understandable. All I'm saying is that if you've got time to investigate a murder then you've got time to see your father."

"Maybe you're right, Unc."

"Shit, I know I'm right. He's your father and no matter what they say he did, he raised you and supported you even when you decided to leave the church and become a chaplain in the Marines."

"I hear what you're saying, Unc, but everything he's taught me, my whole being, has been based on a lie."

"Listen to yourself, Frank. Are you saying you're not going to see the one man that raised you since you were a baby because he lied to you? Hell, I lie everyday, I even get lied to, but you don't see me crying about it."

"It's different for you, Unc."

"Don't give me that crap. You want sympathy, how about you go see your old man? See how much sympathy they're showing him up there in Joliet."

I look out the bay window at the traffic zooming by as if everyone is heading to some all-important destination. I wonder where the road of life is leading me. It's been almost a year since my father was convicted of murdering my partner and I still can't bring myself to face him. The media made a spectacle of the story and it took a few months before the articles and editorials became nothing but small snippets, until the murder, and subsequently the trial, were nothing but old news.

"You think I'm a bad person because I haven't gone to see him, don't you?"

"I don't think that at all, Frank. We all deal with things differently. All I'm saying is that you need to see your father in order to put things behind you and move forward."

"I'll take those words into consideration."

"Good. And while you're at it, let this investigation into your captain's murder rest with the detectives working it."

"Yeah, I'll try."

"Well, I'm sure you'll figure it out, Nephew. I have faith in you."

Uncle Skeet stands, pats my hand, and then leaves me at the table staring out the window at the ever-moving world. I down the cup of coffee, remembering that Uncle Skeet called it being a "pioneer" because only hardcore people who drank their coffee straight had the backbone, persistence, and resilience of a Western pioneer to face the world head-on without fear.

Pioneer.

I like the ring of the word. I realize that if I'm going to find Father Pantone's killer, I'll have to work the case on my own, outside the jurisdiction of the department. Since I don't officially have a badge, I have nothing to lose. And when you're a man with nothing to lose, I guess you're essentially a pioneer out on the Homefront, riding the line between death and survival or madness and peace.

CHAPTER 7

Without the murder book, a three ring binder that possesses the autopsy, evidence and all pertinent information regarding the case, the investigation into Father Pantone's murder is looking more like an aquarium of dead goldfish in clean water. At first glance, one might think that the goldfish died from attrition, but upon further investigation the results clearly point to bacteria growing on the algae at the bottom of the tank as the cause of death.

The murder book is in Kawowski and Lopez's possession and there's no way in hell that I'm getting anywhere near it. I get up from my seat and grab today's editions of the *Chicago Sun-Times* and *Tribune* newspapers off the counter. I open the *Tribune* and flip to the metro section. There's an article about Father Pantone's murder.

The old Uptown neighborhood was rocked early Tuesday evening by the murder of Father Anton Pantone who oversaw services at Saint Helen's Missionary Church. Father Pantone had been a chaplain in the navy for sixteen years before retiring and taking up the cloth as a civilian clergy.

Scanning the page, I skip over the biographical paragraphs of Father Pantone's life. The only thing I need to know about the man, I learned in Iraq.

Detectives found Father Pantone's body after receiving a call from an anonymous source. One source claimed that the father was killed by a shot to the heart. No suspects have been apprehended. Detectives are continuing their investigation.

I close the paper. The department is doing its best to keep my name off the radar. Opening up the *Sun-Times*, I find a very similar article to the *Tribune* except this one quotes a witness as seeing a priest leaving Father Pantone's office just before I discovered his body.

I read the byline.

"Shit. Anyone but him," I say to myself as I rip the article from the paper, fold it and place it in my back pocket. I drop a ten-dollar bill on the table and leave the diner. Outside, the mid-day sun is just beginning to heat up the streets. A nice day like this usually means that crime is going to be high, which also means that every cop on the street is fully aware of Murphy's Law: anything that can go wrong, will go wrong.

I exhale the musty air and then pull the article out my back pocket and reread the name of the reporter on the byline just to make sure I'm reading it correctly. Crumpling the article, I realize that Murphy's Law is already in effect for me. Especially, if it means I have to start talking to reporters like Arnie Ratcliff.

CHAPTER 8

Arnie Ratcliff sits in a corner of the Billy Goat Tavern on lower Wacker Drive with one of the establishment's famous cheeseburgers fitted in between his hairy palms. He's a small man, almost rat-like in his appearance with thin black-rimmed glasses and a balding head. He even nibbles on his burger like a rat, his slim mustache twitching under the brim of his sharp nose.

The lunch crowd, mostly newspaper personnel, jams the small-squared tables by four. The scent of seasoned burgers, grilled onions, and skin-wrapped Polish sausages lament just above the heads of everyone inside the dim eatery.

There are four hostesses scattered about the room with one manning an old-fashioned ring and clear cash register, two behind the U-shaped counter and another at the bar. All are wearing white triangular hats and off-white grease-covered aprons.

I descend the small staircase and make my way over to Ratcliff. I've known the reporter since back in the day when he covered the crime beat. But it wasn't until the arrest of my father that I really came to know Arnie Ratcliff as a hounding news junkie who'd sell his own mother's soul for a good story.

"Hey Arnie," I say, sliding into a seat at his table.

The small man pushes his glasses up from the end of his nose with his index finger. He looks up at me with furrowed brow. "Well, well, well, if it isn't Detective Frank Calhoun, Mister Go-Fuck-Yourself in person."

I did my best not to smile. "How's business, Arnie?"

Ratcliff hunches. "Can't complain. They keep killing and I keep writing. It's a check."

"Yeah, I guess that's the truth."

"Whaddya want, Calhoun? I'm trying to enjoy my cheeseburger."

"I can see that, Arnie. I just thought you might be able to help me with something."

With Ratcliff, I know I have to choose my words carefully. The man can turn a simple innocent sentence into a world-ending statement.

"This wouldn't have anything to do with that murder in Uptown, would it?" Arnie smiles and pushes his glasses back up on his nose. "Because word has it that you knew the priest."

The thing about a crime beat reporter like Arnie Ratcliff is that there is always someone in the department willing to shell out information for little to nothing in return.

"I may have known him," I say, trying to sound as nonchalant as possible.

"Well, I guess our conversation is over, especially if you *might* have known him." Ratcliff takes a small bite out of his burger and grease oozes from the side of the buns. The little man knows he has me by the balls.

I look around the room, suspicious of every reporter, but I'm old news and my face doesn't even give a register. I lean in towards Ratcliff. "All right, Arnie, you got me. I knew Father Pantone."

Ratcliff smiles, showing his tiny teeth. "Care to explain how you knew the deceased priest?"

"Look, Arnie, I just need a name. I don't have time to go into detail about this."

"A name, you say? Would that name happen to be the witness quoted in today's article? Because if it is, you should know by now that a reliable source is as good as a freshman politician."

I tap my fingers on the table. Ratcliff is in the mood for games.

"Okay, Arnie, what do you want in exchange for the witness's name?"

Ratcliff leans in over the table. "So you're working Father Pantone's murder? Aren't you a little too close to the victim to be doing that?"

I say nothing. Any admission of my involvement in Father Pantone's murder puts me on record as an investigating detective.

"Look, Arnie, just give me a name and I'm out of your hair." I clench and unclench my fist in rapid succession.

Ratcliff pushes his glasses back up on his face once again. "And what do I get in return?"

I stop tapping my fingers on the table and stare into Ratcliff's beady dark brown eyes. "There's still a story to be told about my old man and me—one that no one's been able to write."

"Frank, please. Everything that could be written about you and your family has been written. You'll have to do better than that."

I sit calmly back in my seat and crack a smile. "Not everything."

Ratcliff leans in even more. "Yeah, and what's everything?"

"An exclusive interview with me. The real story of how I discovered the truth. Everything about that night of the arrest—the day after, *everything*."

Ratcliff runs his tongue over his front teeth. I've got him, but I need a cherry to top it all off. "I'll even get you an interview with my father."

He smiles. "And how do you plan to do that?

"Let me worry about the devil in the details. All you have to worry about is penning that Pulitzer-prize winning story."

Ratcliff taps the tip of his nose with his index finger. I begin to unclench my fist as I feel my palms becoming sweaty. He pushes his glasses back up on the bridge of his nose with a smile, showing me those tiny teeth of his and says, "The eyewitness's name is Lillian Murphy. She resides in an apartment just above the shoe store across from Father Pantone's office."

I hop out my seat. "Thanks, Arnie."

"Yeah, yeah, yeah, just remember the exclusive."

"I will," I say as I head towards the door.

Outside the tavern, I inhale the bittersweet underground air circulating through the cement labyrinth of the city beneath the city. I've given Ratcliff an exclusive interview with my father even though I haven't seen him in almost a year. I'm not even sure I can pull off such a promise, especially since he's refused to speak to anyone about the incident since his incarceration.

I hunch my shoulders and head north on Lower Wacker Drive towards Grand Ave. to the Red Line train station. I'll deal with Ratcliff when it's time to cross that bridge. I have other things to worry about like a possible witness to Father Pantone's murder.

CHAPTER 9

illian Murphy is a small woman who stands at exactly five feet. When she opens the door to her apartment on Broadway and Wilson, my first thought is that I have the wrong residence. "How can I help you?" she asks, her voice delicate and small like her body.

Her face is slender with a dash of pink blush across her white cheeks as her loose brown bangs hang just over her grayish- green eyes, which seem to keep changing color right before my own eyes.

"I'm Detective Frank Calhoun. I wanted to ask you some questions about the incident that occurred across the street."

I flash my father's old badge.

"You mean the murder?" She's direct.

"Yes, Ma'am, I mean the murder."

Miss Murphy turns from the door, leaving it ajar, "Are you coming in or what?" she asks, her voice echoing down the apartment's hall with every step she takes.

I close the door behind me and proceed to follow the small woman. The apartment smells like pine, the cardboard kind that hangs from the rearview mirror of a car. Ten feet down the hall and the apartment opens up into a spacious living room. An old brown floor model television sits against the north wall, topped with a glass menagerie of turtles. To the left of the television are three large windows and adjacent to the windows is an easy rocker recliner with a ball of yarn and a pair of crocheting needles lying in the seat.

"Would you like something to drink, Mister Calhoun? I have pop, beer, water, juice, and gin."

"No thank you, ma'am. I'm fine."

"Suit yourself," she says turning and walking past the recliner and into the small kitchenette. On the walls hang pictures of a brown haired blue-eyed Jesus, the Virgin Mary and Bob Hope.

"I just have a few questions, Miss Murphy and then I'll be out of your hair."

"Not to worry," she says from the kitchen. I hear the sound of bottles clinging against one another as she opens and closes the door of the fridge.

"Would you mind twisting this off for me?" she asks, coming back into the living room with a beer bottle in hand. I open the bottle and hand it back.

"If you don't mind," I reach inside my coat pocket. "I'd like to take a few notes as we go over the questions."

"Knock yourself out." Miss Murphy takes a long swig of her beer and then she slowly licks the amber residue from her upper lip.

"You were quoted in the paper as saying that you saw another priest leave the scene of the incident. Am I correct?"

"You mean the murder."

"Yes, I mean the murder. Did you get a chance to see the priest's face?

"Nah, I was too far away to see it."

"Then how did you know it was a priest?"

"Because the man looked like a priest. He had on one of those black robes and was wearing one of those white-collar thingys. And had slicked black hair, too."

I jot down the information. "And you saw this priest from this window over here?" I point, making my way over to the recliner. "Were you sitting in this chair?"

"Yeah, I was knitting." She brings the neck of the bottle up to her lips and takes another swig. For someone so small, she's taking it down pretty fast.

"May I sit?"

"Just don't get too comfortable."

I remove the yarn and needles and sit down in the brown chair. It's more than comfortable—it's relaxing. I sit back and turn to look out the middle window. From where I'm sitting, I can see clear across to the west side of Broadway. A panhandler is holding up a sign that reads 'WILL DANCE FOR MONEY' as he stands on a corner shaking his arms and jostling his shoulders in a synchronized fashion.

I look to the building where Father Pantone's office is located and can see the closed blinds. There's a loud boom within the apartment as I whip my head around, turning to look at the doorway that leads down the hall to the bedrooms.

"Billy! Billy! Turn that shit down!" Miss Murphy yells. Her voice seems unnatural coming from her small frame. "It's my boy, Billy. He's playing that damn war game. Something 'Duty or Die' or some shit like that."

I nod my head and then turn back to stare out the window at the chipped painted windowsill of Father Pantone's office. I look back at Miss Murphy. "So you were sitting right here yesterday when you saw the priest?"

"Yep, I was right there knitting my ass away."

"Were you sitting forward in the chair or were you sitting backwards, you know, in a more relaxed position?

"I was ummmm... sitting backwards. Why?"

"Did you have the seat reclined?"

"I don't remember. Why does it matter?"

"Listen, Miss Murphy. I need you to think about this long and hard before you answer. Was the seat reclined?"

Miss Murphy takes a long sip of beer and then holds the tip of the bottle on her bottom lip. She rolls her eyes, closes them, and then reopens them and says, "The seat was reclined. Definitely reclined."

I sit back and pull the lever for the recliner. From this angle, I can barely see over the edge of the windowpane let alone across the street to Father Pantone's office.

I return the recliner to its original position and then stand with notebook in hand. Jotting down notes, I look at Miss Murphy with a questionable stare.

"Are you sure you were reclining in this chair when you saw the priest's face?"

"Yeah, I'm sure. How many times I got to tell you? You think I'm lying?"

"I don't know about lying, but you couldn't have been sitting in this chair when you saw that priest's face. Sitting there, I can barely see across the street and I'm nine inches taller than you. So maybe you need to rethink where you saw that priest."

Miss Murphy takes another long swig of her brew as her eyes dart around the room before landing back on me. "I guess the seat was forward. Yeah, that's what it was. It was forward."

"Look, Miss Murphy, I don't have time for your guessing games. If you like, I can run you in and question you in an Area Four interrogation room. *Or*, you can start telling me the truth."

I stare at the small woman trying to give my most defiant gaze. I keep my eyes locked on her. There's no way I'm going to give her a chance to come up for air. She brushes a few strands of hair behind her ears and looks as though she might blow away if I dare to crack the window.

"Mah! Mah!" a voice from the extended hall cancels out the silence between us.

I finally break my stare and turn to see a tall white male barging down the hallway wearing black jeans and a black tee-shirt with an image of Lil' Wayne on it. His face is like that of a bulldog, fat, meaty and lovable. His eyes are walnut brown and his russet colored hair is cut low into a fade. I place him at the tender age of seventeen or eighteen.

"Billy," Miss Murphy says to her son. "This is Detective Calhoun." Instantly a wall of distrust goes up in Billy's eyes. He drops his head and pretends to pick his nails.

I study the young man for a second before asking, "Did you happen to see anything suspicious occur yesterday during the incident across the street?"

Billy looks up from the floor. "You mean the murder?" Like mother, like son.

"Yeah, I mean the murder." "Nah, I ain't seen nothing."

"Well, that's too bad because your mom saw something."

"She ain't seen nothing, man. She Looney Toons. Ain'tcha, Mah?"

"Well, I don't give a damn what she is. I'm running her in and I just might run you in also. Is that marijuana I smell?" The man-child is silent.

"Okay," Miss Murphy says. "I wasn't sitting in my recliner."

"Mah?! What'cha doing talking to the cops?"

"Shut up, Billy! I know what I'm doing. The truth is I was downstairs, just outside my front door. Trying to sell some old prescription Tylenol 3's to some passing junkies when I turn and see this priest with jet-black hair and a large black mole just below his left eye coming my way. From a distance, it almost looked like one of those tattooed tears you see gang-bangers wearing, but it was a mole. I was so ashamed that when I saw him, I turned and buried my head in the doorway until he had passed."

I look up from my notepad. "You sure he had a mole under his left eye?"

Miss Murphy nods. "Yes, I'm sure of it."

"Thank you. That's all I needed to know."

I show myself out. Halfway down the stairwell, I hear the mother and son yelling at one another. I have half a mind to go back and teach Billy a lesson about how to speak to his mother, but then again, who am I to dole out parenting advice? What can I possibly tell him that the street hasn't already taught him?

Outside, the sun is scorching the asphalt and it literally feels like hell on Earth. Crowds of people rush by, ducking in and out of various storefronts with bags wrapped around their hands. I open my notepad and stare down at the underlined words *mole under left eye*. I bite my bottom lip, tasting the iron in the blood as it courses over my tongue. I once knew a man with a mole under his left eye named Sanchez. He was one of my brothers in the Corps, but unlike Father Pantone there was no love lost between us.

I hail a taxi. When it pulls to the curb, I hop in and say to the driver "North Avenue and Division" and then sit back and wait for the ride to end.

CHAPTER 10

Father Cicero Sanchez heads a monolith of a church in Wicker Park called Saint Peter of Alcantara. It's a large stone cathedral with ruby, sapphire and emerald stained glass windows, each depicting one of the twelve disciples of Jesus. Far up, gargoyles look down on the trendy neighborhood as the last remnants of a blue collar culture fade into the background while the new residential millennials walk and bike these once rough streets. I enter the gothic building. The empty pews, numbering a hundred or more, extend from the back of the church all the way to the altar where a small choir of boys are singing. I turn to my left and make my way over to the three confessionals lined against a wall. They're wooden boxes with angular roofs and crosses engraved into the doors. The middle confessional has its green light on, which means that it's open to see the priest. I step into it and close the door. The small space smells like olive oil and gardenias.

The sliding door to a small mesh screen is pulled back and a voice asks from the darkness. "When was your last confession?"

I smile. It's Sanchez.

"To tell you the truth, I've never confessed. Then again, I never raped a child."

The light from the other side of the screen disappears as Sanchez brings his face up to the mesh.

"Calhoun?" he whispers.

"Yeah it's me, Cicero."

"Outside," he commands.

I stand and leave the confessional while the sounds of the young choirboys' heavenly voices fill the enormous space of the church.

Outside, the traffic noise drowns out the escape of the boys' voices from the church. I stand just beyond the building's doors with my arms folded over my chest. Down below, just beyond the concrete stairs, two pigeons are perched on the sidewalk near the curb, pecking at one another over a piece of stale bread.

The doors to the church fly open and Sanchez storms out. His face is grim, almost like stucco, rough and hard. His bushy eyebrows are furrowed into a unibrow and just below his left eye is the black mole that accents his face.

"Where do you get off coming into my church, making such a wild accusation?" he asks.

"Is that what they are now, Cicero? Accusations?"

"That was another life. I left all that back in Iraq. I've repented and the Lord has forgiven me for my sins."

"Maybe so, but that doesn't erase the fact that it happened."

"Neither does your father killing your partner, but I'm sure God has forgiven him as well."

I step forward into Sanchez's face. My nostrils flare and we lock eyes. "You want to go, Cicero? Is that what you want?"

Sanchez smiles and says, "A few years ago, I would have been all over you, Frank. Showing you a few things about respect..." he takes a few steps back with his arms open and hands up in the air. "...but now I leave it to the Lord to fight my battles."

I stare at Sanchez through squinted eyes. I want to kick his ass so bad, I can taste it. But I have to play it cool, especially if I'm going to get any information out of him.

"I don't know if you've heard, but rumor has it that you were the last person to see Father Pantone alive."

Sanchez turns and looks down at the quarreling pigeons. He puts his hand under his dark robe and pulls out a pack of cigarettes. He pats the bottom of the pack against his palm and knocks out a cig through a tear in the package's corner. He lights the short menthol, exhales a fume of smoke and says, "Is that a fact? And who started this rumor?"

"Doesn't matter, Cicero. I want to know if it's true?"

"Are you trying to imply that I killed Father Pantone?"

"I don't know. Did you?"

"How absurd, Frank. He was my friend, too, you know."

"Save it for your parishioners. All I want to know is if you were there or not?"

Sanchez takes another drag off his cigarette, savoring the scratch from the nicotine itch that grows in the back of his throat. "I might have been there," he says, exhaling the smoke. "But I didn't kill Father Pantone."

I nod my head. I just needed to corroborate Miss Murphy's story to make sure she hadn't pulled Sanchez out of some long forgotten memory.

"Do you mind telling me why you were at Father Pantone's office?"

Sanchez takes another drag off the cigarette and then stares down at the fighting pigeons. The white and brown one is flapping its wings in a rapid succession.

"I can't."

"Why not?"

"Because my vows prevent me from doing so."

"That didn't stop you back in Iraq."

"As I told you, God has forgiven me. Even if I wanted to, I couldn't tell you."

I get the picture. Whatever Father Pantone told Sanchez is privileged information between priests.

"Did he have you come in for a confession?" I stare at the quarreling birds. The black and grey pigeon keeps trying to peck away crumbs from the stale bread as the other bird tries to fight him off with his aggressive wing flaps.

"I can't discuss why Father Pantone and I met."

"Come on, Cicero. If he was really your friend as you say he was, I'd think you'd want to help find his killer."

"Trust me, Frank, I want his killer caught and I pray to God that he is caught. But I also pray that God will have mercy on the killer's soul."

"What?!"

"You have bloodlust in your eyes, Frank. I can see it. I hope God helps you through these troubling times. I know it can be difficult—"

I push Sanchez up against the stone wall of the building. "All I want to know is what did Father Pantone tell you?"

"I can't tell you, Frank. Now you can beat me if you like, but you'll only be doing more harm to yourself."

I hate to admit it but he's right. I release my grip from around his robe as the two pigeons continue their feverish pecking dance and more pigeons arrive atop the church's roof, waiting for a chance to take a peck at the lone, crusty bread.

"Thanks, Cicero," I step away without even a handshake or a meeting of the eyes.

I make my way down the stairs to the car-lined street, then walk a block over to the Milwaukee and Division Blue Line subway station. Sanchez is a dead end. I need to think. I descend the subway stairs leaving the sunlight at my back. With every step, I draw closer to the darkness until I disappear into the void that is the transit terminal.

CHAPTER 11

etective Kawowski watches the hooker in her short neon pink mini-skirt and matching halter-top stride pass his Caprice and cross the intersection of Sheridan and Wilson where he and his partner sit at the corner waiting for the light to change.

At the adjacent corner sits Saint Helen's Church, which becomes a shelter for the homeless at night for those that cling to the four corners of the intersection. The building is a brown-brick fortress with hardwood floors and oak doors. It's the church that Father Pantone has presided over for the last three years.

"How sad is it that Father Pantone was killed less than three blocks down the street from his own church?" Kawowski asks as Detective Lopez pulls the car into park.

"You think she's really in there?" Lopez asks. "You think that kid of hers was telling us the truth?"

Kawowski pops a piece of sugar free spearmint-flavored gum into his mouth. "If not, then we know where to find them both."

They get out of the car and then cross the street. The smell of battered chicken from El Polo Loco on the Southern corner fills the air. There's a handful of Black, White and Latino men standing and sitting on plastic milk crates near the entrance to Saint Helen's. Some of the men pass a brown bag amongst themselves, and even though they realize that Lopez and Kawowski are cops, no one tries to conceal the spirited libation. Kawowski taps Lopez on the shoulder. "Keep it moving,

David," he whispers. "Let the beat cops handle 'em."

Inside Saint Helen's, a large crucifix looms over the altar. The ceiling rises far up into the rafters where the support beams gradually disappear amongst the shadows. The pews, wooden and lacquered brown, are filled with scattered bodies as people bend down on kneelers to say prayers.

"I'll take the east, you take the west," Lopez points, handing Kawowski a three-by-five-inch photograph of Lillian Murphy. The two detectives move down the aisles doing their best to check the faces of the bowing parishioners against the picture they now possess. Every now and then, Kawowski looks across the room and sees Lopez moving in between the pews, arousing the parishioners from their thoughts, just so he can get a good look at their faces. After rounding the church, Lillian Murphy is nowhere to be found and the two detectives meet up near the altar.

"I knew that little fuck was lying," Lopez says.

"Ah," Kawowski slaps his partner across the chest and points up at the crucifix.

"Oh yeah. Sorry Lord, please forgive me." Lopez makes the sign of the cross over his body.

"It doesn't matter. We'll just go back to the apartment and wait for her there."

The two detectives stroll back down the center aisle towards the door. Lopez taps Kawowski on the shoulder. He nods in the direction of the confessionals, "You check those?"

"What do you mean, did I check them? We can't check those."

"Maybe. But we can at least knock on 'em, can't we?"

"Wait, you can't"

Kawowski attempts to stop Lopez, but he's too late as Lopez knocks on the door to one of the confessionals where the overhead light isn't green.

"Don't you see I'm using this?" a fierce female voice jumps out of the booth as if the sound alone could claw out Lopez's eyes.

He knocks again, standing to the side as the door swings open. In the confessional doorway stands Lillian Murphy wearing a canary yellow dress with a large yellow hat atop her head.

"Didn't I say I was using this?" she says to Kawowski, who is standing in her line of sight. She hasn't yet seen Lopez.

"Miss Murphy?" Lopez asks, leaning against the confessional all cool and calm.

"Yeah, who wants to know?"

"Detectives Lopez and Kawowski that's who."

Miss Murphy looks at their badges without even batting an eye. "Yeah, so what?"

"We want to ask you some questions about the incident that took place across the street from your apartment."

"You mean the murder?"

"Yes ma'am," Kawowski says. "The murder."

"I've already told the other detective all I know."

"The other detective?" Kawowski asks.

"Yeah, name's ummm... Corn... Calius..."

"Calhoun?" Lopez interjects.

"Yeah, that's his name. Calhoun."

Lopez looks at Kawowski. They both nod their heads and then turn to walk back down the aisle.

"I guess it's time we see for ourselves if the stories about Area Four are true," Lopez says.

"Be careful what you wish for, partner."

CHAPTER 12

After the Blue Line train rolls out of the subway tunnel near Clinton Station, I check my cell and find two voicemail messages. I have to stick my index finger in my left ear to drown out the noise of the train rolling over the steel tracks.

The first message is from Buddy Heim. He's got a small lead on the key, but nothing solid. The second message is from Captain Haggerty ordering me to come down to the station house immediately.

I close the phone. *What could the captain want with me? I haven't missed a day of therapy, so why would he need me to come in?* I put the phone in my pocket and decide to call Captain Haggerty once I'm home.

As I approach the wire fence to my home, I see Jamal and Janai playing with their toys on the wooden porch. Rays of sunshine splinter through cracks in the tree's leaves and fall upon their faces.

Jamal is the color of mahogany with a stout body. His hair is cut low into a fade with waves running across his head. His eyes are small and bright and his face is round like a melon. At ten years old, his hands are large and meaty like dough, yet rough like cooked clay. He wears a red headband, a pair of red and white Chicago Bulls basketball shorts and a white Nike t-shirt.

Janai is much lighter than her brother with a deep amber complexion like tree sap. She has short microbraids that extend to her ears. Her eyes are the shape of small almonds with slick curly eyelashes that she bats to hide her hazel- colored eyes. She stands up in her pink sundress and says, "Hello, Mister Calhoun. Pretty day, isn't it?"

I have to smile. At seven years old, this little girl has an old soul.

"Yes, it is, Janai. It's a very nice day."

"Hey Mister Calhoun," Jamal says without taking his eyes off the Transformer in his hands.

"Hey, Jamal, how are you?"

"Good," says the boy, flipping the toy over with his fingers working aggressively to turn the robot into a car.

"That's good," I say, climbing the stairs.

"Mister Calhoun, can I read your palm?" Janai asks, batting her eyelids.

"Sure." I have an affinity for the little girl. I reach out my hand to her.

"Your hand is so ashy and old-looking," she says, turning it over so that my palm faces upwards. She drops her small index finger into my large hand and runs her thin, pink nail along the jagged, crosshatched lines. "Your hands are rough. This line right here..." she begins, etching her nail from my index finger to the base of my hand. "...is your lifeline. You've got a very long time to live."

"Really?" I chuckle.

"Wait, what's this?" Her finger stops in the middle of my palm where a patch of skin bulges.

I look down at the bulge, almost mesmerized by the memory it evokes. I was six, standing in the bathroom in my briefs next to my father. He was a tall, muscular man, but skinny in his frame. I watched as he drew the hand razor across his prickly face, essentially changing from a man into Super Cop right before my very own eyes. After my father finished shaving, he left the razor on the edge of the porcelain sink and I picked it up and ran it across the bare skin of my hand.

At first, I didn't feel the cut nor the pain that followed until I saw droplets of blood cover the white-and-black checkered tile floor. It was only then that I cried out for my father, who swept me up into his arms and bandaged my hand.

"Mister Calhoun?" Janai asks, snapping me back into the present.

"What's this on your hand?"

"It's just a scar from when I was a boy," I say with a smile, trying to reassure the child of its innocence.

"Does it hurt?"

"Janai, quit asking so many questions and leave Mister Calhoun alone," Jamal says, finally transforming the robot into a car.

"It's all right," I say, reassuring them both. "No, it doesn't hurt, Janai. Not anymore."

I step past the children and enter the outer foyer and then into my apartment where I rest my back against the large wooden door and trace my finger over the scar.

My father, the Super Cop.

I shake my head, ridding myself of such notions. I have to stay focused. Father Pantone's murderer is out there somewhere and that is all that matters.

I exhale and whisper to myself the motto that Father Pantone taught us young chaplains during the war in order to keep ourselves motivated.

"Only the holy remain," he would say. I push myself up off the door, open my cell and call Captain Haggerty.

Area Four headquarters is located at Harrison and Kedzie on the West Side of the city. It's a brown rectangular monstrosity with dark paneled windows which give the impression that the building is made up of only two floors, but there are actually four. The other two floors of the complex are built underground to house the jail and holding cells. Behind the precinct sits the Area Four courthouse, making the complex a one-stop shop for booking and processing criminals.

When I step through the doors of the Detectives Division, all eyes fall upon me. I haven't been in the office in almost a year, and of all days, it's a bit surprising to find that the six-men squad that make up the division are all in attendance.

I'd worn all black as if I'd just returned from a funeral. I once read that Steve Jobs decided to wear all black because he didn't have time to think about what to wear when there were so many other pressing matters in the world. It was exactly how I felt in regards to Father Pantone's murder.

"Hey Frank, how ya doing?" Fred Lions asks. He's a fifteen-year veteran with salt-and-pepper colored hair and a stomach the size of a medieval stewpot. Other than myself, he's the only other black detective in the whole division.

"Doing good, Fred, how about you?"

"I hear you stepped on some toes," he nods his head back towards Captain Haggerty's office. "Best be on yours."

"Thanks for the heads up, Fred."

I walk across the room, keeping my sight focused on the captain's door. It's not that I don't like the other detectives, but I knew that if I gave them the chance, they'd all be trying to see how I was doing. Meaning that they really wanted to know if the trauma of my father being incarcerated made me a liability as a cop, and more importantly, as a potential partner. When I open the door to the captain's office, I'm surprised to find Kawowski and Lopez seated in front of his desk. I thought I might find Cicero Sanchez filing a complaint, but not the two detectives.

"Detective Calhoun, come in," Captain Haggerty addresses me from behind his desk. He's a broad man with large square shoulders and a neck the size of a pot roast. His hair is the color of sand, which matches the handlebar mustache on his thick face. He holds the stub of an unlit cigar in between his off- purple lips before removing the stub and pointing to Kawowski and Lopez with the cigar jutting from his meaty fingers. "These detectives say you've been working their case. Now I told them that that couldn't be because Detective Calhoun is on psychiatric leave. But then they tell me about this victim, a Father Pantone, and how you two are connected."

I don't know what to say. The only thing I can think of is that they've gotten to Lillian Murphy.

"I wasn't investigating, Captain, I heard there was a witness and figured no one knew about it, so I thought I'd save these two detectives some time and check out the story and see if it was true."

Lopez leans forward in his seat. "And what did you find?"

"Nothing. But I'm sure you two already know that."

I'm gambling that Lillian Murphy didn't confess twice to selling a controlled substance, especially to a boy scout like Lopez. The guy looks as if he'd run you in just for looking at him wrong, which means they haven't found Sanchez yet.

"I'm going to say this once and only once," Captain Haggerty says. "You stay out of their hair. If I find out you've been dabbling in their investigation, I'm going to have your badge. Is that understood, Detective?"

"Yes, sir," I say, giving the room a defeated expression.

"Well, I guess it's settled then," Kawowski says, rising from his seat. He shakes Captain Haggerty's hand and then goes for the door. Lopez follows, smiling.

As I turn to leave, Captain Haggerty calls me back into his office. I can hear Lopez say, "Ohhhh, looks like someone's in trouble."

I close the door to the office and turn back around to face Captain Haggerty.

"Frank, I want you to know that I'm here for you on this whole Pantone thing just like I was there for you when your father went down."

"I know, Captain."

"So who's this Father Pantone anyway?"

"He's just an old friend from my time in the Marines."

"Detective Lopez says you found the body."

"I can't help but be at the wrong places at the right times, I guess."

"Frank, Reynolds' death wasn't your fault. There was no way you could have known you'd be the one to find his body."

"I guess you're right, Captain. I'm just trying to work through it all, you know?"

"You've been seeing the therapist, right?"

"Yeah, I've been seeing her. I'm okay."

"All right. If you need anything, you let me know."

"I will. Thanks, Captain."

After exiting the captain's office, I slowly walk past the line of empty desks as if going through a gauntlet. I go over to one of three black file cabinets against a wall and remove a large green binder from the top drawer. I scoop up a black sharpie and a pen off of Lions' desk and take a stack of pre-punched paper from the copy machine down the hall.

Outside, the air feels thin and the humidity has risen at least ten degrees since I entered the building. For the first time, I regret wearing all black. I cross the street to the Kedzie Blue Line station and take the train two stops east to the medical center. To the north of the station is the Malcolm X Community College, with its black façade and dark windows shining bold against the beautiful sun. To the south is the newly built Strogger Hospital, though everyone still calls it "the County" along with Rush Presbyterian Hospital and the newly built Center for Disease Control.

In between, sits Sal's hotdog stand on Harrison and Ogden. It's a small place where first year med-students and interns grab food on the go while busying themselves with their studies. But since the new hospital is built two blocks behind the old gothic medical building that's still erected on Harrison, Sal's is pretty much empty when I enter it.

I order two Chicago dogs with all the fixings and take a table in the back. After eating the dogs, I pull out all the materials I took from the office and spread them out across the square table. I put the paper in the binder and write FATHER ANTON PANTONE across the top of the page with the black sharpie.

I flip open my handheld notepad and transcribed everything I know about the case into bullet points inside the binder. When I'm finished, the time reads 1:30 p.m. meaning lunchtime is over.

I close the binder and leave Sal's, heading west down Harrison towards the medical examiner's office.

CHAPTER 13

The Cook County medical examiner's building is a wide grey slab of concrete that very much resembles the Area Four building with two floors exposed to the street while the other two floors are underground.

I enter the building, flash the guard on duty my dad's old badge before signing in and walking down an off-white hall to the elevators. I place the binder under my arm while I wait for the elevator. I can't help but hum the tune of "Sweet Home Chicago" as the elevator opens and I press the button marked L2. The doors close and the car descends.

Two stories below, the elevator doors open to the smell of antiseptics and formaldehyde. There's a guard sitting at a desk reading today's edition of the *Sun-Times* newspaper. He looks up when he sees me coming down the hall, nods after seeing my badge and then returns to his paper.

The hall that leads from the elevators to the examination rooms is long and dim as if the environment of the place needed to match the occupants in the slide out freezers. I enter the third room on my right. It smells more like vinegar and bleach than it does anything else. In the center of the room is a long stainless steel table with holes at the head and foot for draining blood. Next to the table are two trays on wheels with various size scalpels, scissors and saws and other tools necessary for performing an autopsy on the human body.

"Mags, you in here?" I call out.

"Give me a sec," her soft voice calls back from somewhere within the darkness of the sterile room.

I walk around the room. The walls are covered with diagrams of the human body. There are two light boxes for x-rays, a plethora of beakers, and vials of blood on a counter.

"Don't touch anything," she calls out to me, her voice much closer than it had been before.

A few seconds later, Maggie McCallon steps out of the darkness and asks, "What's up?" She's three-foot-five with long light brown hair, brown eyes and small brown freckles that adorn her oval face. Her nose is small and her lips are pink and thin. She's wearing a mini white lab coat and holding a can of Pepsi in one hand.

"How's it going, Mags?"

"Just death and more death. What brings you down to the tombs?"

"I need some information on an autopsy."

"You're back on the streets?"

"Not quite."

"Oh," she raises the can of Pepsi to her lips and downs the last of the soda. "So is this some case you just can't let go? I've read there's at least one case that every detective carries with them."

"Nah, nothing like that, Mags. This one's personal."

Mags crushes the can in her small hands. "This isn't about your father is it?"

"No, it's not about him. I just need some info on a victim is all."

Mags walks over to a steel garbage can, which is about the same height as her. She steps on the metal pedal that flips the lid up and drops the aluminum into the cylinder. "You know I can't do that, Frank. It goes against policy."

"Yeah, I know that, Mags. That's why I'm asking for it off the record."

"You're on leave, Frank—maybe you should really consider what that means."

"I appreciate the concern, but this man was like a second father to me. I just want to help capture his murderer. All I'm asking for is a photocopy of the autopsy report. I promise no one will ever know you gave it to me." I stare down into her brown eyes with a puppy dog expression on my face. "Please, Mags? Just a little help."

She exhales and rolls her eyes. "What did you say his name was?"

"Pantone. Anton Pantone."

Mags turns and steps back into the darkness of the examination room. The sound of her pudgy fingers typing in Father Pantone's name on a keyboard resonates throughout the room. She returns a minute later with a sheet of paper. "I don't think you'll need the whole report. The cause of death came from a single shot through the heart. Forensics is still doing ballistics on the bullet, but my guess is that it came from a high powered assault rifle."

I take the piece of paper, fold it in two, and place it inside the binder. "Thanks, Mags, I owe you one."

"Yeah, just remember not to mention it."

"You got it." I smile and then turn to leave.

While waiting for the elevator to take me topside, I check

my watch. It's already 3:00 p.m. My appointment with the department psych is at four. I'll have to look over the report that Mags has given me after seeing the Doc. But one thing is clear: if Mags is right about the weapon being a rifle, then I'm looking at Father Pantone's murder from the wrong angle.

CHAPTER 14

octor Sydney Staples' office is on the outskirts of downtown, near Clinton and Harrison right across from the Greyhound bus station and a condominium complex. The walls inside the office are pastel green. It's supposed to make patients feel calm, but it isn't working. At least, not in my case.

Doctor Staples is sitting in a beige armchair with her slender legs crossed. She has her dark hair pulled up into a makeshift bun and her dark-rimmed glasses sit on the edge of her nose.

"Good afternoon, Detective Calhoun," she says.

"I told you, you can call me Frank."

"Okay. How is everything, Frank?"

"I'm okay." I look around the room while shifting my body in the other armchair. On a wall behind the Doc hang two degrees in gold frames, a Masters and a Doctorate in Psychology. On another wall hangs a painting of Van Gogh's *Starry Night*.

"You sure?" she asks.

"Yeah, yeah I'm good. Look, Doc, would you mind if we rescheduled this session?"

The Doc leans forward in her seat. "And why would you want to do that?"

"I've just got a lot on my mind right now, you know?"

"Well, that's why you're here, so you can talk things out instead of holding it all inside that head of yours."

"I'd rather not if I can avoid it. How about I just see you next week?" I begin to stand up from my seat.

"Detective Calhoun, part of the deal is that in order for you to return to service, you must attend all sessions." I drop back into my seat with my shoulders slouched down. "This is the best place for you, Frank."

"If you say so," I pout.

"Let's begin our session by talking about the recent murder of your friend, Father Pantone."

I look up from the floor. My mouth is slightly ajar. "How'd you know about that?"

Doctor Staples smiles. "Captain Haggerty gave me a call. Wanted to know if you'd actually show up."

"It figures."

"So who was this Father Pantone?"

"Look, Doc, I don't really want to talk about it." Outside, the roar of a Greyhound bus penetrates through the windows of the office.

"Okay, you don't have to talk about it, Frank. How about we move on? Have you gone to visit your father yet?"

I look away and remain silent. Doctor Staples drops her leg from over her knee and sits forward in her chair. Behind the glasses, her eyes are shaped like cat's eyes, mysterious and seductive.

"The only way you're going to get better and beat this thing is if you start to face the truth of the matter, Frank."

"Well that's easier said than done, Doc. It isn't *your* father. You don't have to live with the memory of arresting him for murder."

"And how does that make you feel?"

I throw my hands in the air and look her in the eyes. "How do you think it makes me feel? I'm angry, hurt, disappointed. I could go on for days explaining how I feel, but it wouldn't matter. It's not going to change a damn thing."

"Do you feel the same way about your friend Father Pantone?"

I stare at Doctor Staples, without blinking. "Don't play me, Doc. I'm not some psych ward patient. I told you I don't want to talk about it. Matter-of-fact, I'm done talking for the day."

"If that's the way you feel about it, Frank," Doctor Staples finally says as she begins writing down notes on a legal pad. The room is silent.

Five minutes.

Ten minutes.

Twenty minutes of silence.

For the next half hour, I sit there biting my nails while trying to read Doctor Staples. She might be a psychologist, but I decided a long time ago that if I'm going to get over what my father has done, I'm going to do it on my own. At five o'clock, I rise from my seat.

"Well I guess I'll be seeing you, Doc."

"Yes, you will, Frank. Next week, same time. And I hope that you'll be prepared to speak more openly."

"Yeah, maybe," I say shutting the office door behind me.

CHAPTER 15

I stand outside Doctor Staples' office trying to hail a cab with my version of the murder book under my arm. One of the downfalls of having post traumatic stress syndrome is losing the right to drive. Since a blackout can occur every now and then, I'm deemed unfit to operate any type of motor vehicle. But I don't blame Doctor Staples because her diagnosis is accurate. Besides, I don't want another person's death on my conscience.

After about five minutes, a taxi pulls to the curb. I give the driver my address and then sit back with the makeshift murder book on my lap. It's all I've been able to think about since I stepped foot into Doctor Staples' office.

I run my fingers along the edges of the binder, eager to open it, but I know I need to be sitting down in a quiet place in order to go over every detail, especially the autopsy report.

At the time that I discovered Father Pantone's body, I didn't give any real thought about how he was killed. I just assumed it had been up close and personal, but it looks like I was wrong. The taxi jumps on the 290 Expressway and heads west. The evening is still warm and the sun won't set for another two hours. I rest my head back on the seat and close my eyes as the taxi cruises along with the afternoon traffic taking me home. When the taxi finally pulls in front of my house, the wooden porch is clear of Jamal and Janai. I pay the driver and climb the seven steps to enter my home. I flip on a light in the main hall while passing through the living room into the dining room.

Placing the murder book down on the dark cherry colored dining room table, I go into the kitchen to grab a bottle of Goose Island root beer from the fridge.

I untwist the cap while walking back into the dining room. Sitting down at the table with bottle in hand, I open the murder book to its first page. Father Pantone's name stares up at me as if it were a specter, haunting and unrelenting, reminding me not only that he was dead, but that I allowed his killer to escape.

I take a swig of the dark liquid. It's smooth as it coats my throat. The pure sugar cane gives me a rush as I write down every detail about the case, as I know it so far. When I get to the autopsy, I read it aloud to commit every line to memory.

"Victim was killed by a bullet measuring .224 inches in diameter, possibly from a rifle. The entry point was near the heart. It created a wound that tore through the victim's chest and exited out of his back."

I take another swig from the bottle and then sit back with my hands on top of my head. I try to visualize Father Pantone's office, attempting to see the man before he's killed.

I'm missing something.

I replay the scene in my mind of how I discovered Father Pantone's body, but nothing seems out of place. I flip the murder book back to page one and re-read every note I've jotted down. I stop at the point at which I begin to question Lillian Murphy. I stand up and pull my chair out from under the table, turn it sideways, imagining it to be the armchair in Miss Murphy's apartment. I then lean back in the chair as though I'm reclining and turn my head to the right, like I'm sitting at the window inside the apartment.

I close my eyes and do my best to visualize the Murphy living room and the scene as it had been. I see the windows of Father Pantone's office, the closed shades and then it hits me. When I first found Father Pantone a window was open in the office. I remember the bloodied leaflets on the desk, floating down to the floor like red snowflakes.

I sit up in my seat. If Father Pantone was indeed killed from a distance, then why didn't the killer shoot right through the glass? Instead, the shades were drawn and the window open, which allowed for a clear line of sight right to his heart.

Could Father Pantone have raised the window himself? Probably, but why would he do that when the office had central air? Also, he would've realized within seconds that the breeze coming off the lake would blow the documents off his desk.

I pick up the root beer and knock it back. The sweet elixir makes me feel jumpy. I sit the bottle down, stand, and rub my hands together as I pace back and forth from the dining room to the living room and vice versa.

If the shooter had a clear sight of Father Pantone, then it meant one of two things: someone picked the mark for the shooter, meaning I should actually be looking for two people. Or, the masked man from the closet was the lone shooter as well as someone Father Pantone knew personally, based on the fact that the killer had to be the one to open the window.

CHAPTER 16

Rays of sunshine break through the dreary clouds as the Red Line train pulls out of the subway tunnel. The car smells like malt liquor and strong piss. I sit there, taking it all in, allowing the stench of the car to awaken every one of my senses.

I've been up the whole night and most of the early morning playing out the scenario of how Father Pantone might have been killed. Without the aide of ballistics, I'm building the make of the gun from an estimated guess. The best I can do now is return to the scene of the crime and try to discover the trajectory of where the shot was taken.

I prop my legs up on an open seat. I've managed to throw on some worn gym shoes with brown mud caked into the heels, a pair of blue jeans and an old 1985 Chicago Bears tee shirt along with a light jacket to conceal the holstered revolver strapped to my hip. On the opposite end of the car is a homeless woman sleeping under the weight of what looks to be a hundred black garbage bags.

When the train finally arrives at the Wilson station, I take the stairs down to street level. The avenue is bustling with late morning traffic cutting between the intersections of Wilson and Broadway. A man wearing a blue smock stands on Broadway in the middle of the street, between the white dividing lines, selling newspapers.

I look up at the sky. It's light grey as if it might rain.

I walk half a block north on the western side of Broadway to where Father Pantone's office is located. I cross the street over to a commercial complex consisting of clothing and shoes stores and small curio shops. Located atop these businesses is a line of two bedroom apartments, one of which Lillian Murphy currently occupies. I survey the building, turning from it to look across the street to where Father Pantone's office is located and then back again.

This has to be the building where the shooter took the shot. I start up Broadway heading south and then I make a left onto Wilson and follow it half a block down before finally turning into an alley.

The smell of a dead rat's rotting carcass stifles the morning air. There are six green dumpsters filled with trash. A yellow poster with an evil black rat hangs on a wooden phone pole with the words 'RODENT INSPECTION' plastered over the top of it in red letters.

Behind the commercial complex, I find that all the shops have steel reinforced doors. Walking along the back wall of the building, I look for anything that seems out of the ordinary, which can be difficult seeing as how extraordinary things are always found in Chicago's alleyways.

I walk a straight line until I come to a black metal-mesh fence that leads up a flight of grey wooden stairs to the apartments overhead. Stretched along the top of the fence is enough barbed wire to skin a man alive.

I push at the fence's entrance. It's locked. I bend down to

examine the bolt. There's no sign of forced entry and the lock hasn't been picked because the old paint around the keyhole hasn't been chipped away. If the shooter didn't break in to get to the roof, there had to be another way.

I double back the way I came until I'm standing in front of the Murphy residence. Looking across the street to the building where Father Pantone's office is, I see Kawowski and Lopez getting into their department-issued Chevy Caprice. I quickly do an about-face so that I'm facing the large windows of the clothing store, watching the detectives' reflections in the glass as they drive off heading south on Broadway.

Once Kawowski and Lopez are gone, I turn and ring the doorbell to the Murphy apartment. Lillian Murphy's voice comes in over the intercom as I announce myself and wait for the door to be buzzed. I climb the stairs to the apartment. As I draw near the door, I find it ajar as the scent of green-apple air freshener lingers in the hall.

"Miss Murphy?" I gently knock on the door.

"In here, Detective," I hear her call out from somewhere in the apartment. I enter and the scent of green apple fills the room even more. Nothing has changed in the two days since I previously visited. I move through the living room and into the small dining area/kitchen. There I find Lillian Murphy standing near her recliner wearing emerald green lingerie with a matching silky green open housecoat. Her hair is done up with brown bangs falling down in front of her face, concealing her radiant grayish-green irises. She has her bottom lip tucked in between her teeth, giving the impression of a hungry lioness. "Sorry," I say diverting my eyes. "I didn't mean to walk in on you like this."

"It's okay, Detective Calhoun. Your gaze is very much welcomed."

"Could you please cover yourself up, ma'am?" I ask trying to keep my eyes diverted.

Her small perky nipples push forward from beneath the thin green cloth. "If that's the way you want it," she says, closing the housecoat around her small frame.

"Thank you, ma'am."

"Don't thank me. This is what *you* wanted," she says as if I asked for the private peepshow in the first place.

Miss Murphy pulls out a pack of cigarettes from a pocket on the housecoat. She beats one out of the bottom of the pack and lights up. "How can I help you, Detective? I've already told you everything I know."

I nod my head in agreement. "On the day of the incident across the street—"

"You mean the murder?"

"Yes, the murder. Did anything out of the ordinary happen on that day?"

"This is Uptown, Detective. A lot of out-of-the-ordinary shit happens around here." The woman changes from an Emerald Princess to the Wicked Witch of the West.

"Yeah, I know, Miss Murphy, but I need you to think about this really hard."

The small woman takes a long drag on her cigarette as though the inhaling of the smoke inflates her body. "Come to think of it, there was something about a satellite dish or something."

"What do you mean by satellite dish?"

"Billy said some repair man came by that day to fix some satellite on the roof."

I look around the room, spot the floor model TV decorated with a menagerie of glass turtles and then turn back to Miss Murphy. "But you don't have satellite, do you?"

"Exactly," she points the cigarette in my direction. "But Billy said it was for the store downstairs, so I let it go."

I nod my head as though I understand Lillian Murphy's thinking even before the words leave her mouth.

"Can you show me how the repair man got up to the satellite dish?"

"Sure, right this way."

She leads me through the small kitchen and out the back door and into an enclosed back porch. She flicks on a light switch near the side of the door and the iridescent bulb turns the dark room into a storage space with a door that I conclude leads out to the flight of stairs I saw earlier from the back of the building.

A pile of boxes, mostly Christmas decorations and gaming systems from times past, are stacked up vertically near the side of the enclosed porch door. Adjacent to these boxes is a ladder that leads up to the roof.

"That damn boy! How many times do I have to tell him this is a fire hazard?" She moves towards the boxes.

"Hold up, Miss Murphy." I extend my arm to hold her back. "Where are those boxes normally?"

"They're usually stacked against that ladder over there, but since the repair man was here Billy had to move them."

"I'm going to have to ask that you step back into the apartment and not come into this back area until it's cleared."

"What do you mean not to come through it? Billy has to take out the trash."

"Listen, Miss Murphy," I turn to look down at the woman. "Your back porch is now off limits. It may contain crucial evidence that could help in this investigation."

We move back into the kitchen and then into the living room.

"By the way, where's your son?"

"He went to the store but he'll be back soon."

"Okay," I say turning from the woman as I pull out my cell. I'm about to call Captain Haggerty and give him the lowdown as well as request a forensics team. I move over to the window to try and get some type of privacy in the small room. As the phone rings, I pull down a few window shades with my index finger and peer out the window as I wait for Captain Haggerty to answer.

Below, the street is now bustling with traffic and people. I stare across the way to Father Pantone's office. The building looks very old in the shadow of the clouds. Its terracotta facade looks to be crumbling as the wooden panes of the windows are brittle and cracked like a sea-battered ferry. I wonder when was it built and what was housed in it before it became a commercial space. I imagine it being a dance hall, an insurance office or maybe even a department store.

The clouds overhead break and the sun shines down, turning the brown building into a gothic landmark with ancient gargoyles cemented into the face of the edifice. I hear Captain Haggerty say hello, but I've already dropped the phone as I look up to the rooftop of the brown building and see a glint of sunlight bounce off a lens as a red beam cascades down on the window.

I stare at the shining beam as an image fabricates in my mind:

Rifle. Beam. Scope.

CHAPTER 17

"**D**own! Down!" I yell dropping to the floor.

"What?" Lillian Murphy turns to look at me, annoyed more than anything.

"Down!" I scream, grabbing her hand and pulling her to the floor.

"Detective Calhoun!"

"I don't have time to explain. Just stay on the floor and don't move."

I crawl on my elbows across the green-carpeted floor and into the kitchen. I take a set of keys off a wooden plaque near the backdoor then race out the outer door of the enclosed back porch and down a flight of rickety stairs to the security gate. I unlock it with the keys and step out into the alley. The rising heat has made the stench of the dead rat even more unbearable.

I run down the length of the alley and cross over to the south side of Wilson. Walking briskly down the street, I keep my eyes locked on the roof of the brown building. When I reach the intersection of Wilson and Broadway, I cross the street over to the structure. I walk casually so as not to bring attention to myself. When I finally enter the building of Father Pantone's office, I unzip my jacket and draw my father's service revolver from its holster and wait for the elevator to take me to the third floor.

I watch as the antique arrow over the elevator counts down the floors. It's moving as if it's counting down for a blast off. I massage the steel around the trigger with my index finger. I haven't shot a gun in almost a year. The elevator finally opens and I hit the number three on the panel as I wait for the doors to close. Once on the third floor, I take the stairs up just in case my theory of two shooters is incorrect.

The hall on the fourth floor is dark, even though it's now afternoon outside. The floor is unoccupied and under development. It smells like brand new drywall and fresh paint.

I move to the end of the hall, crack open the door and listen for the sound of someone inside but there's no one. I climb the last flight of stairs and find the door to the rooftop partially open. I move to the edge of the door and peek around it and catch a glimpse of the shooter lying on his stomach.

I duck back behind the door with the gun halfway up near my chest. I take a deep breath and then step out into the openness of the rooftop. The sun is shining down and I can feel the heat burning into my scalp. The gravel slightly crushes under my feet as I creep with one foot in front of the other.

I keep the gun extended and aimed at the shooter. I stop in mid-stride and look down at my feet. My shadow is five feet ahead of me. If I continue on, I'll lose the element of surprise. I take three more steps forward, position myself in a shooter's stance, and yell out "Police! Put your hands up where I can see them." The shooter slowly lifts his hands into the air. "Don't you fucking move!" I yell out as I slowly move towards the shooter.

The asshole places his hands on his head. "Don't shoot. I'm Officer Sato with the special investigations unit. I'm ballistics."

With the gun still trained on the asshole, I pat him down for ID and roll him over. "Show me your badge."

Sato is a medium built Japanese man with spiky black hair and a pointy nose. He uses one hand to pull the chain that has his star attached to it from up under his shirt.

"Shit. Sorry, man." I extend my hand to help pull Sato to his feet. "I thought you were a shooter trying to kill a possible witness."

"You mean the second floor apartment?" he asks, pointing across the way.

"Yeah. Forgive me, I'm sorry. I'm Detective Frank Calhoun, Area Four." I put my gun away.

"Don't worry about it," Sato says, waving me off.

"You mind if I ask you a question?" I ask.

The officer returns his badge to under his shirt. "Shoot," he says.

"Why the roof and not the third floor where the murder occurred?"

Sato smiles. "Distance," he says. "I need to be able to measure the distance between the buildings in order to get an exact trajectory of where the shooter might have been located." I look down at the device I thought had been a rifle and instead find a laser pointer, a single lens telescope and a black box which looks more like a remote control for a kid's race-car.

"How can you figure out distance with these things?"

"Easily," Sato says. "There's an EDM on the third floor." I look confused. "Sorry, I'm talking technical. An EDM is an electronic distance meter. We use it to measure distance between two objects. In this case, I'm using a robotic EDM. From up here, I use the pointer to direct the robot and it locks on to the laser and takes a picture of the object, such as the building across the street. The data is then stored and later compiled into a program that gives us a 3-D image of the crime scene and a possible idea of where the shooter was positioned when he took the shot."

I nod my head, thinking I've got a good idea of where the shooter was located. I move to the edge of the building and look out over the street. Off in the horizon I can see the magnificent skyline that Chicago is known for. My nose itches from the smell of the lake water that is beginning to sweep through the neighborhood. I no longer consider it a refreshing aroma as it's become a scent that I associate with the death of Father Pantone.

Looking across the street to the Murphy apartment I think about Lillian Murphy's seductive ploy. It makes me laugh to think of her laying on the floor, waiting for me to return. She's probably frightened. I'll have to ensure her that she'll be all right and let her know that the police can protect her if she promises to be a witness. And that's when my blood suddenly runs cold as a horrible thought flashes across my mind.

"Oh my God," I say, turning away from the rooftop's edge with eyes wide and mouth agape. I can't bring myself to form any more words as I run towards the rooftop's entrance.

"Hey, where you going?" I hear Sato call after me, but I don't have time to explain.

I bound down the flight of stairs and down the desolate hall. I hit the stairs again, going as fast as my feet will allow. My heart is beating faster than I can control, but I keep moving, pushing myself down the stairs and out the doors and into the front of the building.

The sunlight blinds me at first as I throw my left hand over my eyes. My breathing is hard and sweat covers my head. The jacket and tee shirt stick to my perspiring body. I stand there on Broadway looking up and down the street, wondering which store Billy Murphy could have gone to. I didn't have time to run back to Lillian Murphy's apartment. Besides, it wasn't her that was in danger—it was Billy.

This entire time, the key witness to blowing the case open was under all our noses and now he was out at some store, unaware that his life might be in danger. The sound of tires screeching comes from the north of Broadway. I turn and see a black hearse make a U-turn in the intersection and begin making its way southbound, back up the street. I watch as the car of death passes by and then I turn to look up the street and see Billy Murphy walking with an Aldi grocery bag in his hand.

The boy has his headphones on and is rapping along to the music. This much I can tell by his hand gestures and the movement of his jaw as I try to wave him down. Then I think about the hearse and the fact that I didn't see a funeral procession following it. I reach for my gun and run towards Billy, trying to get his attention.

I see the first bullet hit the wall behind Billy's head, leaving fragments of brick to explode into the air, but the boy is so into his music that he doesn't hear the shot, nor do I, which makes me suspect that the rifle is equipped with a suppressor. I run into the street and let off a shot in the direction of the traveling hearse. People scatter as cars hit their brakes or turn in the opposite direction.

I let off another shot, which hits the back door of the hearse. I yell for the idiot kid to get his ass down, but he's still oblivious to all that is going on around him. "Down, dammit!" I yell. "Get down!"

He finally looks up and sees me trying to wave him down, but my words are too late. The next bullet from the hearse scatters his brains all across the storefront window of the World Tobacco Exchange, which more than likely sold him his first bong.

I keep running and shooting, running and shooting as the hearse increases its speed and heads southbound down Broadway.

My heart feels as though it might burst. The gun is heavy in my hand. My feet become blocks of cement and then my knees give out and I collapse to the ground. My vision begins to fade to black and then suddenly... I'm out.

CHAPTER 18

Alone in the darkness, I find myself running towards the image of a man standing at the end of a tunnel with light at his back. The figure extends his arms, ready to embrace me. I run towards this image wanting to escape the darkness around me. I gain speed, trying to break free of the darkness, trying to reach the figure ahead of me. I close my eyes and run with all of my strength, tearing through the night like a lion after its prey. But the harder I run, the further away the image of the man waiting for me at the end of the tunnel becomes.

After a while I drop to my knees and cry into my hands like a child. The tears run through the cracks in my hands like water until a puddle has formed in front of me.

I look down into the silvery liquid and see the curvature of my nose, the width of my eye sockets, the measure of my triangular chin and angular jaw line. I peer closer into the liquid as the contours of my face change. My nose becomes larger, my eyes remain the same, but my lips are larger and black like a dark cherry. I realize it isn't me—it's my old partner, Blue.

Suddenly a dark hand shoots up out of the puddle and grabs me by the throat. The touch of the skin is cold. I wrap my own hands around Blue's hand and try to pull away, but I can't.

Before I can manage to rise to my feet, I'm pulled into the puddle, drowning on my own tears.

CHAPTER 19

When I awake a few hours later, I find myself staring up at a white ceiling. The cool cotton sheets under my hands feel relaxing. It reminds me of the sheets my father used to put on my bed as a child during hot summer nights in the city. My chest is covered with a paper-thin white and blue patchwork gown, but somehow I've managed to keep on my jeans and gym shoes.

Suddenly, I remember Billy Murphy and the hearse I fired upon and I quickly bounce up from the gurney like a piece of hot toast being ejected from a toaster. I sit up on the side of the bed, rubbing the back of my neck with my right hand.

"Welcome back to the land of the living." I turn around and find Captain Haggerty sitting in a plush cushioned chair with his unlit stub of a cigar in his mouth. His eyes are cold and silver, the eyes of experience.

"How'd I get here?" I ask.

"Paramedics brought you in after you blacked out on the street."

I don't say a word. The last thing I can remember is Billy

Murphy walking with headphones on as bullets whizzed by him. "The kid?"

"Dead, Frank. Dead before he hit the ground." Captain Haggerty stands up from his seat. "And now I have the chief on my ass and a community scared shitless. So, you mind telling me what you were doing in Uptown and why you were carrying a piece?"

I look down at the white tile floor with pieces of rainbow confetti embedded into it. Captain Haggerty doesn't have to say anything further. I understand. My ass is on the line.

"I came Uptown to apologize to Lillian Murphy for the other day. You know, because of the whole Kawowski and Lopez thing." Captain Haggerty nods his head. "So as I start to apologize, I think I spot a shooter on the roof of the building across from the Murphy apartment and I decide to investigate."

"You mean Officer Sato from special investigations?"

"Yeah, that's what I learn after I go to make the collar."

"Then what happened?" Captain Haggerty folds his arms over his chest and chews on his cigar.

"That's when I realize that Miss Murphy's son might have possibly seen the shooter who killed Father Pantone. With that thought running through my mind, I hit the streets as fast as I could, searching for that boy and then—" The image of the hearse making a U-turn flashes behind my eyes lids.

"And then what, Frank?" Captain Haggerty asks, pulling me back into the present.

"And then this hearse starts barreling up the street, shooting at him right in front of me. The next thing I know I've pulled my piece and I'm returning fire."

"Frank, listen to me because what I'm about to say is going to be hard to swallow. Eyewitness accounts are saying you killed that kid."

"What?"

"They say you just started shooting and running up the street like a madman and that it's your bullet that killed him."

"Well the eyewitnesses are wrong, Captain. You know me. Why the hell would I do that? The only reason they didn't hear or see shots coming from the hearse is because the muzzle of the gun probably had a suppressor on it."

"That may be true, Frank, but until the M.E. rules otherwise, I'm going to have to put you under house arrest."

"Listen, Captain, you can't do this. There's a killer out there and I think—"

"No, that's the problem, *you* don't think! You put civilian lives in danger with your reckless actions! Jesus freaking Christ! You're not even supposed to have a goddamn gun! You're supposed to be on medical leave! You've just put this department in a whole shitload of trouble. So for now, you're going to keep your mouth shut, ride the wave and pray to God that kid was killed by a bullet other than yours! Is that understood, Calhoun?"

I lower my head in defeat. It's the second time the captain has had to see me this way and I feel awful. "Yes, sir, very clear."

"Good. Now that we have an understanding, there will be two officers outside this door ready to escort you home when you're ready."

Captain Haggerty turns and exits the room. Once the door closes, I stand up from the bed and look around the room for my tee shirt and jacket.

There's no way I killed that kid... did I? Not even in the sense that I actually fired the shot, but did my investigation into Father Pantone's murder lead to this boy's death? There was no real way of knowing, but a part of me felt as if I did.

I sigh, accepting the fact that Billy Murphy is dead, and roll back my shoulders and stick out my chest like a good marine.

As a former chaplain, I've become a man of war and a man of conflicting minds and ideals. I know that Billy Murphy's death is just one more demon that will haunt me in my dreams sooner than later.

CHAPTER 20

When the squad car pulls up in front of my home, I get a feeling of déjà vu. The last time I rode in the back of one was the night after I arrested my father. That night felt more like a dream as I remember slapping the cuffs around my father's wrists and putting him in the back of the car. Through the whole process of the arrest, I didn't allow it to affect my performance as a cop even after I was pulled from the investigation because I was "too close" to the suspect. Not even when my father screamed his innocence while being processed did I allow his actions and words to affect me because I was trained not to crack under pressure.

It wasn't until I was escorted home that night that I started to feel the effects from arresting my father for murder. My palms were sweaty, my mouth was dry and my heart was beating fast like a drummer hitting a snare. I needed air as I exited the car and it was only after looking up at the two-flat brick building that I grew up in calling home, a place where my father raised me from a boy to a man, that I felt the weight of the world on my heart. I saw my whole childhood become a ripple in time and that's when my first blackout occurred.

This time around I don't feel the weight of the world on my heart as I felt before. This time I feel nothing as I exit the car and stare up at the building where I've spent all of my life.

One of the officers gets out of the car and asks if I need any help getting up the stairs.

Do I really look that old?

I shake my head and turn to look over my shoulder. The uniformed officer is leaning on the patrol car's hood with his arms folded over his chest and a large triumphant smile on his face.

God, what I wouldn't do right now to knock that smirk off his face.

I climb the stairs and enter my apartment. I don't attempt to turn on any lights. I maneuver through the darkness making my way to my bedroom.

I struggle to slip off my shoes. Once they're off, I lay down and stare up at the dark ceiling replaying every moment of Billy Murphy's murder in my mind, looking for ways that I might have done something different in order to save him.

But every option to save Billy Murphy is just a deviation from the truth. He couldn't have been saved because no one realized he was in danger. I continue to stare up at the ceiling with my hands behind my head. I should've stayed out of it. I should've let Kawowski and Lopez do their jobs.

They're the detectives. Not me. Not anymore.

At best, I'm a liability that got an innocent kid killed. I close my eyes and try to drown out the silence in my own life with Captain Haggerity's voice telling me that I need to ride the wave or Cicero Sanchez stating that I have a bloodlust in my eyes. For the first time in a long time, all I can hear are my father's words whispering into my ears: "Long are the days of a weary soul."

After a while I drift off to sleep, where a world is being ravaged by a large sweeping fire that cleanses the land of all living things, leaving behind a charred soil made of rotting corpses.

The ringing of the house phone awakens me. It's one of the last and few relics of my father's past. I fumble for the digital clock on my bedside table and squint to make out the time which reads 4:00 a.m. I drop the clock on the floor and slowly rise from the bed. I make my way across the darkened room and out into the hall.

The phone continues to ring. Halfway down the hall, I stub my toe on a wall.

"Shit!" I let out as the pain shoots through my toe. Hopping on one foot, I make my way into the kitchen where the phone hangs on a wall near the sink. Just as I go to pick up the receiver, it stops ringing. I wait a few seconds. It doesn't ring again. Must've been a wrong number.

I turn from the kitchen and sluggishly head back to bed. I'm halfway down the hall when the phone starts to ring again. I turn and hurry back to the kitchen, this time making sure not to stub my toe on the way. On the third ring, I pick up the phone.

"Yeah?" I say, grumbling.

"Frank?"

"Who's this?"

"It's Cicero."

"What do you want, Cicero? It's four in the morning."

"Yeah I know, but I'd like to talk to you about Father

Pantone."

"I'm listening."

"No, not over the phone. How about you come down to my church tomorrow and we can talk then?"

"Sure, Cicero. I'll be there at ten." I hang up without saying goodbye. Maybe Cicero has come to his senses and realizes that Father Pantone's confession might have also gotten him killed and now he feels guilty. I turn, making my way back to bed when the phone rings again.

Okay, Cicero, now you're pushing it.

I snatch the receiver off the hook. "What now, Cicero?"

"Cicero? Who the hell is that?" Arnie Ratcliff's voice comes back through the receiver.

"Nobody. Do you know what time it is Arnie?"

"Yeah. *Late.*"

"You mean early."

"Depends on when you sleep."

I shake my head even though I know he can't see me. "What do you want Arnie?"

"Just the truth."

"Like that would be the first time."

"Okay, I'll get right to it. I hear that you were involved in that incident in Uptown."

"You mean that murder?"

God, I was starting to sound like the Murphy's.

"Yeah, that murder. Care to comment?"

"It wasn't me. That's my comment."

"You sure? Because I hear—"

Click.

I yank the line from the phone jack and head back to sleep. My comments are for Sanchez and Sanchez only. And like Arnie Ratcliff, all I want is the truth.

CHAPTER 21

Saint Peter of Alcantara is quiet when I enter through its large wooden doors. In fact, the church is completely empty. The pews are polished and bibles have been placed in hutches along the backs of them in orderly fashion next to hymnal songbooks. The kneelers have been swept free of lint and to the left of the entrance the baptism bowl is filled with holy water.

I brush down the front on my trousers and remove my cap. "Ahhh, you must be Detective Calhoun," a voice says from in front of me. I look to the altar where I find a young man in his early twenties. His face is that of a thirteen-year-old, thin and full of pimples. His hair is brown and slicked down.

His eyes are pecan colored and he's wearing a brown and white robe, which tells me that he's an altar boy.

"I'm looking for Father Sanchez," I say, looking around the room. "You know where I can find him?"

"Father Sanchez is waiting for you in his office." The altar boy points to the left where a door is located at the back of the altar. "Straight down the hall and to your right," he says as he turns back to the altar and begins lighting prayer candles. I follow his directions, leaving the young man to his duties.

I hadn't noticed on my first visit, but as I look up at the ceiling, I see an image of a white, curly-haired, blue-eyed Jesus extending a hand from the clouds with his index finger outstretched ready to touch the world and make everything right.

Inside the hall is an exposed brick wall, which makes me feel more like I'm heading into a medieval crypt. The hall smells like the virgin olive oil that the church uses to light the candles. As I descend into the damp corridor, I gently run my fingers along the wall, feeling the grittiness of the bricks as I skip over one of the electrical candelabras that light the passage.

I make a right at the end of the corridor and find a large black door with a wooden crucifix hanging over it. I roll my eyes at the church's dramatics and knock on the door. I can hear the shuffling of feet, which means that Sanchez isn't alone.

The door opens and Sanchez stands in the doorway with a large smile across his face. His dark hair is even slicker than the day before with a shoe spit shine to it.

"Thank you for coming, Frank," he extends his hand. I walk past him, ignoring the gesture. I need to see who else is in the room.

Sitting at a circular table are two other men. One is round like the Pillsbury Doughboy with plum colored cheeks. He's in his early forties with thinning brown hair and pasty white skin. He's wearing the standard-issue white collar and black robe. The other man sitting next to him has piercing blue eyes and has to be in his mid-seventies. His skin is white, wrinkly and waxy. He's wearing a red and black robe with intricate cross-hatched threading. Both men stand and extend their hands. I turn and look back at Sanchez so as to overlook their greeting.

"What's going on, Cicero? I thought you wanted to talk about Father Pantone?"

"I do, Frank. Please take a seat." I reluctantly sit across from the other two men. "This here is Cardinal Gregorian," Sanchez introduces the old man in the red and black robe. "And this is Father Wells. They're here as official representatives of the Diocese."

I lean back in my seat studying the two men. *What was Sanchez up to?*

"So what do you want to talk about Cicero?" I ask.

"Father Sanchez was asked to set up this meeting in the name of the church, Detective Calhoun," Cardinal Gregorian says in his most stately manner.

I look at Sanchez. The man is biting on his bottom lip, which tells me that he has something to say, but he just can't say it. I turn to Cardinal Gregorian. "So why'd the church want to meet with me?"

"Well as I'm sure you're fully aware, Father Pantone was a leader in this community." The old man pauses to let his words carry their full effect. "And as a leader in this community, he also represented the church. That is why we want to hire you to find his killer."

"Is he serious?" I look to Sanchez.

"I am very serious, Detective Calhoun. We are willing to pay you very well for your time."

"Look, Cardinal Gregorian, you don't have to pay me. I already have a job. Besides, there are two competent detectives already working Father Pantone's murder."

"Yes, I am aware of that, Mr. Calhoun. But I don't think you understand the nature of our request."

I lean forward in my chair. "No, I don't think I do. Please explain."

"It's simple," says Cardinal Gregorian. "We all know that Father Pantone was assassinated. It wasn't as if he was some thug gunned down on the street. We also know that no man is an angel, especially one that comes out of the armed services. Father Sanchez has informed us that you and he were once of the same clothe as chaplains, which means you understand how one's past can adversely affect his life after returning from war. To be blunt, Detective Calhoun, there may be things about Father Pantone's past that could come to light, things that the church might not want to go public. And if so, we'd like to know."

"I don't believe this," I say standing up from my seat. "You want me to play big brother while you try to assess the situation and play damage control?"

"We all want the same thing, Detective."

"Which is?" I ask, staring into Cardinal Gregorian's ice blue eyes.

"Father Pantone's murderer."

"No disrespect—but bullshit! You don't give a damn about Father Pantone's murder. All you care about is the church's image." I turn to leave, but stop and look down at Sanchez. "And *you*? I should lay your ass out right here. Be thankful that I respect God's house."

"Wait," Father Wells finally says, rising from his seat. But by then, I'm already out the door.

I make my way through the church, trying to keep my thoughts to myself as I move through the building. I push open the church's front doors and step out into the daylight. Sitting at the curb are the two uniforms waiting to take me home. I completely forgot about them.

I step down the stairs and make my way over to the patrol car. As I enter the back of the vehicle, I hear Sanchez's voice calling after me. I turn and look up to the top of the church's stairs and see Sanchez standing there. His face is low and his eyes have the look of a lonely puppy dog.

"Frank, wait." He walks down the concrete stairs with his arm's wide and his palms open.

"What do you want, Cicero? I'm really not in the mood."

"Please, Frank, we were once brothers in the Corps. We bled for our vows and fought for them. Father Pantone was just as much a father to me as he was to you." I'm silent. I haven't given any thought as to all the other soldiers who'd be affected by Father Pantone's death.

"Please, Frank," Sanchez opens his arms even wider. "Just give me one last hug for old time's sake."

What's Sanchez up to? I don't like that he tried to play me for a patsy, but something about him standing there all Christ-like has me in the forgiving mood.

I close the patrol car door and look up to the top of the stairs where Father Wells stands, looking down on us with a concerning stare. I look into Sanchez's eyes and can see the regret on his face. He's still biting his lip, which tells me that he really has something he wants to say. So I open my arms and embrace him fully.

"Frank," Sanchez whispers into my ear. "I'm going to tell you what Father Pantone told me on the day that he was killed. He confessed to me that he had broken his vow of celibacy. He was having an affair with a woman."

CHAPTER 22

All the way from Saint Peter of Alcantara on the northwest side of the city to my home on the city's west side, I sit in silence in the back of the musty, cramped space of the patrol car dumbfounded by the knowledge that Father Pantone broke his vow of celibacy. I don't want to believe it but after staring into Sanchez's eyes, I know that he's telling the truth. As we embraced, I asked him to tell me who the woman was but he said he didn't know.

The two officers, Richter and Smith, are busy in the front seats talking about the latest rivalry between the Cubs and the White Sox, but I couldn't care less as I think to myself that everything I've known about Anton Pantone is starting to become a lie.

I bite off my fingernails and spit them against the Plexiglas barrier that separates me from the officers. I need coffee, strong and black.

"Hey, could you two get me the hell home already?" I ask, irritated.

"Uh oh, looks like somebody didn't have a good time at

confessional," Smith says. He's in his early thirties with dark hair, a thin pointed nose and black eyes the shape of nickels.

I can see the smug grin on his face in the rearview. I swear one of these days I'm going to knock that grin right off his face. I sit back and say nothing. I need to think and really clear my head. I lean forward in the seat. "Say, you guys hungry?"

"You treating?" Smith asks.

"Maybe. How about we go to Skeet's? You know where that's at, right?"

"Yeah, we know," says Richter, whose store-bought tan is beginning to fade.

They turn the car on to Damen Avenue and head south. I sit back in my seat. I need to talk to Uncle Skeet. He's the only person that can help me make sense of all of this and uplift my spirit at the same time. And right now, I can't see past this crisis of faith.

Skeet's is packed like Monday rush hour on the Eisenhower expressway. All the tables, including the counter, are filled with newfound customers that are slowly trickling down from the recently-built condos surrounding the small sandwich shop. The chattering of daily events overflow inside the restaurant and spills out unto the streets when Richter, Smith and I open the door and enter.

Philicia the waitress is moving from table to table with a coffee pot and notepad in her hand. She smiles at me and says "He's in the back. You'll have to get him yourself though."

I turn to Richter and Smith. "Find yourselves some seats and order what you want. It's on me."

A few uniforms sitting in a corner wave Smith and Richter over to their table. Smith stops mid-stride, turns and grabs me by the arm. "I don't want to have to come looking for you," he says, dropping his voice into a baritone as if I were a convict allowed a reprieve to the restroom.

I let Smith's threat slide. I don't have time for him. I pass a row of tables on the far right wall and then walk through the opening in the counter space and into the back of the kitchen. The smell of cooking grease and lard languishes in the air. Lil' John the cook is at the burner scrambling eggs. The round man flashes a smile of golden teeth and nods.

I return the gesture as I continue making my way through the kitchen and into the back office where I find my Uncle Skeet sitting at a beige aluminum desk wearing a bulletproof vest.

"I thought you were done being a cop?" I say, ducking into the office.

"I could say the same about you. I heard about the shooting up on Broadway."

"Yeah, that..." I drop my head.

Uncle Skeet flaps his hands. "Don't worry about it. I'm sure everything will work its way out."

I take a seat in one of the metal chairs in front of his desk. "Yeah, I hope so."

"So what brings you by?" I stare at the vest. "Oh, this?" Uncle Skeet swipes at the vest. "I just wear it when I'm in the office. Never know when some crackhead or stupid mother-fucker might try and stick me up." He reaches under his desk and then pulls a large black Desert Eagle pistol from underneath.

"But whoever they are, they better have angels on their side, because they got one shot—*and one shot only*—of walking out of this room with my money." I start laughing. Uncle Skeet is definitely a cop that the hood has made. "What's on your mind, nephew?"

I look down at my crusty nails. I've bitten them down to the tips of my fingers. "If you've heard about what happened on Broadway, then you also heard about me blacking out."

Uncle Skeet runs his hand over his hairy chin. "Yeah, I heard. You were trying to save that kid, weren't you?"

"But I didn't, Unc. I passed out. Couldn't handle the stress and I just passed out."

"You're dealing with a lot of shit right now, Frank. You did the best you could."

"No, that wasn't my best. Ever since—" my voice trails off.

"I know, Frank, you don't have to say it. We're all hurting in some way."

I look up from my hands and stare at Uncle Skeet. Again, I've failed to see the pain that everyone else is carrying around with them. Uncle Skeet has been my dad's partner for over twenty years, but even he didn't know the truth about Blue and my father.

"I think I'm walking away from this life, Unc. There's too many lies and too many secrets for me to face."

"What do you mean you're walking away?"

"I mean this city, this place. It isn't my life anymore. Half the time I don't even know who I am. Just existing to exist."

Uncle Skeet rises up from his seat and rounds the desk, looming over me.

"What do you mean you don't know who you are? You're Frank Calhoun, dammit! You're a cop. And don't give me that shit about this not being your city. You grew up here walking these streets just like everyone else. You know the danger that awaits you every day when you walk out that door. Hell, you knew that before you even became a cop. No one said life was going to be easy, Frank."

"But—"

"No buts. We're not quitters, Frank. Your father didn't raise you that way and I damn sure know I didn't. The way I see it, you've got two options: wallow away in self-pity and die. Or, do something about what's going down. I know Captain Haggerty has you under watch, but you're a cop, Frank. And a damn good one at that. They can't take that away from you. You're born into the blue religion whether you like it or not."

———

After leaving Skeet's, I have Smith and Richter take me home. Uncle Skeet is right. They can't take the cop out of me because it's in my blood.

I go into my bedroom closet and grab the set of extra hand-cuffs off the top shelf along with a small microfilm canister of fingerprint powder. I go into the kitchen, slightly lift up the blind that covers the glass section of the backdoor and see the squad car still watching my home.

I turn from the backdoor and step over to the kitchen sink. The clock on the right wall, which is shaped like yolk running from a cracked egg, reads 5:00 p.m. I open the drawer on the far left side of the kitchen sink and pull out a brown paper bag, which I fold and place in my back pocket. From another drawer, I grab a roll of clear tape and stuff it in the front left pocket of my jeans.

After placing a small paintbrush in my other back pocket, I pick up the telephone off the wall and dial a number from memory. The phone rings for while before it's finally picked up.

"Hello?" a young boy's voice answers.

"Jamal? How ya doing? It's Mr. Calhoun. Is your mother in?"

"Hey Mr. Calhoun! Yeah, she's in. Hold on." I look up at the ceiling. I can hear the boy running across the floor and into the kitchen to get his mother. A few seconds later, a voice softer than Egyptian cotton comes in over the line.

"Frank?"

"Hey Gloria. I wanted to know if you could help me with something?"

"Anything for you, Frank."

The way she says it has the carnal pistons in my loins revving. I can picture her standing in her dining room with her long black hair tied into a graceful ponytail while her light skin glows under a lamp's iridescent bulb. The dimples in her cheeks emerge and accentuate the beautiful angular smile she's forming as she speaks.

I cough to buy myself some time so that I can get my thoughts together and explain that I need her to make a batch of her turtle brownies with a very special ingredient.

At first Gloria is hesitant; after all, what I'm asking her to do is criminal. But I assure her that I'll take all fault for her actions. After half an hour of pleading and explaining in very minute detail the execution of my plan, Gloria finally breaks down and agrees. I don't like bringing others into my world, especially people like Gloria but I have no other choice. I have to see this thing through and right now she's my means to an end.

My watch reads 7:30 P.M. when I look out the front window to see Gloria sashay down the concrete walkway to the patrol car that sits just outside our home.

She's wearing red shorts and a white tee shirt tied from the back. Her hair is in a ponytail and bounces against her back. In her hands, she holds a plastic container filled with brownies. I watch as she approaches the patrol car, bending over and bringing the brownies up to the window. I see Richter pass a few brownies to Smith before taking some for himself. After each officer has their fill of the delectable treats, Gloria turns from the car and makes her way back to her apartment. I wait a few seconds and flip open my cell to call Gloria. I thank her for her help and reassure her that no criminal charges will be filed.

An hour later, I step out the front door and stand at the threshold to see if Smith or Richter might make a move but neither one does, meaning the Valium has done its job. I step down the stairs and walk over to the driver's side of the patrol car. Smith's head is leaning against the door with drool slowly oozing from his mouth all the way down to his uniform. I bend over into the open window and turn the key in the ignition. When the car purrs to life, I push the button on the side of the door and roll up the windows a little over halfway and lock the doors. I don't need somebody coming by and possibly stealing their weapons; I have enough death on my conscience as it is.

The night is humid and I take my time walking up the empty street toward the EL train that's located a few blocks away. One avenue over I can hear the sounds of a neighborhood block party where people section off both ends of a street, usually with orange cones or parked cars, and bring out music and food to share with one another. It's ironic that one block away people are out celebrating the joy of life while I'm on my way to an area recently plagued by death.

CHAPTER 23

The moment I step off the red line train at Wilson, my stomach churns. Just around the corner and half a block up, yellow tape sections off the area where Billy Murphy fell. I take a deep breath and tell myself it isn't my fault and catching the killers is the best thing I can do.

I cross over to the East side of Broadway where a few homeless people are mulling about making their way to Saint Helen's. I ring the doorbell to Lillian Murphy's apartment. This is the last place I want to be, but I have to check the enclosed porch for prints. It's the only thing that can possibly lead me to the truth of what happened to Father Pantone and Billy. I wait a few seconds, but don't get an answer. I ring the doorbell again and then decide to yell up towards the window for an answer.

The door finally buzzes and I rush to open it. As I climb the stairs and draw closer to the apartment door, I feel my heart drop. The door is ajar and as I enter the apartment, I find Lillian Murphy slouched down in her recliner with a gallon of Seagram's Gin in her lap and a cup in her hand.

She turns to look at me with sad, grey eyes. They're no

longer changing colors and the fact that they are now a singular tint almost makes me want to cry. She seems to have aged ten years, with wrinkles and bags now appearing under her blotchy eyeliner.

I take a step forward but stop. I don't know what to say somehow I choke out the words, "I need to check your porch." She waves her hand as if dismissing me from her memory and turns to look back out the window at the world that now moves without her.

I move through the small kitchen and onto the enclosed porch. One thing I've learned from my time in the military is that people tend to leave a little piece of themselves be- hind, whether that be a rosary by a solider praying before deploy- ment, a photo of a little girl left by a medic rushing to an emer- gency, or a sheet of scripture from a Bible pulled from the hands of a dead solider. In the end, we all leave something—it's just a matter of taking notice.

The back porch is still in the same condition as when I first saw it. The old boxes are still stacked against the wall near the exterior door. I pull the mag-lite out of my jeans pocket, pop in a new battery and shine the beam on the wooden ladder that leads to the rooftop.

All along the dusty wood, I can see partial fingerprints and full boot prints. I had every intention of telling Captain Haggerty about the prints, but no one on the force is listening to me, especially after I allowed a kid to die on my watch.

I examine the prints closely, trying to find a complete one, but there isn't one. I know a partial print isn't enough to iden- tify the shooter. And that's when it hits me: if the killer had climbed the ladder without gloves, then he probably left a print on the rooftop lid.

I place the mag-lite in between my teeth and start climbing the ladder. After ten steps up, I'm less than six inches away from the rooftop's entrance. I pull out the canister, which is filled with black lead powder and pour a small amount into my hand and flick it against the surface of the rooftop.

After the powder dissipates, I take the brush from my back pocket and gently swipe at the surface. With each swipe of the brush, oval lines start to appear until a group of complete fingerprints are visible on the lid.

I take the tape from my pocket and tear off a piece. Pressing it against the fingerprint, I slowly pull it away until I've lifted the full print off the surface of the wood. I then place the tape on the back of a white index card, put it inside the brown paper bag and climb back down the ladder.

When I reenter the apartment, I find Lillian Murphy downing a cup of gin. The small woman's hair is beginning to turn gray at the edges. Her eyes tell the story of a woman lost.

I drop my head. "Miss Murphy, I'm sorry for your loss."

She stands up from her recliner, rocking back and forth. She looks as though she might fall right over if a light breeze blows through the room. Her mouth is agape as though she's going to say something, but instead she continues to rock back and forth like a small sailboat in troubled water. I force myself to look away. Her accusatory gaze is too much for me to handle. "You," she finally manages to say, raising her arm, which sets her off balance and causes her to fall forward.

I rush to catch her as she falls into my arms. I hold her close to my chest as I stare down into her full grey eyes. All I can see is pain.

"You need to sleep," I say, pulling her up to her feet. "Billy sleeps," she whispers, her words fermented in gin.

I pick her up and carry her down the hall to her bedroom, which is painted a beautiful pastel pink. I lay her down on the queen-size bed and as I rise, she clutches my collar.

"My boy—my boy is dead." I start to pull away. There's

nothing I can say or do for her. "W-wait," she calls out to me, pulling on the end of my shirt. "Please. H-h-hold me. Please... just until I fall asleep."

I stare down into her eyes, trying to find the innocence that she's lost. The very same innocence I lost when I arrested my father and discovered his secret. Outside, thunder cracks across the sky as if God is telling me to be still and comfort a mother who's lost her one and only child.

I sit on the edge of the bed and wrap my arms around her. I pat her head and tell her everything is going to be okay. Rain follows the thunder soon after as I close my eyes and try to fight back the tears that have built up inside me. These are tears of remorse and regret. Tears that I can no longer hold back, as they fall from my eyes for Blue.

CHAPTER 24

At the age of thirteen, Desmond Reynolds was five-foot-ten and still growing with skin so dark, it looked almost blue in the moonlight which earned him a nickname that couldn't be more fitting: Blue.

He and I met at the tender age of nine and our friendship instantly grew, taking on a life of its own. We were inseparable, becoming the best of friends while fighting together against the neighborhood bullies, playing basketball in the back alleys and graduating from the same elementary school together.

"Yo, Frank, you coming?" Blue asked while standing at the bottom of the stairs in front of my home. His hair was cut low into a fade and he was wearing a red and black Chicago Bulls jacket.

"Yeah, I'm coming," I said, running out the door. My hair was cut into a box shape and my eyes were soft and full of light. My arms and legs were thin, but strong like Chick-O-Sticks.

"Where we going?" I asked.

Blue smiled. "Why? You want to tell yo' daddy?"

"Naw, I just want to leave him a note, so he knows where I am."

"Quit being such a wimp."

"I ain't no wimp."

"Yeah, you is."

"No, I'm not."

"Then prove it. Don't leave a note and let's go on an adventure." I bit my bottom lip. I knew I had to let my father know where I was going at all times. "I knew it. You scared." He started to caw like a chicken.

"I ain't scared!" I stepped outside the gated fence and rolled up the sleeves of my Chicago Bears jacket. "Come on, if we're going on this adventure."

Blue straightened out the cuffs of his jacket and we started up the leaf-covered street, kicking stray beer cans and juice bottles as we went. The scent of rain was in the air, but we didn't care.

"So, where we going?" I asked again, opening up a box of Lemon Heads.

"To the donut factory."

"The donut factory? What's that?"

"Just wait and see. Quit asking so many damn questions."

We rounded the corner at the end of the block and walked up the street toward Greater Galilee Baptist Church. In all of my life, I had only been in the church once, the day my father took me to be baptized at the age of six. When I inquired why we never returned, my father stated that 'once is good enough to be washed of your sins.'

"Man, we going to church? I thought you said we were going to a donut factory?"

"We are. Just follow me."

Blue lead me towards the back of the one-story church where a four-foot wall had been constructed to protect the locomotive tracks on the other side. He scaled the wall and extended his hand down to me. "Come on," he said.

I took two steps back and shook my head. "We can die up there," I said. "You can get electrocuted."

"No, you can't. Now give me yo damn hand." I hesitated and Blue furrowed his brow. "Quit being such a chicken shit."

"I ain't no chicken shit!" I returned, reluctantly giving him my hand. He pulled me up, and once over the wall, we walked along the tracks skipping rocks as we went.

"What does this donut factory look like?" I asked, tossing a rock.

"I hear it's ginormous and filled with every donut ever made." Blue was licking his lips as if he could already taste them. "I hear there are trucks filled with donuts that they don't even use."

I skipped a rock across the wooden tracks and then watched as it ricocheted off one of the steel rails and fell over the side of the underpass. We looked at each other with eyes wide, heard the screeching of tires below and then took off running down the tracks.

After a few minutes of running we stopped, doubled over trying to catch our breath. We looked at each other and began laughing, realizing that the car below couldn't have even seen us because of the height of the tracks.

After we had regained our breath, we took up to walking the tracks once again. An hour later, we saw a white smoke stack rising up into the air like a large cigarette and the aromas of dough, cinnamon, yeast, chocolate and warm sugar all mixed in the air around us.

"Smell that?" Blue asked, closing his eyes. "Just imagine how many donuts we're going to get."

"You might not get any!" I said from a distance as I ran towards the factory as Blue gave chase. The donut factory was an off-white building with a platoon of white, boxed-shaped delivery trucks aligned into three rows.

We crawled through an opening in the barbed wire fence. Blue took the lead with his lanky arms swinging by his side. We approached the nearest truck and Blue pulled open its back doors. A scent of sweet dough and an arid sourness escaped from the metal body of the truck as individually-wrapped donuts, cakes and pies spilled out onto the ground.

"See? What did I say?" Blue said with eyes wide.

"It looks like we're stealing," I said, hesitating as I looked at the pastries on the ground.

"We ain't stealing nothing, Frank. I told you this is stuff they ain't using."

"How you know they ain't using it, Blue?"

"Because the side of the truck says disposable, which means they just gone get rid of it anyway."

"Why would they get rid of this stuff?"

"I don't know, Frank. Does it really matter?" Blue bent down and picked up a handful of pastries and stuffed them into his jacket. "You better hurry up and get you some while you can." He ripped open a package of mini-chocolate donuts with his teeth and shoved two of them into his mouth. He chewed it for a few seconds, taking in the sweet chocolate as if it were the first time. The inside of my mouth began to salivate at the sheer expression of joy on his face, but soon after he spat out the doughnut and a tear filled up in my eyes for the loss of that luscious sweetness.

"What?" he said, looking at me quizzically. "I think that one was stale."

Did that mean that all of the donuts were stale? If so, this had been a huge waste of time. I wanted to tell Blue that we should go since we weren't supposed to be here anyway, but then he tossed the packet of donuts and said "You scared now, aren't you?"

"I ain't scared."

"Prove it. Let me see you eat something."

"Like what?"

"I don't know, *something*."

I looked down at the packaged goods wondering which one to choose. There were powdered donuts and cinnamon glazed pies and even a brownie or two scattered about the heap. I closed my eyes and picked up the first package I felt. When I opened them, I saw that it was a chocolate cupcake.

"Let's see you eat it," Blue said with his arms crossed over his bulging jacket. I tore open the shiny wrapping and looked at Blue. "Come on, eat it."

I removed the small chocolate cake from its wrapping, closed my eyes and jammed the cake in my mouth. At first, I chewed quickly, but as the taste of the sweet, white filling spread across my tongue, I began to slow down and savor its taste as serenity washed over my face.

Blue snatched the other cake out of my hand and gobbled it down with a triumphant smile. "See?" he asked with dark chocolate covering his teeth. "That wasn't so bad."

I picked up another package and tore it open. The scent of cinnamon from the apple pie tickled my nose. I bit into the glazed dough and packed my mouth full with gooey gobs of apple filling. I was in heaven.

"Hey, what are you kids doing in here?" someone called out from the front of the truck.

We ducked our heads to the side of the vehicle and saw a security guard approaching fast. I took off running towards the right and Blue went to the left. I looked over my shoulder, and after seeing the guard go after Blue, I turned and pursued the guard. But it was too late—he already had a hand on Blue's collar and began wrapping his own arms underneath Blue's, locking him into a full nelson restraint.

"Let me go, muthafucka!" Blue yelled in protest as he struggled, but it was to no effect.

I stopped in my tracks and watched as the guard wrangled Blue along an uneven dirt trail to a whitewash trailer while Blue's threats trailed off into the distance. I turned and ran back between the square white trucks and up the small bluff and through the hole in the gate and back onto the tracks. Tears began to swell up in my eyes as I walked the tracks alone, praying that I was going in the right direction towards my home. The sun was beginning to set and every now and then I would hear things moving just beyond the brush of forestry that ran alongside the train tracks. I quickened my step, trying to make it home as fast as possible. Blue had been caught, but I just hoped he was okay. There was no telling what those white guards were doing to him.

Probably beating him to an inch of his life.

With the thought that Blue could be dead, I ran home faster than I had ever run before. My father was the only one that could save Blue now.

I burst through the front door with sweat pouring down my face as my clothes clung to me like a wet dollar bill. "Dad? Dad!" I called out, rushing through the foyer and into the living room. I heard my father's voice from the kitchen.

"Okay," said my father into the receiver of the phone. He still had on his blue officer's uniform. "No, don't worry—I'll take care of it and have him home to you soon. No problem." He hung up the phone and turned to me. "Where have you been?" he asked, leveling his eyes on me.

He was a big man with deep dark skin the color of a blue lagoon. The thin black mustache that sat flat across his face always seemed funny to me because it was the only facial hair he had. I knew those eyes all too well. They were his cop eyes, a look I associated with the belt. Self-preservation kicked in.

"Ummmm... n-no-nowhere."

"Nowhere, huh?" he repeated as he moved in closer to me. "Because I think you've been out to that donut factory." My jaw dropped. "I keep telling you, Frank, if you're going to lie, then lie for a good reason! And always cover your lies. Look at you—you've got sugar all over the sides of your mouth." I used the back of my hand to wipe the dried excess sweetness from my lips. "You even smell like a donut!"

One of the drawbacks to having a cop for a father was that I couldn't lie without him detecting something.

"Plus, Regina just called and told me they're holding Desmond down at that factory." I lowered my head. "I'll deal with you after we get him back home. Now, go get in the car."

I walked back through the house with my head down. I was in for a heap of trouble. At least we were getting Blue back. There was no way some flashlight guard was going to tell a real cop we couldn't have my best friend back.

I sat outside the Philmore donut factory in the back of my father's squad car with the windows rolled down halfway. The back of the car smelled as if it hadn't been washed in over a year. I poked my fingers in between the steel grate that separated the driver from the prisoner to keep myself entertained.

Ten minutes later, I saw Blue and my father exit out the door of the security trailer. My father walked proudly with his chest puffed out and a stern look on his face. Blue sauntered along side him with a little smirk on his lips and a swagger in his step as his lanky arms swung like a metronome. I kept my face impassive even though I wanted to smile. The expression on my father's face warned me that any attempt at making a celebratory gesture would only be met with brutal consequences.

He opened the car's back door and turned to Blue. "I don't want to see you two up here again. Do I make myself clear?" Blue didn't say a word. He moved to enter the vehicle, but my father put out his arm to block the door. "I asked if that was understood?"

Blue looked up into my father's eyes, his face beginning to transform into a mask of anger. "Yeah, whatever, nigga. You ain't my daddy—you can't tell me what to do."

As fast as the words leapt from Blue's mouth, so did the reaction of my father's backhand. Drops of saliva and blood flew from Blue's mouth and splattered the gravel beneath their feet.

"Stand your narrow ass up!" my father demanded. He grabbed Blue by the collar and pulled his face close to his. "You better be glad I'm not your father or I'd put my foot so far up your ass, you'd feel it 'til you were thirty." He pushed Blue into the backseat and slammed the door.

The fifteen-minute ride back home seemed like an eternity to me as I sat quietly across from Blue staring out the window. When we pulled up to Blue's apartment complex, I finally let my gaze fall upon him and saw that he was licking his busted bottom lip. My father rounded the car and opened up the back door.

"See you later, Blue," I whispered, but he didn't respond as he got out of the car and began making his way towards the apartment.

My father and I drove off into the night, but I turned to stare out the back window as Blue stood on the apartment stoop with his hands balled into tight fists and a vengeful, defiant expression on his face until he was swallowed up by the night.

CHAPTER 25

awake to a loud crack of thunder as I slowly open my eyes, trying to make sense of where I am. I look down and see Lillian Murphy's head resting comfortably in my lap. She seems at peace while she sleeps. I know that once she awakens, the reality of her son's death will set in and bring her back into a world filled with pain.

I gently lift her head and slide out from under her. Once I'm free, I open my phone to check the time and see that it's 4:35 a.m. I snap it close and do my best to maneuver out of the room without waking her.

In the living room, I stare out the window across the way to Father Pantone's office and a tingle rides up my spine. The image of the building will haunt me for the rest of my life. I take a deep breath and turn away from the window, remembering that Father Pantone's funeral is today.

When I slip out the door of the building, it's still dark out. The streets are desolate as if no other man, woman, or child exists. The quietness that settles across the asphalt jungle makes it feel even more dangerous than usual. Every sound, no matter how small, becomes a sounding board of terror and every shadow that stretches from a luminescent streetlight or store sign becomes a predator lurking and hunting its prey.

Suddenly, I stop in the middle of the street and look in each direction as I get the feeling that someone is watching me. I scan the darkened, hallowed spaces of the empty cars parked along the street but then decide that it's just my cautionary cop senses playing with me. I enter the Wilson street train station and head home.

Officers Smith and Richter are still knocked out when I arrive home at 6:40 a.m. I smile, knowing they're going to be in a lot of trouble when their relief shows up and finds them asleep behind the wheel. I climb the stairs and enter my apartment. The hallway is dark as I turn a corner and enter the living room. Under the cover of darkness, the couch and 27-inch television look more like chunks of cottage cheese than actual furniture. As I make my way through the living room and into the dining room, I suddenly stop mid-stride when I hear someone breathing.

No, not breathing... snoring. I grab one of my high school chess trophies from the dining room cabinet and charge back into the living room, shouting as I flick on the lights.

"Preacha, Preacha! It's me!"

Lying on the couch with his eyes bulging halfway out of his skull is Buddy Heim. "What the hell are you doing here, Buddy?" I've got the trophy held up over my head. "I almost bashed your damn brains out."

"Thank God you didn't," Buddy says, sitting up on the couch. "How'd you get into my home, Buddy?"

"Come on, Preacha. Do you really have to ask?"

"Hand it over." Heim wrestles a key out of his pants pocket and hands it to me. "You ever enter my home again without my permission, I'll break both of your hands. Understood?"

"Awww come on, Preacha. You know you just kidding." Buddy smiles, but I'm impassive. "You got something to drink around here?" he asks, rising from the couch.

"Yeah, I guess so." I turn and walk towards the kitchen, putting the trophy back in the cabinet as I pass through the dining room.

"Been trying to reach you all night," Buddy says from behind me. "I left you like twenty messages."

"So, why didn't you just wait 'til I got back to you?"

"I tried, but I figured I'd swing by and tell you face-to-face." I pull two chilled root beers from the fridge and hand one to Buddy. "So why didn't you wait for me on the porch?"

"I was going to, but I saw the squad car outside. Figured maybe something might have happened. But when I saw the two cops knocked out, I thought maybe you were in trouble, so..."

"So, you let yourself in."

"Yeah but I got so tired of waiting, I guess I fell asleep."

I take a swig from the bottle. "So, what's so important that you couldn't wait to see me?"

Buddy's eyes become large and a wide smile forms across his brown face. "I got a lead on that key you been looking for, but I don't know if you're going to like it."

"What's the lead, Buddy?"

"Remember, I'm giving it to you the way it was given to me."

"Out with it, Buddy. Now!"

"Prince Paul. He knows something about the key and says that if you want to know what he knows... then you're going have to come see him yourself."

I sit the bottle down on the kitchen table. "Good job, Buddy. Thanks for the info. Now if you'll excuse me I got a funeral to get ready for. You can let yourself out."

Sitting inside Saint Helen's for Father Pantone's funeral, I try to do my best to shut out all thoughts of the outside world, but all I keep thinking about is what Buddy Heim told me about Prince Paul's demands. I haven't seen Paul in almost two years, not since Blue and I came across him in the neighborhood barbershop.

When we were kids, Paul would bully me. Now it has me wondering what type of God could be so cruel as to intertwine our fates once again. After all, I'm a homicide detective and Prince Paul is one of the biggest drug traffickers on the west side of the city. I push those thoughts to the back of my mind since there are still more pressing matters like the fingerprints from the Murphy home that still need to be processed.

The pews of the church are filled with a handful of people. The funeral procession consists of Father Cicero Sanchez and two altar boys, gliding steps behind him while holding candles in their hands as they walk down the middle of the aisle towards the altar where Father Pantone's casket lies. I remember what Sanchez told me about Father Pantone having a mistress, so I turn and scan the church hoping to find a sobbing woman. My eyes fall on four women who seem to be taking the funeral proceeding particularly hard.

The first woman is Caucasian and she stands at the front of the church. She's a brunette dressed in an ash-grey business suit. Her face is plushy pink and she stands so erect, you'd think she was born with a ruler down her spine.

The second woman is Asian and dressed in a dark skirt and suit jacket with a red ribbon tied around a lock of her black hair. She dabs at her eyes every now and then with a hand-kerchief.

The third woman, who sits two pews behind the Asian

woman, is pale like a porcelain doll with blond hair. She's dressed in an off-white gown, which almost looks like an old wedding dress.

The last woman sits far in the back of the church. Her head is bowed low as she weeps openly into a black handkerchief. Her head is covered with a shawl, but I can see escaped strands of black hair uncurl in front of her forehead. No woman cries this hard for a man unless it's because of love. She has to be the one. The woman looks up from her dark handkerchief and locks eyes with me. We stare at each other for a few seconds before she stands and begins making her way towards the door as Sanchez stands at the altar about to give the benediction.

Father Pantone will have to forgive me.

I rise from my seat and follow the woman out the doors of the church.

"Excuse me, miss?" I call after the woman as she makes her way down the church's stairs.

The woman stops in mid-step and turns to face me. Her eyes are shaped like cat's eyes and even though she's been crying and her mascara is running, I can see that she's beautiful. Her dark irises are like deep pools of shadows and her cinnamon- colored skin makes her even more exotic as she presses her radiant tan lips together to form the words.

"Yes, how can I help you?"

For a second, I let myself wonder about how soft her lips might be, but then I say: "I think we're grieving the same friend." However, the woman gives no indication if I'm correct or not. I extend my hand. "I'm Frank—"

My introduction is cut short from the sound of screeching tires. We both turn our heads to find a blue and white cruiser coming to a sudden stop. The car is barely in park when Officer Smith jumps out of the driver's seat and heads my way, spitting obscenities as he runs up the steps of the church. I turn back to the woman but she's already down the stairs, heading in the opposite direction of Officer Smith. I start to go after her, but Smith jumps in my way before I can make a move.

"I'm going to kick your ass, Calhoun!" he blurts out with his nostrils flaring and his face turning red.

I smile even though I've already lost the woman, which may prove to be insignificant since I still have the prints in my pocket. But the fact that Officer Smith is the cause of me losing this potential lead makes what I'm about to do even more enjoyable.

I look over Smith's shoulder and see Officer Richter heading our way. "What's wrong, Officer Smith, you oversleep?" I ask sarcastically.

Smith cocks back his arm to throw a punch. I block the attack and counter with a head butt between his eyes.

"Ahhh fuck!" Smith drops to his knees. "My nose! You broke my fucking nose!"

I sidestep the injured officer as Richter comes to his partner's aid. I step down the stairs and walk to the corner of Sheridan where I hail a taxi.

"West," I tell the driver. "Forensics Science Center on Roosevelt and Damen."

CHAPTER 26

ay Charles' "Busted" is playing from a small boom box sitting on a counter when I enter lab #6, where Kevin Masters sits with his eyes glued to a high-powered microscope. He's a medium-sized man with a crayon brown complexion and thin, shoulder-length dreads.

"Kevin?" I call out to him.

Masters lifts his head from the microscope and turns to look at me. "Frank Calhoun," he says, smiling, his lips large and black. "What up, brother?"

We both shake hands and hug. "Is that the genius I hear?" I ask after we part.

"You know it. The one and only. Man, he will be missed." We both shake our heads, saying a silent prayer for the late Ray Charles. "So what brings you by? I'm sure you didn't come all the way down here to listen to my music."

"I need a favor."

"What kind of favor?" Masters' smile disappears from his face.

I look around the lab just to make sure we're alone, before

turning back to Masters. "The kind of favor that's not on the record."

This time, Masters looks around the room and leans in towards me. "What do you mean off the record?"

"Just like I said, Kevin. *Off the record.*"

"What are you saying, Frank? Are you still on leave?"

"Maybe. But then again, I might not be saying anything. The less you know, the better. Just in case this thing blows up in my face."

Masters takes a step back and throws up his hands in front of his chest. "I don't even want to know." He turns back to his microscope.

"Come on, Kevin. I just need for you to analyze a print and give me everything on it if it hits."

"You know I can't do that, Frank. Only active detectives working actual cases can get that kind of information. Besides, there are other cases pulling rank over your request."

"I'm sure there are, Kevin." I move in closer towards him. "I'm just asking that you take a look at *this* one."

Masters turns from his microscope. "No, Frank—you're asking me to put my career on the line."

I take a deep breath. I don't want to have to play this card, but Masters is leaving me no other choice. "All right, Kevin. I understand your concern. But how many times did my old man stick his neck out for you when you were a rookie?" Masters remains silent. "Oh yeah, I know the stories. If my father hadn't gathered new evidence on that Polanski case after you corrupted it, who knows where that murdering SOB might be?"

"That was an honest mistake," Masters refutes.

"I know it was. And I know there's no one better than you in this office. That's why I'm asking you to run these prints and see if you get any hits." I put the brown paper bag down on the counter.

Masters looks at the bag and then turns to me. "Just this once. But after this, I never want to hear about your old man sticking his neck out for me again."

I nod my head and turn to leave. I hate that I guilt-tripped Masters into looking at the prints, but it was the only way. I hope this incident eventually becomes water under the bridge, but when you use a cop killer as leverage it's hard to mend such relationships.

Just outside the forensics building, my cell rings. It's Captain Haggerty.

"Captain," I say looking around, searching the cars parked outside the front of the building. I half expect to see Smith and Richter or some other uniform following me.

"When you can, I want to see you in my office, Calhoun."

"Be there as soon as possible, Captain."

I hang up. Captain Haggerty's request means immediately. My thoughts go to Officer Smith's broken nose. I thought it would take a bit more time before I had to answer for that one, but I guess I was wrong. I walk down Damen Avenue over to Harrison towards Area Four headquarters.

The stroll is at least three miles, but a good walk is what I need. There's a lot to think about such as who was the mourning woman at Father Pantone's funeral? What did Prince Paul have to do with all this? What did the key open? And most of all, where did it lead?

The west side neighborhood near Western and Harrison is filled with beige new-construction condos and pastel blue row houses. What was once trash-filled vacant lots, abandoned factories and decaying homes have now become the set piece for the city's redevelopment project, which just means the gentrification of African-Americans from their homes and neighborhoods.

With the new construction succeeding on the southeast

side of the 290 Expressway, it'll slowly move across the bridge where the last of the Rockwell Garden Public Housing Projects now stand. Soon the tall brick and brown mortar fortresses will all be gone, along with the gangs that control them.

I shake my head as anyone with an ounce of street knowledge can see the pending doom that will occur from the demolition of these housing projects. The war for the city's streets will intensify, homicides will rise and civic leaders will wonder why, not realizing that the very answer lay in their plans for redevelopment.

As I walk through the neighborhoods, watching the transformation from newly built homes and condos to decaying structures of wood and brick I think about my own neighborhood. The gradual sweep west is picking up steam. Who knows how far the redevelopment will reach, but with younger money coming into the city it's only a matter of time before Washington Heights will be graced with some monstrosity made of plywood, drywall and a façade of plaster. I vow at this moment that I'll never sell my home, no matter the offer that should come my way.

By the time I reach Area Four, I've nearly forgotten the reason why I've come into the office. The squad room is empty and Captain Haggerty has his door open. He yells for me as soon as he sees me step inside.

"Close the door behind you," he orders, looking up from a stack of papers on his desk. I try to study his face, but he's emotionless. Whatever he wants, he isn't letting on. "Take a seat."

We sit in silence for a moment while Captain Haggerty sorts through some papers. "I swear, I'm either going to die from a fucking paper cut or from being buried under paper." When he's finished signing his name to the last document, he removes the burnt-out stub of a cigar from his mouth and says

"You're officially cleared in the murder of Billy Murphy. Ballistics pulled the bullet out of the kid and matched it with the one they found in Father Pantone."

I wasn't happy. A death is a death. "Did they track the gun?" I ask.

"The best we've been able to come up with is that the rifle was a Bushmaster XM-15 semi-automatic."

"A Malvo?!"

"That's the one."

I shake my head in disbelief. A Bushmaster XM-15 semi-automatic rifle made sense. The same type of gun had been used a few years ago by John Allen Muhammad and Lee Boyd Malvo as they hid inside the trunk of an old Chevy Caprice while shooting innocent people before they became known as The Beltway Snipers.

Captain Haggerty clears his throat. "Now that you're an innocent man, I think we need to talk about your altercation with Officer Smith."

"There's nothing to talk about."

"Really, detective? Then, tell me why I have an officer with a broken nose."

"I wouldn't know anything about that, Captain. Was there a complaint filed?"

"You know damn well there wasn't a complaint filed," Captain Haggerty says, rolling the cigar around in his mouth. "Remember who you're talking to, Calhoun. Don't try and get fresh with me."

"Wouldn't think of it, sir. The truth is it was self-defense."

"Self-defense, huh?"

"Yes, sir. Ask Officer Richter. He'd verify my story."

"And what makes you think he won't cover his partner's ass?"

"Because he's an honest cop."

Captain Haggerty nods his head. "I'm telling you now that I don't want to hear about any more altercations with my officers, is that understood?"

"Yes, sir." I stand to leave.

"I didn't say this meeting was over. Sit down, detective." I retake my seat. "Now that you've been cleared of the homicide, I'm going to tell you this once and only once—stay out of Kawowski and Lopez's investigation. If I find out you've been interfering in their case in any way, I'll have your badge and make sure your ass is sucking wood down at the county jail. Is that understood, Detective?"

"Yes, sir."

"Good. I'm glad that we have an understanding." I sit quietly like a grade school student waiting for permission to go to the bathroom. "You're dismissed, Detective." I stand up from the chair and move towards the door. "Oh, by the way, take this and put it back where you got it. I don't want to see it ever again."

He tosses me my father's old service revolver, which is sealed in a plastic evidence bag. "Yes, sir, never again."

CHAPTER 27

"Tell me again why we're watching this asshole?" Detective Lopez asks from behind the wheel as he takes a sip of coffee from a cheap Styrofoam cup.

The detective's burgundy Chevy Caprice is parked along a car- lined street, half a block down from Area Four head-quarters.

Kawowski clears his throat and answers without turning to look at him. "Because Calhoun knew our victim intimately and we haven't cleared him from our suspect list yet."

"You know, we could always just interrogate him and get this over with," Lopez says matter-of-factly.

"Yeah, we could. But I want to watch him for a while. He's got something going down and I want to know what it is."

Lopez hunches his shoulders and takes another sip of coffee. "I can't believe you staked out the Murphy residence all night waiting for this prick."

Kawowski is silent.

"The nerve of him fucking a grieving mother after she's just lost her son. Says a lot about a man, you know? You think we should get IAD involved?"

Kawowski finally turns and looks at Lopez. His forehead and eyebrows are furrowed. "*Never*. Unless we really have to. We don't throw one of our own under the bus. Besides, we don't have any evidence to back that kind of play. So for now, we sit on him and see what moves he makes."

"I still think we should reel him in for questioning."

"We'll do that when the time is right. But for now, we sit."

The two detectives sit in silence, watching as uniforms and plain-clothes detectives enter and exit the brown brick building. Lopez turns on the radio and a pop tune comes blaring out of the speakers, but Kawowski reaches over and turns it down.

"Do you ever listen to anything other than this crap?" he asks.

"Look, this kind of music keeps me awake." Kawowski leans back in his seat and shakes his head, mumbling that he needs a cigarette. "I wonder why he came down here to HQ?" Lopez asks.

"Who knows? By the way, did you swing by the M.E.'s office and get that autopsy report on Billy Murphy?"

"Oh yeah, almost forgot," Lopez reaches into the backseat and retrieves a manila folder before handing it over to Kawowski. "Turns out the kid was killed by the same gun that killed the priest. I guess that kinda knocks Calhoun out of the lead as our main suspect, huh?"

"Maybe. But then again, he could've had an accomplice."

"Didn't think about that. Maybe that whole blackout bullshit is just a cover."

"Maybe. We'll just have to wait and see."

Lopez takes another sip of his coffee, when he looks up he sees Calhoun exiting the building. "Speak of the devil, there's our boy now." They both watch as Calhoun stands outside the building on his cell phone. "You think I can take him?" Lopez asks, sizing Calhoun up.

Kawowski doesn't say anything since he's too busy studying Calhoun's profile, watching his hand gestures and filing every detail of the man to memory. "I can take 'em," Lopez says aloud. "I bet I can take 'em."

Kawowski nods his head. Not in agreement with Lopez, but as a way of acknowledging to himself that he has Frank Calhoun committed to memory.

"When we nail his balls to the wall for these murders, I'm definitely going to take him," Lopez says.

"Calm down, tiger. You'll get your chance."

"Who's that?" Lopez points to a silver 1969 Ford Impala pulling up in front of the station. They both watch as Calhoun puts his phone away. He hesitates, looking around before finally opening the passenger side door and hopping into the car. The Impala peels off down the street heading east on Harrison.

"Gun it," Kawowski says. "We don't want to lose him now."

CHAPTER 28

stare across the red leather seats of the '69 Impala at the lanky, light-skinned driver known as Prince Paul. He's six-foot-four with cornrows braided to the back of his head. Both of his arms are covered with tattoos of devils with pitchforks, six-point stars and the words 'THE WORLD IS MINE' covering up a knife wound on the inside of his left forearm. On his right hand is a facial tattoo of a baby girl smiling.

I shift down in my seat. Even though I'm on leave, I know it isn't good for me to be seen with a known narcotics dealer like Prince Paul even if the courts can never find enough evidence to convict him of such crimes.

"Damn nigga, what you afraid of? You looking 'round like people after you or something," he says, gliding his hand back and forth over the leather-wrapped steering wheel. The tattooed smiling girl on his hand looks as if she's shaking her head with disapproval.

"Just drive, Paul."

Prince Paul nods before reaching down on his lap and grabbing a small black remote for the radio. He turns up the volume two bars and the trunk starts to rumble as if there's a pack of mad dogs in the back.

"Turn that shit down!" I yell at the top of my lungs as I reach over and turn off the radio. "I'm not here to listen to your goddamn music. What the hell do you want?"

Prince Paul smiles, giving me his most evil bully grin without showing any teeth as a single dimple implants itself deep within his right cheek. It's a smile that hasn't changed since we were kids.

"I hear you're looking for a key?"

"I got your message from Buddy. So what's up?"

"Well, if you got my message, you sure don't act like it. I told Buddy to tell you to come see me. I guess if I hadn't rolled up on you, we would've never met, huh?"

I stare out the window watching as the neighborhood before me changes from two-flat gray stones and three story apartment buildings into cookie-cutter condos and sky blue town homes.

"Let's hear it, Paul."

"Hear what, Frank? Or should I call you Preacher like everybody else in the hood?"

The car comes to a halt at a stop light at Western and Harrison. I turn to look at Paul and to my surprise sitting in his lap like a fat house cat is a chrome nine-millimeter pistol. My eyes fall on the pistol and then I look at Paul with raised eyebrows.

"Don't worry, it's legal. I got the papers and shit in the glove compartment. Even got a FOID card. Don't want you thinking I'm concealing a weapon. We know how you cops like to get itchy trigger fingers."

"Humph, you sure that's what it is? You wouldn't be trying to intimidate me now would you, Paul?"

Prince Paul flashes his bully grin again while turning the car onto Western Boulevard heading north.

"Nah, this doesn't scare you. I'm sure you've seen bigger. This right here is for those little bitch-ass motherfuckers out here who be trying to pull it." He picks up the pistol and kisses its chrome body. "This here is my bitch, you feel me?"

As we ride across the bridge that separates New Western from the Rockwell Housing projects, I can't help but think about what the fall of these colossal buildings will mean to Prince Paul and all the other factions of gangs running the streets.

As we drive past Building 450, Prince Paul throws a hand up in the air to a few guys standing out in front of the building. To a normal bystander Paul's fingers look to form a 'K,' but it's actually a pitchfork like the ones adorning his arms as if they were a Red Badge of Courage for the Gangster Disciple Nation, an organized crime syndicate that started off as a mere street gang. The guys outside the building return the salutation with a similar hand gesture.

I shake my head. With Building 450 being one of the last remaining towers, it's only a matter of time before Paul has more than enough competition on the streets. He turns the car west onto Jackson Boulevard.

"So what do you know about the key I'm looking for?"

"I might know somebody that *might* know something."

"Who's this somebody?"

"Just somebody I know." Paul cuts a sly grin. "Maybe even someone *you* know."

"I don't have time for these games. Either you know something or you don't."

"Let's just say for now I know something. But it's going to cost you."

"Cost me what?"

"I need a favor."

"What kind of favor?"

"The kind of favor you do for friends."

"We're done. Pull over."

Prince Paul veers the car over to the side of the curb. "What's wrong with a favor between friends?" he asks.

I open my door and step out of the car. "We've never been friends, Paul. And we never will. Keep your damn info to yourself." I slam the door.

"All in due time, Preacher. All in due time," he says, peeling off from the curb and down the street.

I start walking east up Jackson. Prince Paul can keep whatever he knows about the key to himself.

The nerve of that fucker. If I had my badge, I might have considered beating the information out of him—maybe give him some payback for all those childhood lumps, but then again, that wouldn't do me any good.

I stop walking and decide to wait at a nearby bus stop where a young black woman is playing with her beautiful baby boy. The baby takes hold of his mother's index finger and bursts into laughter. Watching the young woman and child makes me think about my own mother who died giving birth. All I can recall are photographs of her light complexion beaming off the face of photos. Her mahogany eyes always seemed full of life. People always told me I had my mother's smile but I knew from experience that I had my father's eyes.

Half a block away, the CTA bus is making its way up the street. I run a hand over my face as if trying to remove it along with all that I know of my so-called life. I glance over at the baby and its mother once more and smile. Life is beautiful, even if I never knew the real love of my own mother.

As the bus comes to a stop and throws open its doors for us to enter, I take a deep breath and mumble the words I know that will keep me moving forward.

"Only the holy remain."

CHAPTER 29

"So how is everything, Frank?" Doctor Staples asks as she sits in her chair with a legal pad and pen resting in her lap.

"I can't complain," I say, hunching my shoulders.

Doctor Staples adjusts her glasses. "Do you think you'll be ready to talk today?"

"I guess we'll have to see."

She nods her head. "Very well, let's get started." I shift in the chair trying to get comfortable. "How about we start with your friend that was killed?" she says.

"Father Pantone?"

"Yes, I believe that was his name."

"What about him?"

"Who was he to you? Was he more than a friend?"

I stare at Doctor Staples for a few seconds, not really wanting to discuss this. "Fine," I huff. "He was a good friend. He was my former captain back when I was in the Navy Chaplain Corps."

She nods her head again. "And is that all he was?"

"What do you mean, Doc?"

"I'm just wondering if this Father Pantone was more than a friend to you."

I bite my bottom lip. "Maybe. Look, the whole Corps saw him as more like a father. He gave us spiritual guidance and helped a lot of us through some troubling times. You've seen the newscasts about the war—I don't have to tell you how hard it can be to know what your moral duty is when you're over there. But Father Pantone kept us in line. So yeah, I guess you could say I loved him like a father."

"So now you want revenge?"

"Not revenge. Justice."

"That's good to hear, Frank. But how do you feel knowing that you're on leave and can't take part in the investigation of your friend's murder?"

"I'm not going to lie. At first I was pissed, but after awhile I got over it. There's some good detectives out there working his case and I'm sure they'll bring his killer to justice."

Doctor Staples jots down a few notes in her legal pad then looks back up at me. "How about you tell me about the blackout you had the other day?"

I stop biting my lip. Captain Haggerty must've given her the heads up. I try to smile to convey that I'm not bothered by the fact that she knows more about me than I do about her, but I'm unable to say if it's working.

"What's to tell?" I hunch my shoulders. "It was a blackout, plain and simple."

"But you haven't had one in awhile, right?"

"Yeah. Truthfully, I thought I had them beat and then out of nowhere, I got this woozy feeling. Next thing I know, I'm waking up in a hospital."

"What do you think brought about this feeling of wooziness?"

I look down at the floor, wrestling with my hands. "I was trying to save a kid. A seventeen-year-old who was a witness to Father Pantone's murder, except no one realized he was a witness until it was too late."

The room is silent. I can hear Doctor Staples writing in her notepad, but I'm a bit afraid to meet her gaze for fear that what I'm about to say might be too horrific for her seminal virgin ears.

"I'm telling you, Doc—I can still see that kid. Walking with his headphones on, not a care in the world and then out of nowhere... splat! He's just gone. Shot in the head. And all I could do was try to run to him, to reach out to this dead boy." I hold out my open palms. "And I couldn't even do that much because I passed out."

"It isn't your fault, Frank."

I look up from the floor and stare into her eyes. "I know that, Doc, but you have no idea how it feels to sit back and watch someone die." I ball up my fist. "To know that I could have saved that kid and didn't."

"You can't blame yourself for what evil men do."

"Can't I?" I stare at her with burning eyes of coal. "Next, you'll be telling me that my father's actions have nothing to do with me either."

"They don't."

"Maybe you're right. But it's something I have to live with. Just like I have to live with the image of that boy's grief- stricken mother. I didn't even know what to say the last time I saw her. I was at a complete loss for words."

"It happens. We all handle traumatic situations differently."

"Not me. I've seen enough traumatic situations in my life. I shouldn't have blacked out. And I need you to help me fix it, so it doesn't happen again."

"This isn't a problem that you can fix overnight."

I lean forward in my seat. "And why not?"

Doctor Staples sits astute in her chair as she adjusts her glasses, "Because your blackouts stem from post-traumatic stress, which takes time to get a handle on."

"So, the blackouts are related to what my father did?"

"Maybe. It could also be from your time spent in Iraq. There are a number of things that could be causing them."

"Listen, Doc." I gesture with my hands clasped together. "Just give me something, *anything* I can focus on to beat this thing. I gotta get back to catching the evil men of this world."

Doctor Staples pauses as if she's looking over her notes. "If you really want to beat this, then you're going to have to face your biggest fear and learn to forgive yourself."

"My father?"

"I'm not sure. Only you know what your biggest fear is."

"Yeah, I do. And I think I can do that."

CHAPTER 30

Outside Doctor Staples' office, I inhale the balmy Chicago air as I think about her advice in regards to facing my biggest fear. For first time in a long time, I feel new and refreshed as if a heavy weight has been lifted off my chest. The Doc was right about one thing: talking things out makes me feel a lot better.

"Frank?" someone calls out to me.

I turn and see Andrew Keys, my old bunking mate from chaplain school, bounding up the street with a green military duffle bag hoisted up on his shoulder like an eighties boombox. He's in his late thirties with sandy blond hair, an all-American-square jaw and green eyes to match.

"You old mastiff," Keys says, slapping his hand into mine.

"Drew? What are you doing here, man?" I ask with a genuine smile.

"Just got in on the Greyhound. Came to show my respects for Father Pantone."

"Sorry to tell you, but the funeral was earlier today. I'm sure you can pay your respects at the burial though."

"Yeah, I'm sure I can."

"Where are you coming in from?"

"Tennessee."

"You must have had a long ride. I see you still carry around that old duffle of yours."

"Yeah," Keys says patting the side of the bag as if it were a dog. "Never leave home without it."

"Hey be careful, I think American Express owns that phrase." We laugh like old school yard buddies. "Man, I'm starving. How about we have dinner and catch up on old times?" Keys offers.

"Sounds good to me. I know just the place."

We start walking up Harrison heading east towards Greek Town on Halstead. For a three-block radius, the air smells like roasted lamb. We find some seats at a quaint bar in the middle of Greek Town's restaurant quadrant. I order a gyro with the works and Keys has grilled octopus.

"You drinking?" he asks.

"Nah, I haven't touched the stuff since leaving Iraq."

"You're shitting me. Not even a beer?"

"Not even a beer. I never really liked the stuff anyway."

"Yeah I know, but I do recall the time you drank twelve cans after that patrol near the Euphrates River."

"Well, that was the first time I saw heads floating in a body of water. Drinking seemed appropriate."

"I guess seeing something like that would make any man drink." We sit in silence for a few seconds allowing our shared experience to sink in. "You ever hear from Sanchez?"

"Yeah, he was at the funeral. He's a priest now. Heads a church over in Wicker Park."

"You're shitting me!"

"Yep, all the way down to the white collar and black robe."

Keys shakes his head. "There's no way a monster like him should be a priest."

"Who you telling? When I discovered he was wearing the collar, I started asking around, seeing if he had been up to his old tricks."

"And was he?"

"Nah. He's as clean as a baby's bottom."

Keys laughs. "That's ironic."

"Yeah, I know. Sanchez was a good chaplain though."

"Yeah he was. Even better as a soldier. At least when it came to raping and pillaging."

"We all lost something in Iraq."

"How so?"

"Because—" I pause and wait for the bartender to place our food down on the bar before I continue. "Because we all went into the service for different reasons. But we all came out changed somehow. Maybe not on the surface, but that war changed us all."

"I guess you're right. Well, here's to change." Keys lifts his beer bottle in the air. I bring my Coke up and we clank bottles.

"To change!"

We shoot back our bottles and dig into our food.

"So," Keys says, wiping his mouth with a napkin. "The million dollar question..."

"Which is?" I respond with a mouth full of lamb.

"Do they know why Father Pantone was killed?"

I shake my head and swallow the food before continuing. "Detectives are still working the case."

"Detectives? Aren't you working it? Last time I heard you were a cop, right?"

"Not me. At least not officially." I can't bear to tell Keys that I'm on leave. Besides, it's none of his business.

Keys smiles and nudges me in the ribs with an elbow. "What does that mean?"

"I'm looking around. But officially, I'm not allowed to work the case due to the fact that we shared a personal relationship."

"Oh I see. Have you found anything?"

"A few things, but nothing pressing."

Keys nods his head. "Man, I really don't understand why someone would want to kill the old man. It just doesn't make sense."

"Some things in this world are hard to explain."

"It's like everyday this world seems to get crazier and crazier. I don't know how you're a detective. How'd that happen anyway? If I recall, you didn't want to become a cop because of your dad. What happened to wanting to save the souls of men?"

I partially laugh. Keys can always put a smile on my face. "To tell you the truth, it was Fallujah that changed my mind."

"How so?" Keys leans in towards me.

"It was after we started walking through the city. A 'city of death' is what Father Pantone called it. Somewhere between stepping foot inside that city and returning to base camp something clicked. It was as if I had lost my faith for a few seconds. But within those seconds, I decided that the only way I could actually help the world and save a few souls was to get evil off the streets. I didn't want Chicago to become a city of death."

"I totally understand, Frank." Keys picks up his bottle of beer and wets his lips. "Nobody else understands. They think the war is all about oil or democracy or a million other things, but nobody has an idea what real war is or what it does to you, you know what I'm saying? How it opens your eyes to the real world around you and gives you a broader perspective on what matters."

I down the last of my Coke. Hearing Keys talk about Fallujah makes me feel as if I'm not alone. With Father Pantone gone, there's no one to talk to about the war except Sanchez. But he'd come through the crucible a changed man, following the path of God. And not every chaplain can do such a thing after witnessing the atrocities of war.

"Bartender," I call out. "Can we get another round of beers?" I'm breaking my code for tonight—I can't allow a fellow chaplain to drink alone, especially on the day of our spiritual leader's funeral.

"Heeeeey! Now, that's what I'm talking about!" Keys bellows with arms wide open as the bartender drops two more bottles of Budweiser down on the bar.

"To Father Anton Pantone!" I declare.

"To Father Pantone!"

I pinch my lips together sustaining the taste of the sour amber brew. The first drop of beer after a long absence is always extra tart. I sit the bottle down on the bar. "You remember that time back in Newport when we got Sanchez, Lee, and Douglas to drink that homemade moonshine we made from orange peels?"

"Oh yeah! Man, we had those damn things sitting for days percolating in their own juices."

"I thought you were crazy when you first suggested it."

"But it worked, didn't it?" Keys says beaming with pride.

"Yeah it worked all right. Neither one of us was willing to try a drop."

"I was willing... once we found somebody else to take the first drink."

"And to think, all this time I thought you were a man of God. You're supposed to walk by faith, not by sight."

"Oh, I did." Keys laughs. "I walked right over to Sanchez's dorm and offered him and his roommates the closest damn thing they were going to get to alcohol."

I close my eyes and rub my hands together. Just the thought

of that day has me cringing and salivating at the same time. "We got down that night. I had never been so drunk in all my life. I was drunk for two days straight."

"You were," Keys says. "I guess we all should have been grateful that it was a few days before we took our vows and Father Pantone showed us leniency."

I take a long swig of my beer. "He was a good man. One of the best," I say.

We raise our bottles again in remembrance. "Bartender!" Keys calls out. "Another round and a shot of Jack. And let's get some Irish car bombs down here!"

CHAPTER 31

opez sits up in his seat when he spots Frank Calhoun and another man exit the bar. He checks the clock on the dash. It's 2:50 a.m. and Kawowski hasn't returned yet with the coffees. He watches the two men stagger drunkenly up the street towards Jackson Boulevard where the restaurant and club crowd are beginning to mix. He has it in his mind to slip out of the car and make it look like he's bumping into Calhoun by coincidence and see what he can learn from their brief encounter, but then he thinks better of it. Besides, Kawowski is the lead on this case, which means he needs to follow the play that's being called.

Lopez cracks the window of the Caprice so he can listen to the two men as they bound up the street singing Cab Calloway's "Minnie the Moocher." Halfway through the second verse, he watches Calhoun stop and lurch to the side of the curb. He can hear the guttural wails from Calhoun as he regurgitates his meal all over the sidewalk.

"This is fucking ridiculous," he says aloud, looking over his shoulder to make sure Kawowski isn't within earshot. He doesn't believe in his partner's play wholeheartedly, but he has to stomach it.

He turns his head and watches a group of women strut up the street. They're all dressed in mini-skirts and halter-tops. He sizes them up, taking into account that he can clearly see the horizon of their breasts bursting from the seams of their Victoria Secret Wonder Bras and the outline of panty lines for those that are wearing them.

"Focus," he tells himself. He turns back to look across the street where Calhoun and his friend have been standing, but finds the curb empty. He leans in closer to the windshield, studying the lit street.

Where the hell have they gone?

He opens the door and steps out of the car, scanning the block, but there's no a sign of them.

"Shit!" he yells out, slamming his hands against the top of the car's roof.

He turns and looks back down the street to where the group of women are now entering a club. He sees Kawowski beginning to walk up the street with two cups of coffee in hand and a smile on his face. It's a smile that he knows will fade once he tells him that they've lost Calhoun.

CHAPTER 32

The yellow taxi pulls to the curb of my home.

"You sure this is the address you want?" the Indian driver asks for the tenth or eleventh time as if Keys and I have somehow made a mistake about the address due to the fact that we're both intoxicated.

"Yeah, we're sure," Keys says, handing the driver a ten-dollar bill on the $9.50 fare. "Keep the change," he states in a snide manner to let the driver know that we don't appreciate his assumption about the location of my neighborhood.

Upon exiting the car, Keys wraps his arms around my waist and hoists me up under the shoulder as we slowly make our way up the flight of stairs to the doorway. He stands me up against a wall in the outer hall and removes the house keys from my pocket.

"Y-you-you're ma brotha," I drunkenly blurt out. "Ma brotha from anotha motha."

"I'm your brother, Frank. Which key opens the door?" He jingles the key ring in front of me.

"Keyyyyys!" I say. "Fa-Fa-Father Pantone had a key."

"Yeah, what kind of key?" He asks while shoving key after key into the deadbolt.

"Some kind of special key."

"Do you know what it's for?"

"Noooo! But I'm gonna find out! And when I do—" I hold up a balled fist. "I'm gonna kick the guy's ass who took it from me."

"Slow down, champ. I'm sure you will."

Keys finally finds the correct door key and pops the lock. He guides me into the apartment. "Where's the light?" he asks.

"Right wall, as soon as you turn this corner to the living room."

He flips on the light and I cringe like a vampire to sunlight.

"Let's get you to bed, buddy."

"That's what I'm going to do to that guy that took th-that-that key from me. I'm gonna—I'm gonna lay him down like a dirty whore."

"I'm sure you will, partner."

Keys leads me through the living room and into the dining room. We turn to the left and he directs me to my bed where he sits me down on the edge of it. He bends down and unties my shoes while I place a hand on his shoulder.

"You ma brotha no matter what, Drew. We took our vows together. I'll always be there for you."

He smiles. "I know. You're my brother too, Frank. Bound by our vows eternally." Keys lifts my legs up onto the bed. "Sleep well, my friend." He pulls the covers up to my neck and tucks me in.

I watch my friend depart through the open door. I can't help but think about all the good times we've shared while attending chaplain school. As I watch Keys close the bedroom door, a last slit of light from the dining room enters and falls across my face. As I lay, I remember the day that he, Sanchez and I graduated from chaplain school and how Father Pantone told the three of us that we were the best he had ever instructed and that he expected us to go out into the world and create change.

CHAPTER 33

awake in darkness. I lay in bed listening to the quietness of my own home. My head is pounding something fierce as I slowly sit up. The bare wooden floor is cold under my feet and gives me the jolt I need to get up. I rise while stretching and find that I'm still dressed in the clothes that I wore the night before.

Stumbling out of the darkness and into the brightness of the dining room, I attempt to shield my eyes from the light. My head feels as though it might erupt. I walk past the dining room table, heading for the bathroom. But I spot something out of the corner of my eye which causes me to stop and turn back. Sitting atop my dining room table, I find my makeshift murder book sprawled open.

"Drew, you here?" I call out, not hearing a response. I go into the living room and find it desolate. The couch is barren, not even a folded blanket can be found. I look around the room puzzled and walk back through the dining room and down the hall to the kitchen.

"Drew, you here, man?" I ask again.

The kitchen is also empty and dark. I look at the phone on the wall and notice the green light blinking at the top corner of the receiver, indicating that I have a message. I pick up the phone and dial in the number for the voice mail. There's a second or two of silence before it rings and then I input the four-digit pass code. The dial tone of the phone clicks and the first message that comes through the receiver is crackling.

"Detective Calhoun, this is Arnie Ratcliff again. I've heard everything about the Murphy murder and I wanted to know if you wanted to give your side of the story. I can be reached at—"

I delete the message. I'd lain down with a dog and gotten up with one of the biggest fleas in the city. This was just the beginning and I knew Ratcliff would be unrelenting.

The second message is from Masters. He's got a hit on the prints that I removed from the Murphy residence, but he says the discovery isn't good. He starts to leave a call back number but I don't have a pen. I remember there's one in the dining room next to the murder book. With the phone cradled to my ear, I run into the adjoining room to grab the pen off the table and begin to write down Masters's phone number in small print on the palm of my hand. After transcribing the number I walk back into the kitchen to hang up the phone and turn to look over my shoulder at the murder book.

Why is it open? I was almost certain I'd left it closed, but maybe I was wrong. I walk back into the dining room and over to the table. I stare down at the open murder book at a question I'd written a few days ago at the top of a new page: WHO WAS FATHER PANTONE'S MISTRESS?

It's a valid question that's only come into existence based on Sanchez's confession that Father Pantone broke his vow of celibacy. But why was the murder book open to this page? I can't remember leaving it open, especially knowing this entry could reveal Father Pantone's deepest secret.

Drew. It had to be him. But why? I study the book curiously and see a folded sheet of paper sticking out from the side of the binder. I open it to see that Drew has written something.

Dear Frank,

Sorry I had to run, buddy. Needed to pay my respects before I caught the bus out of town. It was great catching up with you. Next time I'm in town, I'll look you up.

-Drew

I fold the letter close. Keys has come and gone like so many others in my life. It's to be expected—you don't become the son of a cop killer without alienating just about everyone you come into contact with.

I reread the question about Father Pantone's mistress once more and can't help but wonder who she might be? My gut tells me it was the woman I followed out of the church, but she's long gone. At least, I have the shooter's prints now, which means this investigation is heading down a new road where the killer doesn't even realize that the noose is closing in around his neck.

I close the murder book and head for the restroom to grab two aspirin before my head splits open. I swallow them down and give Masters a call back to find out what he's discovered.

CHAPTER 34

"What do you mean dead?!" I yell into the receiver of the phone as I sit at my dining room table with the murder book in front of me.

"Listen, I ran those prints like you asked," Masters says. "And they came back belonging to a dead man by the name of Mitch Bigsby."

"Listen, Kevin—this guy can't be dead. I pulled those prints myself. They were fresh."

"Maybe at one point they were, but his military records show that Sergeant Bigsby died in Iraq over two years ago."

"Did you run the prints through VICAP?"

"Didn't have to. Once I started to run it through the national database, I got a hit within an hour."

I sit silently trying to put the pieces of the puzzle together. I whisper a monotone thanks and hang up. I drop my head into my hands. There's no way that Bigsby was on that rooftop three years ago. Those prints were fresh and I was absolutely certain of it.

I turn to a clean page in the murder book and date it before writing a detailed explanation of when and where I pulled the prints as well as an explanation of what Masters discovered in his findings. After every detail is written down I sit back and stare at the sheet of paper.

What am I missing? Whatever it is, it isn't in the murder book. I pick up the phone and redial Masters' number. After a few rings, he finally answers.

"Masters here."

"Kevin, it's Frank again. I need you to fax those Bigsby documents over to me if you can."

"Sure thing, Frank."

I give him the fax number and say my goodbyes for the last time. After hanging up the phone, I sit for a few minutes tapping my fingers on the murder book. I tell myself that I should've gotten dressed and gone down to the forensics building for the papers instead of having them faxed. Even though it will be faster, I'm dreading the fact that the machine is in my father's old office.

I stand up from my seat and take a deep breath, reminding myself that the only way I'm going to beat these blackouts is if I start to face my fears. I walk over to the door, place my hand on the doorknob and take another deep breath. I turn the brass handle and open the door.

The smell of old newspapers and *Musk For Men* cologne drifts out of the bedroom-turned-office. I flip on the light switch near the door and the room illuminates with an orange hue. Three of the four walls are occupied with bookshelves filled with various books on crime investigation and literary classics such as *Middle Passage* by Charles Johnson. In the right corner of the room is a desk with a lamp on top of it along with a magnifying glass and a pencil. On the opposite wall is the fax machine and an old manual typewriter.

I move over to the desk and study the newspaper clippings

tacked to the wall above it. One article is about my father receiving a commendation for his time as an officer. The second clipping is Uncle Skeet and my father smiling after they saved some children from a burning building. The last clipping is a headline from the *Chicago Sun-Times* that reads *LIFE AFTER DEATH*. I don't know what it means, but I think back to what Mags said about each cop having a case that they can't let go. My guess was this was the one my father couldn't let go.

I pick up a dust-covered pencil and turn it over in my hands. There are teeth marks all along the body of the pencil and I envision my father biting down on it as he sits back in his wooden armchair, trying to unravel some secret to a case.

I put the pencil back down on the desk, doing my best to place it within the confines of its dusty layout. I reach over and switch on the fax machine. The piece of equipment purrs to life with blinking red and green lights. It beeps before two sheets of paper appear on the receiving tray. I pick up the fingerprint analysis forms that Masters has sent over and glance over them. I step over to the door, flick off the light and exit the room.

Upon returning to the dining room table, I open up the murder book and place the forms in-between the rings of the binder. Then I turn to page one of the fingerprint forms and read every detail aloud to commit it to memory.

CHAPTER 35

After reading the fingerprint analysis forms and discovering that Sergeant Mitchell Bigsby's last known residence was in New Lenox, I decide it's time to follow the paper trail. Everything Masters told me over the phone about him matched up, right down to the official military seal of classification which didn't disclose any personal information such as his background in the armed services or next of kin. Bigsby's records read like a Watergate file, full of blacked out names and locations. The word "classified" told me two things: one, if the Pentagon wanted a lock on all his records, it meant Bigsby's personal file was as hot as enriched uranium. And two, before long shit was sure to hit the fan.

Upon stepping out my front door in a white polo shirt and khakis, I find Jamal and Janai sitting on the porch.

"Hey guys," I say, surprised they're out so early. "Hey Mister Calhoun," Jamal blurts out.

"We're going to the zoo!" Janai squeals with excitement.

"The zoo, huh?" I nod my head. "And where's your mom?" "She's upstairs getting ready," the little girl giggles.

"Well you tell her I said hello."

I bound down the stairs and just as I'm about to walk out the gate, I hear Gloria coming out the front door. I turn around to see her standing at the top of the stairs wearing a pair of navy blue Capri's along with a blue and white striped polo. Her curly bangs fall across her forehead as small specks of sunlight break through the tree line and cover her light skin, giving it a golden-honey hue.

"Gloria." I speak her name softly as if any other way would be disrespectful.

"Hello Frank." She presses her lips together and smiles. "I see you don't have your babysitters anymore."

I chuckle. "I guess they figured I was all grown-up and could walk the streets by myself."

"Well, that's good to know."

"Mister Calhoun, would you like to come to the zoo with us?" Janai asks with glee in her voice.

I stare at Gloria. "I'd like to, but I can't because I've got some important business I've got to tend to. Maybe next time."

"You be careful out here, Frank," Gloria says in a playful manner.

"Yes, ma'am. You all have a great day at the zoo."

I open the gate and step out, holding it open for the family to follow behind. Once Gloria and the kids are safely inside their car, I wave goodbye and start down the block towards Madison Street where I plan to catch the number 20 bus to my Uncle Skeet's. Walking down the street, I catch sight of hustlers standing on corners waiting to serve addicts as I pull out my cell to make a call.

Two young men in large white tee-shirts who can't be older than seventeen slap box in the middle of a small street with jeans hung low off their asses. The crowd surrounding them is made up of young boys and older men who cheer on the slapping fighters. If I had a badge I might have dispersed the crowd before the slapping turned into fists or escalated into something even deadlier, but since I don't, it means I have no authority on these streets. So I just keep walking, leaving the situation to possibly turn into a powder keg.

After a few rings, the phone is picked up on the other end and a groggy voice comes in over the line.

"Gunz here. Who's this?"

"Petey, it's Frank Calhoun. Sorry I woke you. I keep forgetting Hawaii is five hours behind?"

"What's up Preacher?" Gunz sounds annoyed.

"I need some info, Petey. And you're the only one who can get it for me."

"How so?" Petey asks with a drowsy slur.

"You got a pen?" I hear Gunz exhale with frustration over losing sleep as he sits the phone down and begins to fumble around for something to write with.

He's one of the few souls that I was able to save from these streets. A few years back, he was a young kid stealing electronics, mostly laptops and handheld devices from riders on the city's trains and buses. I came across him in K-Town selling a stolen laptop, back when I was a minister still trying to save the souls of the neighborhood thugs. It took more than one encounter for the young man to trust me, but one faithful night I got a call.

"Preacher, it's Gunz," he says into the receiver.

"Gunz?"

"The black Steve Jobs of K-Town."

"Oh yes. How can I help you, young man?"

"I got caught up and I need some help. They tryin' to send me up to county and a frail nigga like me can't survive in a place like that."

"But you realize that the county jail is part of the doing the crime, don't you?"

"Preacher, you get me out of here and I'll go to whatever church you want me to go to."

"What if it isn't church?

"I don't care. Wherever you want me to go, I'll go."

"Is that a deal?"

"On my dead mama's grave."

"Then, I'll be right down."

That night, I came to his aid with the help of Blue who had just become an officer of the law and convinced him to enter the Navy, where he became an intelligence officer on the U.S. Carrier Alabama.

"Okay shoot," Gunz says finally coming back on the line.

"The name's Bigsby. Sergeant Mitchell Bigsby. He served in the Marines, not sure what unit."

"Mitchell Bigsby. Got it."

"I need everything you can find on this guy, Petey. His file is coming up classified, so I'm going to need this intel to be below the radar."

"Gotcha."

"Thanks Petey. I'll let you get back to your beauty sleep."

"With a face like yours, maybe you should consider getting some extra nap time too."

———

Skeet's is crowded as people sit in their cars outside the restaurant, enjoying cheese grits, scrambled eggs, a side of bacon and toast in a Styrofoam container while washing it down with juice, soda or liquor. Inside, the place is full of energy.

Philicia, along with a light-skinned woman and a Puerto

Rican woman with the complexion of a bright yellow school bus are moving around the place like ballerinas while balancing plates of food in their hands.

I scan the room for a seat, but there are none to be found. I spot Fred Lions and his partner Jeff Bishops sitting at the counter, enjoying their breakfast.

"Be right with you, sugar," the light-skinned waitress says, passing by on her way to the kitchen.

I nod and begin cutting across the room, making my way towards the counter. As I cut in between tables, I come across a large crowd of uniformed officers. Sitting amongst them are Richter and Smith.

"I'll be damned!" Smith says, hitting the table with his bare hands. "This is the fucker that broke my nose!"

The other officers quickly rise from their seats and eye me. I look for a detour but the bodies of the officers block the spaces in between the other tables.

"I was hoping we'd run into each other again, Calhoun."

I pivot on my right foot, ready to throw the first punch. All the officers' faces are contorted with anger as they roll up their sleeves as if they want to avoid getting dirty. Their arms flex with controlled muscle, which tells me they aren't rookies, but experienced men who know how to leave a mark on you without leaving one on themselves. The wall of blue begins to close in around me and Smith soon takes the lead, breaking off from the group to confront me head on.

"I'm going to enjoy this," he smiles. "We're going to show you what it means to play on the same team."

There's a commotion from the back of the group as officers are pushed to the side, making a path for Lions and his partner Bishops to enter the circle.

"I thought that was you, Frank," Lions says, scanning the faces of each officer.

Bishops stands calmly near his partner with his hands at his side, balled into fists.

"If you patrolmen haven't noticed, we're all on the same team here. It's the scumbags out there we ought to be fighting," Lions says, pointing towards the window that gives a clear view out into the world. "But if you boys want to play it that way, then let's get it on."

He drops his blazer to the floor as his muscles bulge under his pink button-down shirt. The place is silent as the remaining customers either clear out or wait in anticipation for what is going to happen next. I stare into Smith's eyes, but the cocky patrolman isn't backing down since he knows we're easily outnumbered three-to-one.

"If you feel froggy, then leap," I taunt.

The quietness is suddenly broken by a loud knock which makes every head in the place turn towards the kitchen. Standing behind the counter with a nightstick in hand is my Uncle Skeet with a red bandanna tied around his head. Standing a few feet to his side is Philicia armed with two large knives, looking ready to go to war for my uncle.

"I'll have you all doing traffic duty before I see any of you disrespect the badge!" he shouts out over the restaurant. "The only person in here that's *ever* going to lay a hand on my nephew is me. Now, if any of you got a problem with that, then you'll have to take it up with me. And I promise you—*you don't want to take it up with me.*"

Smith turns to stare at me, smiling with the bridge of his nose taped up. The silly bastard is going to try it. He takes a step forward, but stops when Richter places a hand on his shoulder. "Let it go, Ryan. The old sergeant's right."

Smith stares at me long and hard before shrugging off his partner's hand and returning to his seat. The other officers follow suit.

I turn to Lions. "Thanks Fred. It's good to know I still have some friends in the department."

"Isn't it?" Bishops says sarcastically as he returns to his seat at the counter.

"Don't worry about him," Lions says. "There's still a few in the department that haven't let go of what your father did."

I nod my head, understanding all too well. We stroll over to the counter where Uncle Skeet is still standing with the nightstick in his hand. "Boy, I hate to say it, but everywhere you go trouble seems to follow."

"Story of my life, Unc."

"Sit on down. What can I get you two detectives for helping out my nephew?"

"We're good," Lions responds with a wave of the hand.

"The least I can do is get the check," Uncle Skeet offers. Lions gives a small shrug and a nod. No way was Lions turning down the idea of a free meal.

"So what did you do to get those boys' panties all twisted in a knot?" Uncle Skeet asks.

"Had a run-in with one of them and broke his nose. I guess he didn't get the message the first time around."

"Frank, you better be careful," Lions warns. "You know how it is to be in the uniform. Those boys ride together no matter what."

"Thanks for the reminder, Fred. I'll have to remember that the next time around. Unc, we need to talk."

"Sure thing, Frank. I'll see you in the back."

I wave goodbye to Lions and step around the counter, through the kitchen doors and into the back office.

"So what do you want to talk about?" Uncle Skeet asks, standing behind the desk with his back to me as he replaces the nightstick on the wall rack.

"I need to take a little trip and I need you to drive."

"A trip, huh? And what kind of trip would we be going on?"

"It's local. A little south is all."

"You sure? Because if you haven't noticed, I've got a business to run."

"Yeah Unc, I'm sure. I wouldn't ask if I could drive myself."

"I know, I know. I guess I could leave Philicia in charge for a few hours."

The fact that Uncle Skeet is willing to leave her in charge of the restaurant says a great deal about their relationship, which I'm certain to be intimate after her knife display a few moments earlier.

"So where we going?" Uncle Skeet inquires.

"New Lenox. There's a dead man I'm hoping to find alive down there."

CHAPTER 36

As he zig-zags in and out of traffic, Uncle Skeet drives like he's still a cop in a cruiser with sirens blaring. A quick peek at the speedometer reads 75 mph and the dial is still revving up on his red Mustang GT.

"You might want to slow it down a little, Unc. The speed limit is fifty-five."

"I thought you said you needed to get to New Lenox in a hurry?"

"I do. But I'd rather not get there in a body bag."

The traffic on the Dan Ryan Expressway is light during the mid-day afternoon, I'm glad we're beating rush hour. Uncle Skeet slows the car down to a moderate 65 mph as we cruise heading south.

"So tell me again why we're going to New Lenox?" Uncle Skeet asks.

"I'm hoping to find Father Pantone's murderer there."

"But didn't you say this Bigsby character was dead?"

"He is. At least on paper."

"Frank, you know I'll back you on anything, but I have to

ask—what makes you think this guy is still alive, especially after the Pentagon has already ruled him dead?"

I suck my teeth and look out the window at the passing cars. "I just have a feeling that some of the answers to my questions lie in New Lenox."

"So you're telling me that you have no proof that this guy is actually alive? Or even if he's the shooter you've been looking for?"

"Look, I wouldn't have asked you to drive me if I could have done it myself." The frustration rises in my voice.

"Don't jump down my throat, okay? I'm just trying to connect the dots. See it as an outsider would see it."

I drop my head. "Sorry, Unc. I didn't mean any disrespect." I need for him to know that he's as necessary to this investigation as the road that we travel on. We sit in silence for a few miles before I speak again.

"Truthfully, I think Sergeant Bigsby might actually be dead, but those prints I pulled don't lie. Which means that either he and Jesus have something in common, or at the very least, the killer is connected to him in some way."

Uncle Skeet nods. "So what happens if we find what you're looking for?" he asks.

"What do you mean what happens?"

"Let's say we come across whoever you're looking for—what do you think is going to happen when they see you coming?" I'm silent. I didn't think about the possibility of anything going down. "I bet you're not even packing, are you?"

"Just my old man's retirement piece," I say.

"At least you aren't stupid enough to go out on a limb with your dick in your hand and no protection. I've got a few things in the trunk in case we need something a little more powerful."

"What type of things?"

"Nothing you need to concern yourself with."

I give a shrug and switch on the radio, tuning it to 107.5 WGCI, a predominantly hip-hop and R&B station. A fast tempo song comes blaring out the speakers, but Uncle Skeet quickly turns the tuner to 102.3, an old school station that plays classic R&B. "Now if you're going to ride in my car then you're going to ride to something a little more easy going," he says as a bass riff for the Temptations' "Papa was a Rolling Stone" churns its way out of the speakers. "Now that's what I'm talking about."

Uncle Skeet bobs his head while tapping his fingers against the steering wheel. I sit back in my seat and stare out the window, as the song forces me to think about my father having another son not even a block away from my own home. I close my eyes and tell myself not to think about him because I need to keep my mind focused on the task at hand. My gut is telling me that I'm on to something, but I'm not sure what. All I know is that the truth lies in New Lenox.

Uncle Skeet shakes me awake as he pulls the car to the curb of a cul-de-sac.

"We're here?" I ask groggily.

"Up the street a ways. The house you want is up there." He points through the windshield to a tree-lined street of beige houses with a few SUV's and minivans parked out in the driveway of the homes.

"Why'd you park all the way down here?" I ask sitting up in my seat.

"We need to get ready."

"Get ready? What are you talking about?"

"You'll see." Uncle Skeet opens his door and I do the same as he proceeds to round the car before opening the trunk.

Inside are two pump-action 12-gauge shotguns, a pair of bullet-proof vests and a tackle box full of ammo.

"What the hell do you have all this stuff for?" I ask.

"In case of situations like the one we're about to walk into. We need to be ready for anything. Lord knows your father wouldn't forgive me if I let something happen to you."

I lay my hand on my uncle's shoulder. "Listen, Unc. I appreciate what you're trying to do, but I won't need any of this. This is just a routine questioning."

"What do you mean *I*? I'm going in there with you."

"No, you're not. You're not an officer of the law anymore and I can't put you in harm's way."

"Shit, I was in harm's way before you learned to piss in a pot."

"That's why I need you to trust me and sit this one out."
"But—"

"Trust me."

"Okay, Frank. This is your show, so I'm going to let you run it. But if you're gone for too long, I'm coming in there with guns blazing."

I smile. "I wouldn't have it any other way."

I step around the car and begin making my way up the street towards a two-story house with brown shingles on the roof and a red mailbox that looks more like a homemade bird-house. This cul-de-sac is a stereotypical American suburb with its conforming beige and tan colors and its symmetrical two story single-family homes that include a two-car garage. If it wasn't for the Bigsby name written across the side, finding this place would have been like a needle in a haystack.

I ring the doorbell and a few seconds later, the door opens and an older gentleman wearing a black truckers hat stands in the doorway. The image on the hat is a man pulling the cord to the truck's horn while the words 'BLOW ME' explode from the truck's bugle in bright yellow letters. The man has a gruff brown beard with matching brown eyes.

He looks me up and down. "Sorry, but I believe in Jesus," he says, ready to close the door in my face.

"I'm not a Jehovah's Witness," I say, flashing my father's old badge. "I'm Detective Frank Calhoun."

The man eyes the badge and relaxes a bit. "Sorry about that, detective. Every now and again, we get these witnesses coming through here talking that nonsense about Jesus being just a man."

"I understand."

"So how can I help you... uhhh, what was your name again?" "Calhoun, Detective Frank Calhoun. Could I possibly step inside?"

"Oh sure, sure. I'm Francis Bigsby, but I'm sure you knew that already, right?"

Mr. Bigsby invites me inside his home. The front room is painted white with paintings of baby angels hanging on the walls. The furniture is also white with wooden legs and arms painted gold.

"Right this way," Mr. Bigsby says, ushering me past the front room and into the living room, which is covered in a forestry looking wallpaper. Above the fireplace, hangs the head of a deer and a large wooden cabinet is open, revealing a TV and VCR player.

"You can have a seat," Mr. Bigsby says, pointing to the brown leather couch. "Would you like something to drink?"

"No, thank you. I just have a few questions and then I'll be out of your hair."

"Sure thing, ask away."

I pull out my notepad and flip it open. "Mr. Bigsby, do you have a son by the name of Mitchell Bigsby?"

"I *had* a son by that name."

"Had?"

"Yes, he died in Iraq two years ago." Mr. Bigsby rises from his seat and moves over to the fireplace. "May I ask why you're asking about my dead son, detective?"

"Your son's prints came up in an investigation and I'm just doing my due diligence, you know? Crossing my T's and dotting all my I's."

Mr. Bigsby nods his head. "Well, as you can see my son couldn't be involved in your investigation—"

I stand up from the sofa and sigh. "I'm just trying to cover all the tracks, sir."

"I understand." Mr. Bigsby places his hand on the mantle of the fireplace and slides a dark box off of the stone surface. "This is his purple heart."

He hands the black box over to me and I open it. "It's very honorable," I say, staring down at the gold and purple heart-shaped medal with an image of George Washington engraved on it. "I'm sure it makes you and your wife proud to know your son gave his life for this country."

Mr. Bigsby looks down at the floor before replying in a soft whisper. "My wife's been gone for quite some time. And no, I'm not proud that my boy threw his life away for this stupid ass war." His voice rises with a stern tone to it. "In fact, I told him not to go but after 9/11, he felt he had a duty to serve this country. Now don't get me wrong—I love our troops and believe in them, but this is one war that none of them should be fighting in."

I nod my head and hand him back the medal. I understand more than he realizes.

"And to think, the last thing we said to one another was so hateful," he says softly with his finger lamenting over the dark felt box.

"I'm sure he didn't die with a heavy heart, sir."

"Maybe so. If anything, he died with an angry heart." I look at him quizzically. "How so?"

Mr. Bigsby takes a seat on the couch. He picks up a framed family photo from the side table and stares down at it. His hesitation, and the fact that he's taking deeper breaths than before, tells me that he's reached the apex of his emotional climb and is a dam about to break. I just have to wait for him to come to a resolve, and whatever he's holding back will come spilling forth like a raging river.

Exhaling, Mr. Bigsby says in a low voice as if he's about to say a prayer. "My wife Allison was on one of the planes that struck the twin towers." I don't say a word, just nod my head and allow him to continue. "After her death, my son and I began to drift apart. He became self-absorbed and isolated. I'm a trucker, so I couldn't be here with him twenty-four hours a day. Before I realized it, I didn't even know my own son. He had become obsessed with Al-Qaeda."

He pauses as he looks down at the framed photo. "One night, I came home to find him on the computer watching these Al-Qaeda executions. It was the most dreadful thing I'd ever seen. I mean, there are innocent people, soldiers, construction workers being beheaded. And he's just watching this filth like he's studying it or something. I didn't recognize the look in his eye. After that, I tried to get him help, but it was already too late. He had made up his mind to enlist in the Marines."

Mr. Bigsby stops talking and stares down at the photo, outlining the figures with his finger. The love for his son and wife is undeniable and heartbreaking. It makes me think of my father and how my feelings for him have transitioned to resentment since his conviction. Mr. Bigsby clears his throat as the flooding memory recedes and everything returns to normal.

"I am truly sorry for your loss, Mr. Bigsby. I apologize for having you reopen such hurtful wounds."

"It's okay, Detective. I know you're just doing your job." He places the frame back on the side table and rises from the couch.

"Thank you for your time, sir."

We shake hands. "The pleasure was all mine. I hope you find your man."

"Yeah, me too."

He walks me back through the house and shows me to the door. "Oh, by the way, may I have one of your cards?" He pauses. "Just in case I remember something that might be important."

I study him curiously before handing him a card and turn to leave. I can tell he's holding something back, but he isn't yet ready to let go and I don't want to push it, especially since I'm not supposed to be working this investigation in the first place.

Back in the car, I fill Uncle Skeet in on what I've learned. "So you're letting it go?" Uncle Skeet asks.

"Not entirely. I'm not sure how Sergeant Bigsby is involved in all this, but I think his father knows something."

Uncle Skeet starts the car. "Where to? Back to the city?"

"Joliet. Since we're in the area, I think it's time I see my father."

CHAPTER 37

The rain clouds that occupy the afternoon sky are light grey. I stare up at them, watching as they slowly drift towards the stone castle of Joliet Correctional Center. I tap the roof of the car to let Uncle Skeet know that I'm going in.

"You sure you don't want to come?" I ask one last time.

Uncle Skeet doesn't even turn to look at me as he stares at the concrete fortress. "I'm sure. Once was enough for me."

The prison is designed to look something like a medieval castle with long turrets that rise into the sky and massive brick towers that overlook a barbwire-fenced-in-yard with guards posted at the ready with rifles.

Entering through the first outer gate, I'm stopped at a checkpoint by a white guard with rough blue eyes. I sign in and show him my identification. The guard runs a metal detecting wand up and down my body as well as across my arms and legs. I know the procedure so I left everything except the ID card in the car. After passing through the first checkpoint, a steel-plated door opens and I step into a small space where two black guards stand on either side of a metal detector.

"Detective Frank Calhoun. I'm here to see a prisoner by the name of Joe Calhoun." I show the guards my ID.

One of the guards radios the request while the other watches the sensors on the metal detector as I pass through it. After clearing the checkpoint, I'm led down a long corridor and into a private visitor's room. The room is half the size of a cell and lit by fluorescent track lights encased in metal mesh cages. I take a seat at a metal table with a stainless steel chair on either side of it. The room smells like sweat and cheap cologne, letting me know that a lawyer and client meeting must have taken place before my arrival.

I tap my fingers on the table as I wait for the guards to bring my father down from lockup. My stomach feels tight as if someone's wringing a wet towel around my abdomen. I haven't seen my father since the night I arrested him and I don't really know what to say to him or what he might say to me.

The metal door to the room opens and a guard steps into the space followed by my father, who's wearing an orange jumpsuit. His hands are big and thick and shackled to his sides along with his legs. A salt-and-pepper beard covers his face and extends down past his chin. He's the black Confucius. His eyes are hard, distant and dark and the once lovable smile I remember gracing his face is gone, likely wiped clean forever. He looks slightly older than fifty-five, as if prison has somehow aged him beyond natural limits.

Another guard steps into the room and closes the door behind them. They lead my father over to the table, sit him down in the metal chair and run the manacles on his legs into a steel hoop cemented to the floor.

I study my father while the guards work to secure his restraints. Staring into his brown eyes, I look for the man I knew before everything went to shit. I do my best to picture his handsome clean-shaven face and square jaw that reminds me so much of Blue's.

When the guards have finished securing my father, I show them the badge and request that the hand restraints be removed. The guards comply and I order them to leave the room—I want to be alone with my father.

Once the metal door to the meeting room closes, my father leans forward in his seat while rubbing his wrist and forms a large tar-stained smile. "My boy. Finally come to see yo' old man, huh?"

I stare at him for a second, wondering if the guards have brought down the right man. This man can't be my father. He never smiles unless he's doing his job. Sensing the emotions written on my face, my father drops the smile and leans back in his seat.

"It's me, Frank. Your father—the man you arrested and put in this shit hole."

"That's not my fault. I was doing my duty and following my vows. Didn't you teach me that?"

My father nods. "I guess somewhere along the line you picked up some new lessons, huh?"

I'm silent for a second. This isn't how I wanted us to start. "How are they treating you in here?" I ask.

My father smiles half-heartedly. "How do you think they treat ex-cops in prison? I spent the first six months in solitary confinement because some motherfucker tried to run a shank through me. The warden told me that confinement was for my own protection. Whatever the hell that meant."

"And what about now?" I sound more concerned than I thought I would.

"I'm good. After I got out of solitary, there were still guys looking to take their shot at me. Just when I thought I'd be fighting these assholes everyday, I find out that T-Rex is running things in here."

I look at him confused.

"You know T-Rex. Used to run that dope spot before what's his name took over..." My father starts snapping his fingers. "You know who I'm talking about... Paul. Yeah, Prince Paul. That's his name."

I slowly nod remembering T-Rex. He's a tall dark man with jagged teeth and small evil eyes. He'd been Prince Paul's mentor back in the day and schooled the young hustler in the ways of the dope game.

My father smiles before continuing. "One day I'm in the yard when these two ugly, gorilla-looking motherfuckers roll up on me. Before anyone can throw a punch, I hear my name being called out from across the way. I look up and see T-Rex standing there with a gang of dudes behind him. These dumbasses didn't know me and T-Rex go back a ways. Needless to say, I haven't had trouble since."

I study my father even more. I know that prison can change a man, but my father has done a complete 360 from the straight- and-narrow patrol officer that he had been on the outside.

"Enough about me though," he says. "How have you been?"

"I'm good. Just trying to put my life back together."

"That's understandable," he says before pausing. "I need you to know something, Frank—I didn't kill Desmond."

I lower my head. To hear my father still claim his innocence after the evidence convicted him of the crime pisses me off. I look up at him.

"You still can't call him Blue, can you?"

"That may be what he liked to be called, but his name was Desmond. That's what his mother named him and nothing—"

"I know what his mother named him!" I yell.

My father stares down at his fingernails, looking them over as if he's considering cleaning them. I pause briefly and regain my composure before continuing.

"Look, I didn't come to argue with you."

"Then why'd you come, son? It's been almost a year and I haven't heard one word from you. Suddenly you show up... and what? I'm supposed to be happy? You want me to thank you for finally coming to visit? Well, allow me to show my gratitude. Thank you for putting me inside this—*this hellhole*."

"You put yourself here."

"I didn't murder Desmond. Why would I—" He stops short of saying what I want him to say.

"Don't stop now, Dad. Say it. Why would you *what*? Why would you shoot a fellow officer? Why would you murder your own son? Say it, Dad. *Say it!*" I scream with bated breath.

He rests his hands on the table and lets out a loud exhale. "It's pointless, Frank. You have your evidence and your own point-of-view of how it all went down. There's nothing more to say about it."

My nostrils flare. "I guess you're right—there's nothing else to be said about it. But I've got one question for you. Back when I was thirteen and we went off to that donut factory across the tracks when Blue got caught. His mother called you and when we went to pick him up, you chastised him, threatened him. But you never laid a hand on me. Why?"

My father leans back in his seat and closes his eyes. "Oh yeah, I remember that day. You two almost got yourselves in a lot of trouble. But Desmond wasn't even appreciative that I had come to pull his ass out of hot water, so I had to show him what it meant to be appreciative."

"But you knew then that he was your son, didn't you? Yet, you took your anger out on him and not me."

My father shakes his head. "That's not how it was, Frank. You were my son. My one and only."

"Then what was Blue?"

His head drops and he sighs once again. "He was a mistake. Just a terrible mistake."

I stand up from my seat. For the first time in my life, I want to hit my father.

"Look, Frank, I'm not going to sugarcoat it for you. You're a grown man and that's just the truth that you're going to have to accept. Desmond was your friend—but nothing more."

"I can't believe you can sit there and say that after DNA proved he was your son, too."

My father sighs. "Again, Frank, we'll just have to agree to disagree on this. We're never going to get anywhere because you're just as headstrong as your mother."

"Don't you dare bring her into this!" I shout. "She died giving birth to me. And she loved you all that time, not realizing you were just a cheating asshole. You bring her into this again and I swear I'll break your face in two."

I have my finger so close to his face that I can feel the heat from his mouth. My father pushes back from the table and folds his arms in front of his chest.

"You know, they say after being on the job a long time, you become cynical of the people and the world you're supposed to serve and protect. After a while, you start to forget your vow of justice. Before you know it, you become a number—just like me."

"I'll never be like you."

"You sure, son? Because a second ago, you were ready to smash my face in. That doesn't sound like the behavior of a law-abiding officer to me."

I sit back down in my seat. My father's right. I'm on the edge of becoming a monster, a bad cop that abuses his shield.

"Son, you haven't done this cop thing long enough to understand the red line between crossing over to the other side. But trust me, when you come to that moment, you'll know it. You'll see an image of yourself, staring back at you in your victim's eyes. I pray to God that you have as much restraint as I did with Desmond."

I stare at my father for a long time and yell for the guards.

"Already? Well, that was fast. And I was so sure you came to finally hear the truth."

"I already have the truth."

"Yeah? Is that what it's called? Damn. And here I thought I taught you better than that." For the first time ever my father shows a chink in his armor. He turns his head away from me as the two guards enter the room. "I just want you to know that I forgive you, Frank. One day, the truth will come to light and when it does I want you to know that I won't hold this against you."

I say nothing, watching as the two guards re-shackle my father's hands and disconnect the chain from the steel loop in the floor as they stand him up.

"Later, son," he says solemnly.

I remain silent as the guards march my father out of the room and back into general population. I can hear the chain links of his restraints clanging like ghost echoes of past prisoners, reminding me of the heavy price that's to be paid for crossing the line between duty and revenge.

CHAPTER 38

"So how'd it go?" Uncle Skeet asks after I've entered the car.

"I don't want to talk about it."

"Sounds like it went as well as could be expected." He starts the car and turns out of the gravel-covered parking lot and onto the road heading back to Chicago. He switches on the radio as the rain begins to fall.

I stare out the window, watching as the side of the road fills with puddles of water. My father's warning about me becoming him and crossing the line, shakes me to my very core.

I turn to my uncle. "As cops, do you think we can cross the line? You know, become the monsters that we're sworn to serve and protect against?"

Uncle Skeet turns down the radio. He washes a hand over his face and licks his lips. "I definitely think it's possible to become the monsters we fight against. I mean, we're all human. Cops are no exception to that evolutionary fact."

"You ever come close to crossing that line?"

Uncle Skeet tightens his grip around the steering wheel and

stares forward, watching the road. He clears his throat before giving a reply. "There was this one time your father and I had taken on a domestic disturbance call. At the time, we had been on the force for a few years, saw some things—it's not like we were fresh out the academy. We pull up to this apartment building and out runs this woman, butt-naked and covered head to toe in these grisly, bloody cuts. They say she had been cut like a hundred times or something. It was if Freddy Krueger had gotten to her or something." I shift in the seat uncomfortably as the image burns into my mind.

"We wrap her up in a blanket and wait for the paramedics to arrive on the scene. After they arrived, we entered the apartment to apprehend the suspect. The place was immaculately clean and was full of all these African paintings and pieces of art. We go into the bedroom and find this coked-out Jamaican cat with a bloodied razor blade in between his teeth. He didn't even move. Just had this big, dumb smile on his face. And before I knew it, I just—I just lost it. I was on top of the guy, smacking him with my pistol. I mean, I really lost it. Seeing that woman all cut up like that just sent me over the line. If your father hadn't pulled me off that fucker, I probably would have killed him."

"Ever come close to doing anything like that again?" I ask.

"I've seen some horrible things in my lifetime, but nothing has driven me to cross the line again like I did in that apartment."

I stare out the window watching the rain slap against the windshield. If Uncle Skeet was able to cross that line, then there's no telling what I'm capable of.

Just then, my cell phone rings. "Calhoun here," I say, continuing to watch the rain fall.

"Hey Frank, it's Petey. Got a minute?"

"Sure, Petey. Shoot."

"Well, I did some digging like you asked and pulled Sergeant Bigsby's file. Want me to read it to you?"

"Sure, let's have the short version."

"Turns out that Bigsby died in an ambush in the Ambar Province of Iraq almost three years ago."

"Tell me something I don't know."

"He was part of a special team of Marines training Iraqi security forces as a marksman."

My stomach tightens into knots. The case is starting to breathe again.

"Frank, you still there?"

"Yeah, I'm here."

"This guy's file goes on for quite a while."

"Is there any way you can fax me over what you have?"

"Yeah, but it'll take a while."

I give him the fax number. "Thanks Petey. I owe you one."

"Yeah, you do, Preacher."

I hang up.

"Sounds like you got a bite," Uncle Skeet says.

"Maybe. That was one of my contacts in the service. I had him pull Bigsby's military records, so he's gonna send it over."

Uncle Skeet whistles. "You sure you want to look through that file?"

"No, I'm not sure... but I have no choice."

"Just be careful. It looks like you might be heading down a road filled with a lot of dark corners. There might be someone that doesn't want it to see the light of day."

I nod as the rain begins to fall harder, making the road ahead blurry and almost invisible to the naked eye.

CHAPTER 39

When Uncle Skeet finally drops me off at home, it's already dark. Across the street, a few teens are sitting out on their front porch playing music and looking mischievous. Some play cards on the steps while others battle rap or sing-along to the music spewing out of a speaker that's been placed in an open window.

Nights like this remind me of a time when Blue and I would sit out on my porch and talk about our dreams and fears.

I smile. *Those were the good old days.*

I climb the stairs and enter my home, making my way to the kitchen. I open the fridge, take out a bottle of root beer and down the brown liquid. The sugarcane will keep me going as I ready myself to read Bigsby's file. As I turn to leave the kitchen, the phone rings.

I turn back around and pick the receiver up off the wall. "Calhoun here."

"Hi, Frank, it's Gloria. I, um, wanted to know if you would like to join us for dinner?"

"Well, I would—but I've really got a lot of work to get to tonight."

"Oh. Okay, I understand," she says defeated.

What was I doing? At the very least, I owed her a dinner after all she'd done for me. "Actually, I'd love to have dinner. Just let me get freshened up and I'll be right up."

I hang up the phone and sit the open root beer bottle down on the kitchen table. I'll have to get to Bigsby's file after dinner.

Twenty minutes later, I'm standing inside Gloria's apartment. The last time I was in her place had been about a year ago to unclog her toilet. I scan the room, making mental notes to myself about the subtle changes that she's incorporated into the overall décor of the apartment. There's a new oil painting of a flock of sheep being led up a mountain by a black, long-haired shepherd. The painting complements the brown contemporary love seat and chair she inherited from her deceased grandmother as the clear plastic still clings to the furniture.

The living room now comprises of a beautiful brown couch and two matching armchairs. When she first moved in, she didn't have anything other than a dining room table and a few chairs. She's come a long way.

"Hey Mister Calhoun," Jamal says, coming out of his room with his head buried in his Nintendo DS.

"Hey Jamal. Where's your mom?"

"In the kitchen." He cocks his head to the side. "You can go back there if you want."

I smile. "Thanks."

The boy says nothing as he nods his head and walks past me into the living room. When I enter the lemon-colored kitchen, I find Janai sitting at the kitchen table with flour covering her round face and her hands deep in a bowl filled with dough.

"Hi, Mister Calhoun," she smiles, showing a gap where one of her teeth has come out.

"Hey Janai. What's that you got there?"

"I'm helping Mama make biscuits."

"Biscuits, huh? That's cool."

"Oh, hi Frank," Gloria says, pulling her head out of the fridge with an arm full of jars and vegetables.

"Let me help you with that." I move over to her, taking a handful of jars and sitting them down on the table. "It looks like you're about to cook a feast."

"Just throwing together a little something."

"Thanks for inviting me. I appreciate it."

"You're very welcome. Now as our guest, I don't expect you to be in the kitchen. So you can head in the front room and watch a little TV. Dinner will be done soon."

"You sure?"

"I'm sure. Besides, I've got Janai to help me."

She kisses her daughter on the head and begins to tickle her small belly as the little girl explodes with laughter. I smile and turn to walk out of the kitchen and back into the living room. Jamal is lounging in one of the armchairs with his legs dangling over the side of one of the arms with his attention still focused on the video game in his hands.

I take a seat on the couch and instantly feel a bit nervous. I run my sweaty palms over my jeans and look over at Jamal, wonder what he's playing. As a kid, I obsessed over video games. I remember the endless nights of laying in bed, plotting out various scenarios on how to beat a boss or pass a level.

I smack my knee. "Those were the times," I whisper to myself.

"What did you say, Mr. Calhoun?" Jamal asks without looking up from the device in his hand.

"Nothing, Jamal. Just thinking about back in the day when I use to play video games like you."

"You were a gamer?"

"Don't sound so surprised. I'm not that old, you know."

"Yeah, but you don't seem like a gamer. I mean, you always talking about books and stuff."

"There's nothing wrong with reading books *and* playing games. You don't have to like one over the other. If you think about it, whoever made that game in your hand had to go to school and learn something out of a book."

For the first time that night, Jamal looks up from the screen and gives my statement some thought. "Yeah, I guess you're right," he says simply before returning to his game.

The aroma of fluffy buttered biscuits begin to fill the apartment. I sit back against the couch and do my best to relax. I can't understand why I'm nervous. Perhaps the thought of sitting at a full table enjoying a home cooked meal scares me somehow. Or maybe it's just the thought that everything that comes into my life somehow ends up destroyed which is something I don't want to happen to Gloria and her children.

"Dinner is ready," Gloria calls from the dining room, carrying a yellow ceramic bowl of buttered potatoes. "Jamal turn off that game and go wash your hands," she commands, sitting the bowl down on the table as the boy does as his mother asks.

"Can I help with anything?" I ask, standing up from the couch.

"All you can do is take a seat at the table."

Gloria whips a few strands of hair behind her ear and turns to go back into the kitchen. I take a seat at the table and watch as Janai and Jamal set it with placemats and cutlery. After everything is said and done, the table is covered with a bowl of green beans and potatoes, a pot of corn, a pan of roast beef with a side of gravy and a basket of buttered biscuits.

Janai sits next to me while Gloria and Jamal sit across from us. "Frank, would you mind saying grace?" Gloria asks.

We all bow our heads and hold hands around the table as I clear my throat. "Father God, we thank you for allowing us to have this meal and for giving Gloria the skills to make such a gracious meal. We ask that you allow this food to nourish our minds, bodies and souls, in Jesus name. Amen."

We begin passing the entrees amongst ourselves. Once everyone has a plate full of food, I decide to break the ice by asking Janai about the zoo.

"It was great!" she exclaims. "I saw lions and monkeys and one monkey threw fe—fec—uh, *poo* at Jamal." The little girl cracks up with laughter.

"It's not funny," Jamal says bluntly, crossing his arms.

I laugh along with the little girl and Gloria joins us. "Don't worry. At least you weren't hit with any of it, were you?" I ask.

Jamal continues to pout, shoving a biscuit into his mouth as we all laugh some more.

"Mister Calhoun, why were the cops sitting outside our home?" Janai asks.

"They were sitting out there to protect me."

"Why?"

"Janai," Gloria starts. "Quit asking Mister Calhoun so many questions."

"It's okay. I don't mind answering them."

"You don't know these kids. You give them an inch and they'll take a mile."

I nod and address Janai. "The police just wanted to make sure I was safe from some very bad men. And now that I am, they're gone."

"Cool," she says, returning to her food.

I look up and across the table at Gloria. Her hair falls to her shoulders and her smile seems to melt the butter on the food as much as it does my heart. I quickly look away when I catch Jamal staring at me with a set of piercing, brown eyes. I understand why the boy looks at me with such spite. After all, he is the man of the house and here I am standing before the doorway of his home, knocking to be let in.

After dinner, the kids go off to bed while I help Gloria clear the table. I plug the kitchen sink with a stopper and begin running dish water. I squeeze in some detergent and watch as the suds form and begin to rise up out of the water. Gloria clears the last plate of food and hands it over to me. She smiles and I return one of my own. Our fingers touch for a brief moment and a spark pops between us.

"You shocked me," she says.

"I was going to say the same thing about you."

"You know you don't have to do the dishes," she says, picking up a dry towel from the sink.

"I know, but I'm use to busting suds."

"Really? I don't take you as the cleaning type."

"I dabble a little bit, here and there. When your father's a cop who always works the night shift, you have to learn how to take care of yourself pretty quickly."

"I know what you mean there. I grew up in a house of seven."

"Seven? Wow!"

"Yep, four sisters and two brothers."

"I take it you're the oldest?"

"No, the youngest. If I didn't know better, I'd think you were trying to call me old."

"I wouldn't dare." I say, surrendering my hands which are covered in white, foamy bubbles.

She giggles like a schoolgirl charmed by the sight of a beautiful butterfly.

I hold out my hand and playfully blow a patch of suds into her face.

"Oh, now it's on," she says, scooping up a handful of bubbles and tossing them at my face.

I jump back while reaching for the sink's faucet extension.

"You wouldn't," she says, frozen by the dripping nozzle. "You know a woman's most precious asset is our hair."

"Yeah, you're right," I reply, smiling as I lower the nozzle.

Just as she relaxes, I raise the nozzle and begin spraying her with water.

She shrieks, rushing towards me and attempting to fight the gushing stream. "Oh, I'm going to get you, Frank Calhoun!"

When she's within arm's reach, she grabs the nozzle and we begin wrestling for control of it as water sprays in every direction. We laugh hysterically and draw closer to one another. Water drips from our soaked clothing and we allow our grip on the nozzle to loosen as we stare into each other's eyes, finally succumbing to the tension that's been surrounding us for months. I let the nozzle fall to the floor and bring my hands up to Gloria's arms and gently massage her muscles. I feel her breath on my face as I bend forward and kiss her on the lips.

She falls into my arms as her lips envelope my kiss. I embrace her, wrapping my large arms around her body as she claws at my chest. I can tell that she wants this as much as I do and it feels amazing to finally have her within my clutches.

But before I can fully enjoy it, terrible thoughts flash across my mind. I start to think about my life and the possible danger that I'm inviting into hers. I can't move forward, knowing that there are things in my life I haven't yet overcome, like Blue's death and my father's betrayal.

I pull back and stare into Gloria's eyes. "I can't, Gloria. At least not right now," I whisper.

She searches my eyes for answers and then she nods her head before turning to the side to let me pass. I step past her and make my way down the hallway to the front door. To my surprise, I find Jamal standing at the hallway's entrance hugging the doorframe, staring at me with a malicious gaze.

I walk past the boy without saying a word. My heart feels heavy as I step out the front door and down the stairs to my own apartment. I fish around in my pocket for my keys, but stop when I hear someone open the front gate. I turn around to see Kawowski and Lopez.

"Detectives, how can I help you?" I ask.

"We'd like to ask you some questions," Kawowski says.

I give a sigh. After the fiasco with Gloria, I just want to spend some time alone and go over Bigsby's file but I know if I make things difficult, they'll respond in kind. "Ask away," I say simply.

"Oh, no," Lopez says smiling. "We need to ask you these questions downtown."

CHAPTER 40

The interrogation room in the downtown office of the Chicago Police Department smells like oranges. I guess somebody forgot to pass on the memo to the cleaning crew about using Orange Begone to scrape gum off the surface of the tables since it takes away from the overall sweatbox appeal of the room.

I don't see the logic in Kawowski and Lopez leaving me in the room alone to sweat it out like some common criminal and I'm damn sure they know it.

I do understand why they bought me downtown at this time of night though. They know there won't be any brass in the offices to get in their way and Internal Affairs is gone for the night. Plus, downtown is neutral territory because no single area precinct can claim it, making the interrogation room holy ground if the questioning goes south or leads to a confession. This means no one can say that the investigation is flawed due to precinct loyalty or that the questioning of a fellow officer without his superiors present is unethical.

I sit up in my seat as the door to the interrogation room finally opens and Kawowski steps into the room carrying a manila folder and a cardboard cup holder with two Styrofoam cups.

"Sorry to take so long. Had an issue with the AV equipment," he says simply.

I don't say a word as I stare across the room at the two-way mirror. It's operational procedure throughout the department to record interrogations in case a suspect sues the city for abuse, but it's also used to secure a confession in case a witness or criminal later recants during a trial.

Kawowski takes a seat and then hands me one of the Styrofoam cups. "Cream?" he asks, digging inside the holder.

"Black is good for me," I say.

"Suit yourself, cowboy."

Kawowski treats his coffee with cream and sugar before taking a sip. He leans in towards the mic on the table and states the date and time as well as badge and case number.

He pulls his seat up a little closer and looks me in the eyes. "On the day of Anton Pantone's murder, why were you at his office?"

"You already know why. Do you really want to do this again?"

"Yes, I really do. Now if you will, please refresh my memory."

I sit forward in my seat. "As I told you before, Detective Kawowski, he called me and said he had something to tell me. When I arrived at his office, I found the door ajar. I decided to investigate and that's when I found Father Pantone sprawled out on the floor behind his desk."

"Is that when you decided to call the proper authorities, Mister Calhoun?"

"It's *Detective*. And yes, that's when I called it in."

"What did you do then?"

"What do you mean what did I do?"

"I mean, did you just sit there and wait for emergency services? What did you do after making the call to the proper authorities?"

"Look, I'm a detective just like you. I know how to do my job. The first thing I did after realizing that Father Pantone was dead was retrace my steps and back out of the room. I sealed it off. It was clear to me that it was a crime scene at that point."

Kawowski takes another sip of coffee and then continues with the questioning. "The same night that Father Pantone was killed, you returned to the crime scene. Why?"

"As I stated earlier, I returned to the scene to retrieve my house keys."

"And why didn't forensics come across those keys of yours?"

"I don't know. Maybe they missed 'em. You'd have to ask them that question."

"You stated that you were attacked by an unknown assailant who rendered you unconscious until Detective Lopez and I discovered you the next morning. Do you know why anyone would have been in Father Pantone's office after he was killed? Or what they might have been looking for?"

"To tell you the truth, I wish I did. All I know is that I went up to the office to retrieve my keys and some guy jumped out of the closet and attacked me. I passed out due to a medical condition related to stress, which I've been treating."

"I see. Tell me, Detective Calhoun, do you know what this is?" Kawowski asks, opening the manila folder in front of me and sliding a photo of Father Pantone's collar across the table.

I pick up the photo, stare at it and then sit it back down on the table. "It looks like a priest's collar."

"It is. In fact, it's Father Pantone's collar. See anything different about it, Detective?"

I pick up the picture again and fake like I'm studying it. I know what Kawowski is getting at, but I have to play the part of the village idiot. "It looks like the collar was ripped open," I say finally.

"That's correct. Forensics said it was a little makeshift pocket. But collars don't usually have pockets—any idea what Father Pantone might have been hiding?"

I slide the photo back over to Kawowski. "No idea. Why would I know?"

"I just thought you might have some idea since you served under him a few years ago in Iraq. Figured this secret pocket-in-the-collar business might have been some military thing you good old boys cooked up over there while fighting—oh wait, that's right... you didn't actually fight anyone, now did you? You played more of a pacifist role."

I give a light chuckle. "War is war, Kawowski."

"Well, maybe you can answer this: why were your fingerprints found all over the collar?"

I sigh. "My prints were probably found on the collar since I removed it from his neck when I tried to administer first aid."

Kawowski nods slightly as he smooths out the mustache across his face. "Maybe so, Detective. Maybe so. On the day that Billy Murphy was killed by a drive by shooter, why were you on the rooftop at Father Pantone's office despite being told to stay away from the investigation by your superior officer?"

"This is a free country and I can go where I please. But if you really want to know, I'll tell you the same thing I told my captain. I was at the Murphy residence apologizing to Miss Murphy when I mistook Officer Sato for a sniper. During the apprehension, I realized that Miss Murphy's son was the one actually in danger."

"And how'd you figure her son to be in danger, Detective?"

"Just felt it in my gut."

"Your gut, huh?"

"That's correct. It's something that a detective uses and learns to trust. I figured you Area Two boys would have learned that by now since you don't seem to know anything else."

Kawowski takes another sip of his coffee and grimaces. I can tell he's starting to realize I'm two steps ahead of him in his own investigation.

"Do you know a Sergeant Mitchell Bigsby?"

I pick up my cup and rattle it around in my hand, trying to stir the non-existent sugar at the bottom of it. Now that Kawowski has started to show his cards, any sudden change in my posture or tone in my voice will be open to interpretation by Detective Lopez, who is watching me intently from the other side of the two-way mirror.

I take a long sip of the coffee and clear my throat. "Doesn't sound familiar."

"You sure, detective? Because this individual's prints were pulled from the Murphy residence along with trace amounts of black fingerprint powder."

I sit forward in my seat. "And what's that gotta do with me?"

"Well, it's simple—how does a man who's been dead for nearly three years suddenly show up near a crime scene that just happens to also have been accessed by you, Detective Calhoun?"

"How the hell am I supposed to know how a dead guy's prints popped up at a crime scene?"

Kawowski smiles. "You're good, detective. So tell me this. On the night of Billy Murphy's murder, where were you afterwards?"

I study Kawowski. He's still holding an ace, but I can't tell what it is.

"I was at home."

"Really? Well that's funny, because I could have sworn I saw you leaving the Murphy residence at about five in the morning that night."

I almost drop my cup. I had a feeling someone was watching me that morning, but I can't let on that he's correct.

I look Kawowski dead in the eyes. "Couldn't have been me."

"And how is that?"

"Because that night, I was under protective custody with two officers sitting right outside my front door. You can check with my captain if you like."

I'm betting that Smith and Richter didn't report being drugged, so I'm confident that my alibi is airtight. Kawowski rises from his seat and steps around the table with his hands behind his back. He looks up at the two-way mirror and slits his throat with his hand, giving Lopez the signal to kill the audio and video.

He bends down on the side of me and whispers into my ear. "I know you were at the Murphy residence and I know you were the one who planted those prints. I don't know why and I don't know what you and Father Pantone had going on, but when I figure it out—*and I will figure it out*—I'm going to nail your ass to the wall."

I turn and look at Kawowski. "I'm telling you right now you're barking up the wrong tree."

"Well let me tell you something, Calhoun. I know that you killed Father Pantone, and once I talk to your father, I just may know why. So I'm giving you one last chance to confess and make this right."

"I already told you that you're barking up the wrong tree. Especially if you think my father had something to do with it."

Kawowski stands and moves back around the table to retake his seat. "We'll see. Being that he was your father's spiritual counselor and all down there in Joliet. I'm betting your old man has quite a bit to say about that."

I sit forward in my seat with my mouth slightly ajar, as I stare at a smiling Kawowski who's just played his ace.

CHAPTER 41

t's a quarter after eleven when I finally return home from the interrogation. Kawowski drilled me good and I'm sure that he and Lopez were combing over the film, looking for any telling signs that might reveal a hole in my alibi. I've got to hand it to Kawowski— that last bit of information about Father Pantone and my dad has me boggled.

The most alarming thing that I learned from the interrogation is that all of their leads are beginning to point back to me, which means they're sizing me up to take the fall.

I call Uncle Skeet. Even though it's late, I need to check with him to see if he can run me back up to the prison first thing in the morning. When I hear his voice come in over the line, I apologize for the late call and get right to the point.

"I just learned that my dad and Father Pantone had a relationship. I need to find out what kind of relationship. It might have something to do with Father Pantone's murder."

"Frank, I can tell you right now that their relationship has nothing to do with the murder."

"And how do you know that?"

I hear my uncle sigh through the receiver. "Because Father Pantone was only counseling your dad."

"What do you mean counseling?"

"He worked at the prison one Sunday a month and became your father's spiritual counselor."

"So you've known about them all this time? Why didn't you tell me this before?"

Uncle Skeet sighs again, but this time his voice is low and steady. "Because you had just lost a man you looked up to and I knew you weren't ready to face your father yet. So I decided not to tell you."

I lean against the kitchen sink. The room feels warmer than usual. "How could you keep this from me, Unc?"

"It's not that big of a deal."

"It might not be a big deal to you, but it's a *huge* deal to me."

"I was just trying to protect you from unnecessary pain. I'm sorry."

His voice is genuine and sincere, but it doesn't mean I have to accept his apology. I feel defeated and confused. "I'll talk to you later, Unc."

I hang up the phone and look around the kitchen. It feels like I'm standing in someone else's home. Uncle Skeet said he withheld the information on my behalf, but I highly doubt that. I suspect he really withheld it to protect my father.

I sit down at the kitchen table and my blood feels like it's boiling. I hate being lied to. I'm guessing this is the information that Father Pantone wanted to share with me on the day he was killed.

"Dammit!" I yell in anger, slamming my palm against the table. I've done so much to distance myself from my father, but it seems inevitable that our paths will continue to cross.

I stand up and walk down the hall to my father's office. I push open the door and stare around the room, taking in the ambience of his ghost. I clinch my fist together as I think about how the two men I love most likely sat across from one another and discussed my life openly, like old friends talking about sports. I grab a shelf full of books from the bookcase and throw them to the floor. I sweep my hand across the small desk, scattering pens and loose thumbtacks across the room.

Who were they to discuss my life?

I rip picture frames off the wall. Sending an image of my father and the late Harold Washington to the floor. There's an image of my father retiring from the department, holding his badge in one hand and a smile across his face. I whisk the picture across the room and it smashes against a wall shattering the glass frame into a hundred pieces, which oddly enough feels exactly like my life.

My life.

The words spark a rage within me as I turn around and grab the desk with two hands and begin to lift it off the floor, ready to overturn it and dismantle it into pieces. Then the fax machine beeps and I turn to my left to bash it with my fist. But instead I see a grainy black and white image of Sergeant Mitchell Bigsby staring up at me. In the midst of everything that's occurred, I forgot that Petey faxed over Bigsby's military file. With my anger beginning to subside, I snatch the papers from the fax's cradle, turn off the light and close the door on my father's past.

CHAPTER 42

After a few hours of reading Bigsby's file, I stare down at the papers scattered across my dining room table and wonder what I'm actually looking at. Bigsby's entire military career is displayed on the table, but huge blocks of his life in the Marines have been doctored as full sentences and paragraphs are completely blacked out within the file.

I press my forefinger and thumb against the bridge of my nose. My head hurts, so I rise from my seat at the table and head to the bathroom where I pop two aspirin from the medicine cabinet. I stare at myself in the cabinet's mirror. My face is long and bags are beginning to form under my eyes and my body is starting to feel the effects of a lack of sleep which I desperately need so I can go back through the files with a fresh pair of eyes in the morning.

I turn from the medicine cabinet and walk back up the hallway, through the dining room and into my bedroom. My cell phone rings and I remove it from my pants pocket to stare down at the number on the small screen. The backlight shows that the call is coming from an 815 area code. I don't recognize the number, so I hit the silent button and allow it to go to voicemail as I fall face first onto the bed with my clothes still on.

CHAPTER 43

t's snowing in the middle of July. Or at least that's what it looks like as white phosphorous rains down from the skies of Iraq. The bombs explode over the city of Fallujah like skyrockets on Independence Day. From a distance it's an amazing image—but up close, it's as gruesome and terrifying as one might imagine. The streets are covered with charred bodies scattered about the city, awaiting the Marines and Chaplains of Charlie Company to inspect them.

Wearing protective suits, we move through the burned-out city in formations of three, huddled together with Marines whose rifles are at the ready, but it's the soul-shaking screams of mothers and the agonizing cries of their babies and children as they're exposed to the powdery, flesh-eating substance that takes us all by surprise. It's always this lingering memory that shakes me out of my nightmares and pulls me back into reality.

I open my eyes to the darkness surrounding me, aware of the nightmare that I've just endured. My stomach churns with hunger as I sit up on the side of the bed and pinch the bridge of my nose as I squint to see the time on the digital clock that reads 5:25 a.m.

I sit there for a second, gathering my thoughts when a beeping sound comes from my cell phone. I turn and search the ruffled sheets as the phone beeps again. I finally wrestle it free of the sheets and discover a voicemail.

My stomach growls again, so I kill the screen on the phone and take it with me into the kitchen where I prepare a PB&J and a bottle of root beer. I bite into the sandwich and globs of jelly slide down my fingers as the phone beeps again. I place the sandwich on the table, dial the voicemail and enter my pass code. The message plays and I recognize the voice, but I can't quite put a face to it. After a few moments, it hits me: it's Francis Bigsby.

I replay the message back in its entirety just to be sure that I'm hearing him correctly. The phone crackles and his voice comes in over the line.

"Ummmm... hi, yeah, ummmmm.. hi, Detective Calhoun. I've been meaning to call. After you came by my house, I started thinking about some things. A few days before you came by, I reached inside my mailbox and there was an envelope stuffed full of cash. I thought maybe someone put it in the wrong box by mistake.

"I waited for days, watching the news—but nobody claimed the money. When you first showed up, I started to think that maybe you were here for the money, but when you started asking questions about my boy, I began to suspect something a lot more sinister—you know, like maybe... and I know this is going to sound crazy... but I think my son might be alive." I drop the phone and rush into the living room and start sifting through the military papers, tossing them across the table and onto the floor until I come across the pages I'm looking for.

The official military investigation had been conducted by a

Major Connelly and he indicated that Sergeant Bigsby's unit had come under heavy fire from members of Al-Qaeda in Iraq.

I read on:

The investigation into the Hiditha incident that caused several Marines to lose their lives, was due to an Improvised Explosive Device (IED) which caused the Humvee they occupied to flip over. This investigation is now closed.

It is believed that the insurgents' IED killed all the Marines in the Humvee instantly except for one. Video evidence shows that the insurgents captured Sergeant Mitchell Bigsby alive and executed him by way of beheading. It is this investigator's belief that his body will never be recovered.

I reread the two paragraphs again just to be sure I'm reading it right and my stomach begins to churn with nervous excitement. I pick up the report again and read on.

The incident would later be known as the Haditha Massacre after fifteen Iraqi civilians were killed in retaliation for the murder of Sergeant Bigsby and his unit. During the initial investigation, it was believed that the fifteen Iraqis were insurgents, but new evidence has suggested that the victims of the massacre were Iraqi civilians. After the massacre, Captain Anton Pantone lead a coalition to rebuild trust with the Iraqi people. However, the region became unstable and he was ordered to evacuate.

I sit the file down on the table. There it is—Father Pantone and Bigsby's name together in black and white, but what did it all mean? There's only one man that can tell me what I need to know and I'm going to get the truth, even if it kills one of us.

CHAPTER 44

A green wrought-iron fence with angels holding broad swords pointing to the heavens surrounds the rectory that's next to Saint Peter of Alcantara. The Wicker Park neighborhood is quiet as I stroll up to the gate, ring the security buzzer and ask to speak to Father Cicero Sanchez.

The voice that comes back over the intercom is deep and reminds me of Barry White. "Father Sanchez has not yet risen for the day," the voice says.

"I don't care. Tell him it's Detective Frank Calhoun and that it's an emergency!" I yell into the intercom.

I stand outside the gate for a whole five minutes before I'm finally buzzed in. A pock-faced guard no older than twenty-three meets me at the security booth just beyond the entrance. He brushes his long hair behind his ears and asks to see my identification. I hand it to him and sign my name in the logbook as the guard hands my I.D. back. "Third floor, make a right. It's the last room on your left."

I thank him and take the stairs two at a time. On the third floor, small dangling yellow bulbs light the hall. I walk the length of the floor until I come to the door of Father Sanchez's room. I knock gently, afraid that my raps might echo throughout the hall and wake the other occupants of the building. Finally, the door opens and Father Sanchez stands in the doorway in an all white gown.

"Frank, what brings you by so early?" he asks sleepily.

"You do, Cicero. I've got some questions I need to ask you."

"Come in. Can I get you some tea or something?"

"No, I'm good."

The room is small, illuminated by a single dome light. There's a bed, a desk for writing and a dresser for storing clothes.

"So how can I help you?"

"Do you know a man by the name of Mitchell Bigsby?"

"Should I?"

"He was a sergeant in Platoon 321, Charlie Company."

"Can't say I remember anyone by that name," Sanchez says rubbing his chin.

"After Fallujah, my tour in Iraq was over with and I returned home. But you stayed on with Father Pantone. What did you two do after Fallujah?"

Sanchez takes a seat on his bed. I move over by the door and press in the lock.

"Oh heavens. I didn't know," he whispers quietly to himself.

"Didn't know what, Cicero?"

He pauses for a few moments with his face twisted in horror before speaking again. "I didn't know that the woman you followed out of the church was Father Pantone's mistress. At least not until just now."

"Wait, you know that woman?"

Sanchez looks up from the floor and stares into my eyes. "I *knew* her. In another life, back in Iraq. She just looks so different." He pauses again, looking to collect his thoughts as I study his demeanor. "Her name is Afsaneh Shaban. I helped Father Pantone smuggle her into the country."

"What do you mean you helped him smuggle her into this country?"

"Just as I said, Frank."

"How? Why?"

Sanchez rests his face in his hands. "After Fallujah, everything started to look grim. Our original company was broken up and Father Pantone and I were reassigned to a new company. We tried to look on the bright side, but the nightmares just kept coming— they still do sometimes. Anyway, one day while out on patrol in the city of Adhamiya, we were trying to build relationships with the people. One of the marines let his gun go off by accident and it hit a little girl in the arm. The people were already leery of our presence, so tensions were high enough. But when that little girl got shot, everything just exploded into a powder keg.

We tried to pull out, but the people wanted blood. They started protesting and before we knew it, we were about to massacre them in order to save our own lives. We didn't want to, but it was us or them. At the last moment, Afsaneh Shaban stepped in. She quieted the protesters and helped get us out of there in one piece."

"That still doesn't answer my questions, Cicero."

"I know, Frank, I know. But you had to hear that story to understand how powerful she was in that small town. And many other towns like it across Iraq. But... she was also dangerous. Dangerous... because of who her father was."

"And who is her father?"

"Afsaneh Shaban is known in Iraq as Rasna Hussein. She is one of Saddam's daughters from his many marriages."

"Wait, what? I've never heard of her."

"And you won't because our country still considers all Husseins a threat."

"So you helped this Rasna Hussein escape Iraq and set her up with a new life and a new name so she wouldn't be considered a threat?"

"Yes, but I swear to you, I didn't know about their affair. I hadn't seen Rasna in quite some time. I noticed her at the funeral, but like I said—she looked so different. It wasn't until now that I put two and two together."

"What about Bigsby? How does he play into all this?"

"I told you I don't know him."

I grab Sanchez by the collar of his gown, pull him up off the bed and throw him against the door. "Don't play me, Cicero! I want to know the truth right now!"

"I already told you everything I know."

I press my forearm against his jugular. "How'd Bigsby's prints end up at the Murphy residence? Did you kill Father Pantone?"

Sanchez grabs my left hand and wrestles his hand up under my arm. He plants his right foot on the back of the door and pushes off it. We fall forward onto the floor with a loud thud vibrating off the surrounding walls.

"You're going to tell me what you know, Cicero!" I demand through clenched teeth. "Even if I have to beat it out of you!"

We wrestle on the floor like rabid dogs, but this time I'm a bit more wiry and prepared for such a scuffle. The security guard knocks at the locked door and rattles the doorknob. I roll on top of Sanchez, pin his arms under my knees and hit him across the face.

"You're going to tell me what you know about Bigsby, Father Pantone and the Haditha Massacre!"

The guard slams his frail shoulder into the frame of the

door and calls out from the other side. "Father Sanchez, are you all right?"

I look down into Sanchez's eyes. "I know you know, Cicero. In November of 2006, a marine by the name of Mitchell Bigsby was kidnapped and killed by insurgents after an IED blew up the Humvee he was in. The following day fifteen Iraqis were killed by Marines in retaliation, which they called the Haditha Massacre. I want to know why you planted Bigsby's fingerprints and what it has to do with Father Pantone?"

Sanchez rubs his tongue against his busted lip. "I already told you I don't know. I wasn't even in Iraq during the Haditha Massacre. I was already back here in the States, readying things for Rasna's transition."

"Bigsby's file said Father Pantone was the official peace negotiator during the whole upheaval."

"What file?"

"Never mind that."

I stand up over Sanchez as the security guard's voice begins to strain through the door. "Father Sanchez, please say something. Are you okay?"

Sanchez sits up. He slightly touches his lip and grimaces. "I'm sorry that I can't help you, Frank. But if you want to know what happened at Haditha, maybe you should ask Rasna."

I cut my eyes at Sanchez. "You know where she is, don't you?"

He gives a heavy sigh before looking me in the eye. "She's up in Little India by Devon. Stays in an apartment. 5824 North Washtenaw."

"If I find out you had something to do with Father Pantone's murder, I'll be back and I'm not going to take it so easy on you."

I turn and open the door to a crowd of priests and the pock-faced guard. "I've called the police," he says. "And they're on their way."

"Good," I reply, stepping past the crowd. "Because I *am* the police."

CHAPTER 45

Devon Avenue between Broadway and McCormick is considered Little India due to the culmination of Indians, Pakistanis, Iraqis and Middle Eastern inhabitants that live in the area. I step off the 149B bus at Western and Devon in the heart of the community where the strip is full of shops and restaurants with bright neon signs and digital displays. Rasna's apartment is on Washtenaw Street, a few blocks up. I zip up my light jacket to conceal the pistol I have tucked at my waist and stroll up the block.

The air smells like curry. There are men standing outside a few shops and sitting at corner benches reading Arabic newspapers and discussing the day's events. All the men watch me with an awareness that tells me I don't belong.

Even though I'm black and have witnessed discrimination firsthand, I understand the cautionary stares are not because of the color of my skin, but a deeper emotional scar that's been left by 9/11 when racial attacks against Middle-Easterners were at their highest. Anyone who steps foot into Little India who isn't of Middle-Eastern descent is typically scrutinized with sly, distrustful stares. I observe the men as I pass by a busy grocery store with a chaotic parking lot, full of beeping cars trying to make it in and out of a very small one-way opening.

I turn down Washtenaw and head up the block towards the apartment building. I read the addresses as I go, studying the bungalow-style homes and two flat greystones that make up the neighborhood. The building where Rasna lives is a three- story structure connected to two other buildings that have a similar design, except they've been renovated into condos.

I ring the doorbell and wait for a response. When Rasna Hussein's voice comes in over the intercom, it's as soft as I remember.

"Yes, who is it?"

I hesitate for a second and then bend towards the intercom. "Ummm... hi, the name's Frank Calhoun. I, ummmmm... I was sent here by Father Cicero Sanchez."

The door buzzes. I open it and climb the stairs to the third floor. Rasna Hussein is standing in the doorway wearing a black cardigan pullover and a pair of faded jeans. Her hair curls down past her shoulders and falls between her breasts. Her eyes are dark like olives and shaped like almonds. If Sanchez hadn't told me she was one of Saddam's daughters, I would've never believed it.

"You," she says, readying to close the door.

"Wait," I say, reaching out a hand as I leap up the final three stairs. "I'm here because I need some information about Father Pantone."

She keeps the door cracked as she studies me. "I'm not sure I can be of any help." Her English is perfect and refuses to betray her secret.

"Please, can we talk inside?"

Rasna studies me a few more seconds then slowly opens the door. I step into her apartment and she leads me into the living room where she takes a seat on an old beat up couch. There is also a wooden rocking chair and a side table with an old record player on top of it with a built-in speaker.

I start in fast. I don't want to give her a chance to start telling me lies.

"Father Sanchez told me everything. I know who you are, Rasna Hussein."

Rasna stares at the floor. "So the truth has finally come out. Well good—maybe it's time I stop hiding." She holds out her arms with her hands balled into fist. "I am ready to face the judge and return to Iraq where I belong."

"I'm not here to arrest you, Rasna. I just need some info about Father Pantone and a man named Mitchell Bigsby."

Rasna drops her arms and stares up at me. "That name sounds familiar. What is this about?"

"As far as official military records go, Bigsby was taken hostage by insurgents after an IED flipped his Humvee in Haditha. After his capture, he supposedly died by beheading."

"I remember. My people were out for blood after the Marines stormed the city and killed innocent civilians."

"But in the aftermath of Haditha, Father Pantone quieted the storm of the people. He couldn't have done that unless he had someone that the people would listen to—someone like you."

Rasna stands up from the couch and walks over to the small side table. She lifts the record player and removes a small photo hidden underneath it. "You don't understand. Anton was really over there trying to help my people. He was a comfort during very dark times. When those Marines died in Haditha, he knew that the relationship between the Iraqis and the Americans was in dire strain, so he asked me to speak to my people. I did as he asked and kept them calm. But it was *his* Marines that could not hold their tempers in check.

"So during the dead of night, they raided the village and killed fifteen innocent men, women and children. The thought of peace was long gone. Too many innocent people had died."

"So the storm came anyway?"

"And I was branded a traitor because my people felt that I had allowed the Americans to brainwash me. Anton and I were marked for death."

"So in order to save you, Father Pantone had to smuggle you into the country."

She nodded. "It was during the month before Haditha that the two of us fell in love. It just happened. Before we realized it, everything we were working towards was coming apart at the seams."

"Do you think this is what got Father Pantone killed?"

Rasna looks up from the photo in her hand. "I guess I never thought about it, but it could be."

"Maybe someone in the area recognized you two?"

She shook her head. "No, Anton never came here. When we met, it was always in a secret location, far from both of our worlds."

I nod my head. "I see. I'm still not sure how Bigsby plays into all this."

Rasna looks confused. "I told you—his death was the catalyst for the Haditha Massacre."

"I understand that, but I think you know more than that. I think you and Cicero are using Sergeant Bigsby as a cover," I say sternly as I take a step closer.

"Cover? I don't understand." She searches my face for a clue.

"I think you do. I think you and Cicero killed Father Pantone."

Her eyes grow wide at my accusation. "We would never!"

"All I want to know is *why*? Was it so you and Cicero could continue a secret love affair?"

"That is preposterous!" she yells with a furrowed brow.

"Is it?" I lean in towards her. "Or did you kill him for something more tangible?"

"I loved Anton. I would have never harmed him."

The way she says Anton is like a whisper between lovers, but I refuse to let up. "Really? Then tell me about the key he hid in his collar."

"Key?" Rasna brings her hands up to her mouth. "No—oh no! It can't be."

"It can't be what?"

"The key belongs to—"

Before she can answer, the doorbell rings and breaks the flow of our conversation. I turn to look at the intercom box next to the door. It rings again and Rasna moves past me to hit the speech button on the device.

"Yes, who is it?"

A choppy, static voice comes back over the intercom. "Satellite repairman, ma'am."

Rasna looks at me and then back into the speaker. "Sorry, I don't have a satellite."

I move over to the window, pull down a section of the blinds and look down onto the street. The curb is filled with parked cars, but I don't see a utility van parked out front that looks anything like a repairman's van.

I look at Rasna as I hear the stranger continues over the intercom. "Sorry, ma'am. I'm here to remove the old satellite that's on your roof. I got a call from your landlord."

I turn back to the window and move further to my left to see if the van might be parked down the street, but all I see are empty parking spaces. Something isn't right and I can feel it. Just as I realize what's going on, I call out to Rasna, but it's too late. I turn from the window just as she hits the buzzer to open the door downstairs.

"What?" she looks at me puzzled.

I unzip my jacket and pull the pistol from my waist. "We've got to go."

"What are you talking about?" she asks.

"A key witness was killed by a phony cable repairman. That same man likely killed Anton—and now, I think he might be after you."

I grab hold of her hand and lead her through the apartment to the back door.

She snatches her hand away. "Why don't you just stand behind the door and wait to arrest him when he walks through it?"

I consider her suggestion, but I'm sure there are at least two assailants, if not more. There's no telling how many could be making their way up the stairs. "I'd be putting you at risk. I can't have that on my conscience. Now let's go."

I push Rasna out the back door and down the winding staircase. We burst out the door of the enclosed porch and into a garden filled with colorful flowers. The beauty of it surprises me since it's such a rarity that a garden like this would exist behind an apartment building in the city.

"Where are we going?" she asks.

"I'm not sure. I just have to get you out of here."

We move through the garden towards the back gate and into the alley. I look up and down and it's clear. I remove my cell phone from my pocket and dial 911, but I can't get a signal. I try again, but get the same results.

I look up from my phone and see the same black hearse that shot Billy Murphy speeding our way. I grab Rasna by the hand as I push open an adjacent gate to a home and rush through the toy-covered yard. I can hear the hearse's engine revving and its tires screeching to a complete stop. We keep moving, jumping over plastic building blocks and maneuvering around a large dollhouse.

"Don't stop!" I yell to Rasna as I grip her hand even tighter. I can feel her pulse beating like a paddle stick and ball.

We move through a paved gangway as I'm still trying to get a signal on my phone. When we come out the other end of the gangway, we're on a street filled with brick bungalow homes and large green lawns. I look up the block and it doesn't appear that the hearse has come around yet. I pull Rasna across the street and we enter another gangway.

"Wait," she says, breathing heavily. "I need to take a rest."

"Rest?! Are you shitting me? These men are trying to kill you!"

"That's what you say—how do I know you're telling the truth?"

"You don't." I grab her by the hand and drag her along. We enter a backyard where a porcelain birdbath sits in the middle of a lavish green lawn, before Rasna snatches her hand away from me.

"You're crazy!" she says through pattered breaths. "Maybe *you* killed Anton. How do I know you're not his killer?"

"Because you're still alive." I clutch her hand once again as we move through the yard. I stop and turn to look through a small window on the house's garage. I'm hoping to find a car, but the garage is empty.

"Dammit!" I yell, hitting the door with my palm.

I check my phone for a third time, but there's still no signal.

They gotta be jamming it.

I lead Rasna into another alley where black plastic garbage containers are aligned next to the square garages. I scan the alley and there's still no sign of the hearse.

"We need to figure out a strategy. We can't keep running from these guys and I've got to get you into protective custody."

"No!" Rasna yells, backing up. "I won't go. I'm dead if I do. Don't you see? It's your own government that's after me."

"Look, I don't have a choice—"

I hear the revving of an engine as I turn around and see the hearse speeding towards us. I push Rasna towards the gate of a nearby house, but it's locked.

"Run!" I yell, pushing her in the opposite direction of the speeding hearse.

"What about you?"

"Just run, dammit!"

I turn my back on her and stand in a shooter's stance with my knees slightly bent and the gun held tightly within my hands. I let off a shot and the bullet whistles in the warm air as Rasna runs down the alley. I continue letting off shots as the hearse barrels down on me with the bullets ricocheting off its body. The car veers slightly to the side and hits me with its rear fender, throwing me against one of the aluminum garage doors. I drop the gun and cough hard as the blow knocks the wind out me.

The hearse screeches to a stop. As I struggle to catch my breath and get up from the ground. I hear Rasna scream, which gets my adrenaline pumping. I reach out for my gun, but feel the tread of a large boot stepping on my fingers instead.

"Ahhhh fuck!" I cry out as I raise my head to see who is stepping on my hand. But my sight begins to wane.

No, it can't be happening. Not now—not another attack.

I feel the rhythm of my heart increase and the barrel of a pistol is pressed to my head. The cold steel feels hauntingly refreshing compared to the summer's heat. I close my eyes, hear the cocking of the hammer and everything goes black.

CHAPTER 46

The *I Gotcha Faded* barbershop is crowded one early Saturday morning when I step through its doors. Blue is sitting in Ike's chair. We've been partners on the homicide division for almost four years. In fact, it was Blue who convinced me to join the force after returning from Iraq.

"What took you so long to get here?" Blue asks with his head bent forward as Ike runs the buzzing clippers across the back of it.

"Had to look over some applicants for the apartment in my dad's building."

"Why don't you just take it? You know you want to be closer to your daddy anyway. We know how proud he is of you for becoming a cop."

"Moving back home? I can't see that with binoculars. I'm a grown man. What I look like moving back home?"

"You know you want to."

"I have a better idea. How about I let you rent the apartment and you can keep an eye on my old man for me?"

"I'm good."

"I thought so."

I take a seat on the right side of the small shop, which is filled front to back with black barber chairs, black washing sinks and three televisions mounted along the left wall. I pick up a magazine from the stack on the table near the line of sitting customers and begin flipping through it. At one end of the shop, a group of young men are discussing the latest rumors of NBA players to be traded.

The door to the shop swings open and in walks T-Rex and his newest protégé, Prince Paul. I close the magazine and sit it back down on the table. T-Rex is a tall, coal-colored man who always keeps a toothpick in his mouth and an evil smirk on his face. He's wearing a black Carhartt vest, a black Timberland skullcap, black jeans and black Timberland boots. Paul follows behind him with a large puffy coat and sagging jeans. His skin is radiant red from the cold.

"What down, people?" Paul asks with a hop and limp in his step.

I steal a glance at Blue. We both know T-Rex from our old neighborhood and we've grown up with Paul. We also know the complications that narcotic detectives have incurred with getting something to stick on T-Rex. The man has lived through his share of gang wars and come out the other side with just two bullet wounds and a three-inch jagged scar down his left arm from a knife fight.

T-Rex is the last of a dying breed of OG's that have seen gang life when it was strong and vibrant on the streets. He's lived through so much in fact, most people believe he has a guardian angel watching over him. But to Blue and I, he's trouble walking and it's only a matter of a time before he's arrested or someone kills him.

As the two men cover the length of the shop, they keep their eyes on us. It isn't a secret that Blue and I are homicide detectives and over half our caseload is filled with murders that we know T-Rex is involved in, even if we can't prove it.

"If it ain't big bad T-Rex," Blue says. "And here I thought a baller like you would have his own personal barber by now?"

"I'm just like everybody else, trying to make a dollar out of fifteen cents," T-Rex replies, rolling the toothpick around in his mouth.

I stand up from my seat. I know exactly where this is going.

"Don't you mean you're trying to make more drug money?" Blue asks, turning up his lip and frowning.

"Look, I'm just here to get my hair cut, officer. That's all." T-Rex throws his hands up in front of him.

"That's *detective* to you," Blue counters as he holds up a hand for Ike to stop cutting his hair. He rises from the chair with the barber's tunic still covering his body. I flank him on his right as we advance towards T-Rex and Prince Paul.

"Come on, guys—they just want to get cuts," Ike says, fully aware that all parties involved are packing.

All four of us stare at one another like we're part of a western showdown. Paul smiles at me and I return the gesture before grabbing Blue by the arm. "They're not worth it," I whisper into his ear.

T-Rex rolls the toothpick around in his mouth again, smiles an evil grin and gives Paul a light tap on the arm. "We bouncing. We'll come back later when it's a little more hospitable up in here."

The two men walk back through the barbershop and out the front door.

"Why do you let people like T-Rex get to you, Blue?" I ask as he walks back to the barber chair to retake his seat.

"Because they're garbage and it's people like them that are killing our kids with this drug shit."

"But when you fly off like that, we lose our edge."

"Probably so, but I wanted them to know that this barbershop won't become a part of their evil world. I wanted them to know that they won't be protected here."

"I understand that but—"

"No buts, Frank. Besides, people like T-Rex and Paul will always give us another shot to bring 'em down."

"I guess you're right."

Blue retakes his seat in the barber's chair as Ike continues cutting his hair. "Any leads on that double homicide over on Lake Street?" he asks.

"Still nothing. Nobody's coming through with anything," I say.

"Yaw'll talking about that double murder that happened at the Transport Club over on Ashland?" Ike asks.

"Yeah, that's what we're talking about." Blue looks at me. As detectives we have to be leery of everyone, but also keep our eyes and ears open for leads.

Ike starts to cut Blue's hair again before speaking. "I heard a dude in here the other day talking about that club. Said he merked two dudes because he caught them out back kissing and hugging on some gay shit."

"What did he look like?" Blue asks.

Ike looks around the room at the other men sitting in the chairs waiting on haircuts. "Shit, you know I don't be checking dudes out like that. It ain't really none of my business anyway, you know what I'm saying?"

We both shake our heads. We understand completely what he's saying. The barbershop is like the Catholic church; one can come to fellowship with other people, tell stories and even confess to crimes outright without the rest of the world finding out, because there's an unwritten rule between every patron and barber to keep everything that is said inside the walls of the barbershop.

Outside, a car comes to a screeching halt. I rise from my chair with my hand resting on the butt of my gun as I turn to look at the doorway as my fifty-four-year-old father heads towards it. His eyes are large and menacing. He's wearing a dark blue jogging suit with a CPD headband to protect his ears. He comes barreling through the barbershop door as he points to me. "I just got a call that you're butting heads with very important people."

For it to be nobody's business, word spreads quickly. "Nah, things are good, Dad. We got it under control."

"We?" he questions.

"Yeah, Blue and I."

"I should've known." My father turns to stare at Blue who is just now rising from the barber's chair. "Desmond, don't you go dragging my boy into something you two can't get your assess out of!"

"So we're just supposed to let drug dealing assholes like T-Rex walk around like they own the city?" Blue questions.

"I didn't say that. All I'm saying is you've got to learn to choose your fights."

"So I guess we should look the other way when it comes to people like T-Rex, huh?" Blue asks.

"Don't patronize me, Desmond."

"This isn't like it was back in your day. We don't take under the table." Blue steps past my dad, intentionally bumping him on the way out the front door and into the cool day.

"What did you just say to me?" my father asks, following Blue out the door as I follow close behind.

He grabs Blue by the shoulder and spins him around. Instinctively, Blue pulls his piece.

My father throws up his hands. "Whoa, is that how it is? You'd pull your sidearm on an unarmed officer?"

Blue is silent as he stares into my father's eyes.

"Blue! What the hell are you doing, man?!" I yell.

They lock eyes and for a second, I'm afraid I may have to draw my own weapon to keep the peace. "Blue! Put it away!" I demand.

My father bites his bottom lip—his tell that he's thinking about making a move. I slide my hand towards my holster.

Damn you if you make me do this, Blue.

"Put the weapon away, Desmond," my father commands, using his parenting voice. I haven't heard it in a few years, so it takes me by surprise.

Blue licks his lips and snorts. "Sorry, Frank. Force of habit." He re-holsters his gun. "Don't you ever put your hands on me again," he says to my father before turning to me. "Ask him why he doesn't want us talking to T-Rex. Ask him about all the money he's taken over the years from that asshole."

"I've never taken a thing!" my father protests.

"You've taken a lot of things from what I hear. My mother told me all about you."

"What are you talking about Blue?" I ask.

"Nothing, Frank. You know what? I just need to clear my head. I'll meet you back at the office."

Blue walks up the street towards his car.

I turn and look at my father. "Dad, what's he talking about?"

"Nothing, Frank. It's nothing at all. Just let it go."

My father jumps into his car and drives off leaving me to re-enter the barbershop. I have to wait until it's nearly empty before I have an opportunity to pull Ike to the side and question him about the suspect he mentioned from the Transport Night Club shooting. He gives me a name: Diondre Hill.

Back inside my car, I pull up the name of the suspect through the I-CLEAR computer system, hoping to get a hit. The computer screen turns blank and then a color photo of Diondre Hill appears on screen. His hair is braided into two thick corn rows, which curl up behind his head like ram's horns. His nose is narrow but wide near the nostrils. His eyes have dark rings around them as if he's never slept in his life and his lips are black, chapped and peeling.

Below the photo is a detailed report of Hill's priors, which consist of assault with a deadly weapon, possession of a controlled substance and aggravated assault which tells me two things: Hill is a dangerous individual and it'll probably be better to catch him on the streets instead of trying to catch him at his last known residence.

I start up the car and turn onto Homan Boulevard as I head south towards Jackson. I punch in the speed dial number for Blue's phone, but all I get is the voicemail.

"Dammit, Blue, where are you?" I hang up the phone and place it back into my pocket. It looks like I have to ride this lead solo.

CHAPTER 47

The part of Chicago known as Holy City is located in the East Garfield Park neighborhood on the city's west side. When I roll into the neighborhood, it's still daylight out and the once littered sidewalks are now covered with three inches of snow. However, that doesn't stop the thugs from hitting the streets as the hustlers are like postal workers; neither snow nor rain nor heat nor the gloom of night will keep the couriers from the swift completion of their appointed rounds.

As I approach the intersection of Jackson, I see a crowd of young black teenagers break off from the corner they've been occupying and begin walking westward up the street. I pull the unmarked car up along side them and roll down the window.

"Any of you know a Diondre Hill?" I ask.

The group of young men shake their heads no. They're all dressed in puffy black coats wearing dark skull caps with cardboard brims sowed into the fabric and their hats turned to the left.

"You sure?" I ask, studying their faces. All their eyes are filled with hurt and hate.

"Yeah, we sure," one of the boys finally replies.

"All right."

I roll up the window and drive on down the street. I'm sure they know Hill. After all, Holy City is his stomping ground and the fact that all the boys have their hats turned to the left tells me that they're part of the Vice Lord street gang, which Hill is also an associate of.

I make a right turn onto Central Park and decide to hit a block and come back up Homan. Halfway up the street, I spot Hill walking with his hands inside his jacket pockets. I ride past him casually, taking the time to study his face. He looks younger than the picture I have on the computer screen, but the narrow bridge of his nose and wide nostrils are undeniable. Slowing the car's speed, I watch Hill in the rearview. I know my best option is to collar him while there's still light out and he's out in the open. I round the car into a U-turn as he begins to cross the intersection of Jackson and Central Park. Pulling up the street slowly, I try not to give away my intentions but Hill takes off running towards the elementary school on the corner.I should've seen this coming. Hill is a veteran of the streets. The moment our paths crossed he could feel me coming.

"Fuck!" I let out, shooting up the street with a single blue light on the dash blaring and the horn wailing.

Hill hops a fence and begins sprinting towards the Garfield Park housing complexes on Congress Street near Independence Boulevard. I punch the gas pedal as I veer the car onto a curb and speed through a vacant snow-covered lot.

So much for trying to catch Hill out in the open. If I don't play this right, what should have been a routine questioning could easily become a shootout. Even worse, it could transform into a hostage situation since there's a senior citizens home located right beside the housing complex.

I pick up the radio receiver and call for backup as I keep one hand on the steering wheel. Hill runs through the snow-covered lot like a Clydesdale in a Budweiser commercial. Just ahead are the four two-story housing complexes that make up the Garfield Park apartments. There's no telling who Hill might know in those apartments or what type of weapon he might be able to get a hold of. I drive the gas pedal of the Caprice into the floor as I hit a pothole that sends me bouncing up out of my seat.

Hill zigzags across the white field and then cuts in between a fire hydrant and a light pole before slipping into the recesses of one of the buildings. I hit the brakes and before the car can completely come to a stop, I barrel out of it with my gun drawn. The air tastes bitter and sour like it's been released from a moldy abandoned building. The snow crunches under my shoes as I move towards the building with my flashlight and gun crisscrossed in front of me.

"Diondre, I'm Detective Calhoun. I only want to talk to you," I say to the silhouetted opening within the building's exterior. There's no answer. I can hear the sirens approaching, so I'm certain that backup will arrive soon. The buildings are located right across from the off-ramp at Independence, which allows me to also hear the cars and semis on the 290 Expressway zooming by.

I move into the empty open hall and find that the lights are out in the stairway. I sweep the beam of the flashlight underneath the space of the concrete stairs, but all I find is a used condom and some trash. I'm about to climb the stairs when I hear three squad cars pull up to where my car is idling, so I decide to pull back. There's no need to put myself in harm's way when I know that Hill is cornered.

Daylight has faded when I step out of the building and walk over to where the patrolmen are standing. I brief the officers on the situation and instruct them to create a perimeter around the building. I take an officer with me as we go door-to-door inside the quadruple apartment complex asking the residents if they know the suspect while reminding each one of them the consequences of harboring a criminal. It's the best I can do without having a warrant. I've heard the stories of cops breaking down innocent citizens doors without a search warrant and I vowed never to cross that line. Diondre Hill might be my shooter, but I'm not his judge or his jury.

As we come away from the last apartment door slamming shut in our faces, I stand on the open terrace of the stairs and stare out over the 290 Expressway. There are six continuous lanes of car lights moving back and forth on the road. There's no way that Hill ran out the front end of the building and got away. I was on his ass. I'm sure of it.

I rest my hands on the steel grated banister and roll my neck around in a circular motion. As I bring my head up to a twelve o'clock position, I notice a partial metal ladder bolted into the concrete wall that leads to the roof. I tap the patrolman and point up to the rooftop. The officer nods and trains his gun on the ladder before following it up towards the square metal opening in the roof's landing.

"Diondre, this is Detective Calhoun. We know you're on the roof and we have the place surrounded. I just want to ask you some questions—but if you force me, I'll have to call in tactical air support who will shoot you first and ask questions later. So you have two choices. You can come down on your own and do it my way. Or we can do it your way and let air support handle it. It's up to you."

A few seconds later, the rooftop covering is removed and Diondre Hill climbs down and gives himself up. I let the uniforms run him in as I try to reach Blue on his cell phone again, but still there's no answer. The voicemail kicks in and I hang up.

"Where the hell are you, Blue?"

I hop into my car and reverse out of the snow-covered lot and back onto Central Park Avenue. The windows are just beginning to defog when the radio crackles with an operator's voice. I pick up the mic and respond. "Say again Central?"

"I repeat. Shots fired at 4416 West Senate Street. All units respond."

That's my father's address. But it can't be. I give dispatch my badge and car number. I want to confirm the address, so dispatch reads the numbers and street back to confirm that it is definitely my father's home. I spin the car into a U-turn and start heading south.

CHAPTER 48

When I pull up to my father's two-flat apartment building, the outer gate is open and my father never leaves the gate open. I'm the only officer on the scene thus far, as I rush up the stairs and find the front door also ajar. I remove my weapon from its holster and step slowly into the apartment.

"Dad, it's me. I'm coming in!" I yell. My voice bounces off the hallway walls.

Every light in the house seems to be on and as I move further into the apartment that I'd grown up in, seeing everything with new eyes makes it almost unrecognizable. The burgundy couch where I used to watch Saturday morning cartoons is now worn and dust-covered. The ancient floor model Magnavox television's tube is dark and dead. I move into the dining room where the china cabinet beams with crystal figurines that my mother use to collect, along with my old chess trophies.

"Dad! You here?" I call out.

I hear someone shout my name from the kitchen. I enter

cautiously with the barrel of my gun jutting out in front of me. Inside the kitchen, I find the back door open and Blue sprawled out on the kitchen floor like a broken toy soldier lying in a pool of his own blood. I quickly re-holster my weapon and bend down by my partner's side. I open my phone and call emergency services.

"I need a bus for an officer down! Don't worry, Blue, I've got you. Help's on the way." I scan his body looking for other wounds other than the two slugs I see rupturing his chest. I apply pressure to the wounds with my hands in an attempt to stop the bleeding.

"Blue, where's my dad?" I ask through clenched teeth.

Blue slowly opens his eyes with a whimper. "F-F-Frank."

"Yeah, I'm here. Who did this to you, Blue?"

"Father." He points up towards the ceiling.

"Yeah, where is my father?" I look around the kitchen, but everything about the room seems like a blur to me.

"Frank," Blue says tightening his grip around my wrists. "I need to tell you something, b-b-but I don't know if-if it matters now."

"Tell me when you're better, buddy."

"It can't wait. I want you to know that I love you, man."

"I love you, too," I say as tears begin to fill my eyes. I apply more pressure to the wounds as if I can close the openings in his chest with my bare hands.

"Frank, there's something you've got to know."

"If this is about you sleeping with Trina back in high school, I forgive you, man. That's old news."

"No, Frank... listen to me. You and I... are brothers."

"Yeah I know. We've been telling people that for the longest. Yogi and Boo-boo, remember?" I chuckle.

"No, I mean for real. Your father... is my father."

"What? You-you're delirious, man."

"My mother told me... told me the truth. H-H-He's my father, too."

I look down into Blue's teary eyes and feel deep in my soul that he's telling me the truth. I look around the kitchen again and it feels like the walls might disintegrate along with the floor and give way to me falling out of this nightmare I'm currently in.

"Where is he, Blue? Where's Dad?" I ask as my voice breaks.

"Dad." Blue smiles pointing towards the ceiling.

I grab Blue's hands and press them against the wound in his chest. "Apply pressure. I'll be right back. I've got to find Dad."

I stand and wrap my bloodied fingers around my gun. I'm about to go back through the house and check the bedrooms when it dawns on me that the back door was inexplicably open. I step out onto the wooden back porch and scan the small yard. I see the garage light on and hear the revving of the car's engine. I jump down the five stairs and rush over to the garage. Kicking open the door, I'm instantly overtaken by carbon monoxide fumes that have entered my lungs. The smell of motor oil and exhaust fumes fill the cramped space. I duck my head back outside the garage and take a deep breath and then re-enter to find my father unconscious behind the wheel with his foot dead against the accelerator.

I run to the driver's side door and pull on the handle, but it's locked. I knock out the window with the butt of the gun and unlock the door as the carbon monoxide fumes are causing my lungs to burn. I grab my father under the arms and pull him from the car. My legs feel weak and I know it's only a matter of time before I succumb to the fumes.

I drag my father out of the garage and into the cold night before we both collapse on a fresh bed of snow. I double over on my knees, coughing as I try to free my lungs of the poisonous gas. I look over and see my father's tobacco-colored face and notice that he isn't breathing, so I began to administer CPR. The coldness of the night feels like it's biting at my skin as I press my lips to my father's mouth and exhale all the air in my lungs into his. I interlocked my fingers, one hand on top of the other and press down on his chest while keeping rhythmic count.

The cries of the squad car sirens are now in front of the house, but I can't stop and go for help. Every second counts. I continue the CPR procedure until my father finally coughs out the toxic fumes and begins gasping for air.

"Frank," my father says between coughs. "My son."

I stand and instantly feel light-headed. I steady myself against the garage before running towards the house, leap up the five stairs and enter the kitchen. Blue is still spread out on the kitchen floor with his hands resting on his unmoving chest. I fall to his side with tears filling my eyes as I scream to the heavens, mourning my brother.

While I was outside giving my father CPR to bring him back from the clutches of death, Blue died alone on the cold hard kitchen floor. Uniformed officers systematically fill the kitchen and crowd around us with guns drawn as I try to revive Blue with a hug, even though everyone else can tell that he's already given up the ghost.

CHAPTER 49

The slobbery lick from an animal brings me out of my dream. I open my eyes slowly as I feel a black and white Welsh Corgi's warm tongue slap against my face. I stare up into the eyes of the dog and it reminds me of a puppy I received for Christmas one year. Tragically, I let it freeze to death because I forgot to bring him back inside after it relieved itself. I close my eyes and try to think, and that's when I remember Rasna Hussein. I open my eyes, sit up and look around the empty alley for my gun, but all I find is a frail Indian woman with a bindi dot on her forehead, wailing her arms wildly.

"Shoo!" the woman says. "Shoo, you bum. Get out of here before I call police."

I slowly rise to my feet and balance myself against the dented garage door. I remember everything now. The chase, the hearse and even the gun to my head.

"I call police, bum!" the woman yells.

"Yeah, yeah, I'm going lady." I fan a hand at her. I don't have time to explain that I am the police and my head is beginning to throb and ache. I turn and start walking up the alley.

Out on Devon Avenue, traffic crawls as people walk up and down the street. I approach a curb and hold out my hand for a taxi as three simultaneously pass me by. At first, I tell myself it's due to the color of my skin, but it's most likely my appearance as my shirt is covered with dirt and the shins of my pants are worn as if I've been breakdancing on them. I understand now why the old woman thought I was homeless.

After about a minute of hailing taxis with little success, I drop my hand and cross the street to wait at the bus stop for the 155 going east. While waiting for the bus, my phone beeps indicating that I have a voicemail. I dial the mailbox and listen to the message. The voice is deep and unknown.

"Detective Calhoun, we have the woman. If you try and get help, we will dismember her. In twenty-four hours, we will release her unharmed if you comply. We will be watching."

I save the message and then close the phone. I was right about them jamming the cell phone signal and the message also confirms my theory about the possibility of there being two shooters. The time of the message lets me know it was sent two hours ago, meaning I have twenty-two hours to find Rasna Hussein or she'll disappear off the face of the earth, along with Father Pantone's killers.

CHAPTER 50

I take a seat on the Red Line train heading south. Next to me is a young man with headphones, bobbing his head to music. The image reminds me of Billy Murphy right before he was killed and a feeling of dread sweeps over me. I shake my head and do my best to concentrate on what I know about the investigation.

The killers could be extremists who have vowed to kill Father Pantone and Rasna Hussein because of their relationship, but I doubt it. The killings are more calculated and don't seem like the work of terrorists, who usually go after larger numbers in order to create hysteria. That's how they fuel attention towards their cause.

I have a pretty good idea that I'm dealing with professional killers instead of terrorists, but this new knowledge only begs to create new questions that need answers like how did Bigsby's prints end up in the Murphy home if he died in Haditha? There's something that I'm not seeing, something that I can't see, but I'm not sure what it could be.

The rear door to the train car opens and a tall man with a dark complexion and rough brown dreadlocks steps into the car, carrying a cup in his hand. He walks up the aisle asking for loose change while jingling his cup. I turn a blind eye, not because I don't care for the man's plight, but because I know he'll be right back here tomorrow and the next day and the next until he dies.

The kid with the headphones taps me on the shoulder, letting me know that the next stop is his. I rise from my seat and let him pass. As the kid stands at the train's doors bobbing his head to the music, I drop my head and think about Billy Murphy. The poor kid died on my watch because I couldn't protect him, and now Rasna Hussein is in the hands of murderers because I couldn't protect her. *What good am I?*

I lift my head and watch the coin jinglier make his way back up the aisle. He's passing his cup from left to right, from passenger to passenger as he walks. When he passes by the kid with the headphones, he stops and kneels down. I follow the man's hand as he picks up a ten-dollar bill that's fallen out of the kid's pocket. The man taps the boy on the shoulder, but the kid ignores him. He taps him harder and finally, the boy turns around with a fist balled up but at his side, readying to defend himself. He removes his headphones and to his surprise, the coin jingler hands him the crinkled bill.

The boy and man nod to one another as the coin jingler continues on down the aisle asking for change. I sit back in my seat, nodding my head. If this kid who reminds me so much of Billy Murphy can be reached by a total stranger, then there's a possibility that I can too. But first, I've got to see Doctor Staples in order to confirm this theory.

CHAPTER 51

The call comes in to Kawowski's phone as he sits at his desk inside the homicide division at Area Two headquarters. He's playing back the audio from the previous night of his interrogation with Frank Calhoun when the phone rings.

"Kawowski," he says picking up the phone on the first ring. "Detective Kawowski, this is Detective Jim Bauer of robbery and homicide over at the Three."

"How can I help you, Detective Bauer?"

"I just caught an attempted murder case in which a priest by the name of Father Cicero Sanchez was shot and I found your card in his possession. Mind clueing me in as to why?"

Kawowski stands up from his desk with the phone cradled to his ear. "My partner and I questioned Father Sanchez about the murder of another priest that occurred in Uptown."

"I see. Well, maybe we should get together soon and compare notes."

"That sounds all right to me. If you don't mind me asking, where was Father Sanchez when he was shot?"

"At his church in Wicker Park."

"Thanks. I'll be in contact soon, Detective Bauer."

Kawowski punches down the stabilizers to the phone and listens for a dial tone. He punches in Lopez's cell number and waits for him to answer.

"Lo... Lopez here," he says, out of breath.

"David, it's Mike. You out running?" Kawowski asks. "Nah, I'm at home. What's up, Mike?"

"Remember that priest Sanchez that we questioned?"

"Yeah, the one with the huge mole under his eye."

"Yeah, that's the one. I just got a call from a detective over at the Three in robbery and homicide. Said Father Sanchez has been shot."

"Get the hell out of here."

"Yep. And that's not all. They found him shot inside his own church."

"That's a big fucking coincidence."

"You're telling me. I'm heading over to the church, so meet me there. And tell Teresa the mail clerk I said hi."

"Sure, Mike. Shit. See you soon."

Kawowski hangs up the phone and then pulls his glock from its holster and checks the magazine to make sure it's full. He slaps the clip back into the gun and re-holsters it.

There are no coincidences in a murder investigation. Father Sanchez's attempted murder is somehow tied to the Pantone murder case and there's no time for him to waste comparing notes with Detective Bauer when the murderer he's after is so close at hand.

There's yellow tape sanctioning off the doors to Saint Peter of Alcantara as a crowd of people stand before the gothic building holding candles. Kawowski pulls his car to the curb. He hates candlelight vigils, because of all the depressed faces that he has to look into, knowing that at the time there's nothing that can soothe their broken hearts.

He steps out of the car and looks at the teary-eyed parishioners who all turn and stare at him. He takes a deep breath, exhales and starts walking towards the crowd, accepting the fate that has been placed on his shoulders. He stops in mid-stride and listens as a loud buzzing sound shoots up the tree-lined street that resembles a dying engine or the amplified sound of an electric hair clipper. All the saddened parishioners turn their attention away from Kawowski and look in the direction of the buzzing to see a red Mitsubishi speeding their way. Kawowski smiles and continues on towards the church. Normally he hates Lopez's car with its modified muffler, but at this moment he can't get enough of it.

He ducks under the tape and enters the church through the large wooden doors. Inside, the candelabra lights are brighter than the first time he and Lopez visited the church. The hundred-plus pews are now empty and there are two canvas lights set up near the altar with a ten-foot perimeter of yellow tape encompassing it, which marks exactly where Father Sanchez fell.

Kawowski runs his finger along the tape as he studies the blood splatter on the floor. The crimson liquid fell in large blotches before trailing across the surface and ending near the foot of the altar. There's also a long streak of blood across the altar's marble face and then the trail ends. Kawowski comes to the conclusion that Father Sanchez was probably shot at close range, meaning he likely knew his attacker. The trail of blood also confirms that the impact of the shot spun Father Sanchez around as he fell upon the altar before sliding down to the floor, left to bleed out like a stuck pig.

"Can I help you?" the scrawny security guard from the

rectory asks as he steps out of the back room of the church and into the main room.

"Detective Kawowski." he says, holding out his badge.

"Sorry about not standing guard—had to use the restroom," the guard replies.

"I won't tell if you don't," Kawowski says, studying the pock-faced man.

"Any idea when the officers are coming to relieve me? I've got band practice."

"I don't, but I'm sure it'll be soon. Sorry." Both men turn as the doors to the church open and in walks Lopez. "Don't worry about him, that's my partner," Kawowski says to the guard.

When Lopez finally notices the security guard, he begins stepping down the aisle with a hard press walk of a man that means business.

Kawowski clears his throat. "I never got your name?"

"Dave Matthews. And yes, like the singer." The guard sounds a bit dour.

"Okay, Dave. Were you around when Father Sanchez was shot?"

"Kind of."

"What does that mean?"

Lopez walks around the crime scene. He eyes the guard and then turns back to studying the blood splatter. It's best to let Kawowski do the talking for now.

"I was in the area. I work security over at the rectory."

"So you weren't inside the church when he was shot?"

"No, I was busy at the rectory on the phone, trying to keep my job after some guy attacked Father Sanchez in his bedroom earlier."

Kawowski asks while cutting his eyes at Lopez. "What do you mean *some guy*?"

"He said he was a cop."

"What did he look like?" Kawowski asks, opening his notepad.

"Average height. Maybe about six feet or so. Black with a gruff beard."

"Anything else noticeable about him?"

"Not that I can remember."

"Thanks Dave." Kawowski turns away from the guard. "I'm sure your relief will be here soon."

He joins Lopez near the altar and then the two detectives start down the aisle back towards the entrance.

"You know who that sounds like, don't you?" Lopez asks.

"Looks like Calhoun's been busy."

"I want a shot at him this time when we bring him in," Lopez says smashing his fist into his palm.

"He's all yours, partner. Matter of fact, how about you take lead and let's see what pans out?"

"Now that's what I'm talking about. You know we're about to bust this case wide open, don't you?"

"I hope so."

Kawowski pushes open the church's doors as a beam of sunlight falls across their faces. The two detectives shield their eyes with their hands. Standing before them are the parishioners with questioning eyes.

Kawowski pats his partner on the back. "Your audience awaits."

CHAPTER 52

I storm through the doors of Doctor Staples' office and march past her receptionist.

"Hey, where do you think you're going?" the receptionist asks, jumping up from her seat. She's a heavyset woman with dark brown hair and light skin.

"I need to see Doctor Staples immediately," I say.

"You can't just barge into her office."

"Watch me." I blow past her as the receptionist turns and runs back towards her desk.

I force open the door to Doctor Staples' office just as the receptionist's voice comes in over the telephone's loudspeaker. "It's okay, Laura," Doctor Staples says. "I'll handle this. Could you please call back the previous caller and let him know I've got an emergency patient I have to see?"

"Yes, ma'am."

"Thank you." Doctor Staples rises from her chair and greets me with a smile. "Detective Calhoun, what brings you by? Our next appointment isn't until next week." She looks me over with a quizzical stare, likely thrown off by my appearance.

"I know, but I had to see you. I've got a life-and-death situation on my hands right now."

"How about we take a seat and you tell me all about it."

"Don't have the time for that."

"Then I'm not sure how I can help you."

"You said last time that if I faced my fears, I'd stop having these blackouts."

"Well, that's part of the diagnosis. But I don't see where you're going with this, Frank."

"I faced my fears, Doc. I went and saw my father."

"I see," Doctor Staples nods her head. "And what did it feel like to see him for the first time?"

"At first, I felt calm as I sat there studying him, trying to find some resemblance to the father I had once known."

"And did you find him?"

"No, it was as if he was a new man."

"Well, you know as well as I do that prison can do that to a person."

"Yeah, I know. I just never thought it would happen to my father."

"You said you felt calm when you saw him. Why do you think that is?"

"I don't know. Maybe because he's my father and I don't think he'll ever do anything to harm me, so I don't fear him or see him as a threat."

"Exactly. So why do you think he is what you fear?"

"Because I had another blackout. Just a few hours ago."

"What were you doing before the blackout?"

"Well, if we're being honest, I was trying to save a woman from being kidnapped."

"And when that boy was killed what were you doing then?"

"I was trying to save him from being killed. Where are you going with this, Doc?"

"And what were you doing when your partner died? The first time you blacked out was right after his death, during your father's trial. When you testified against him, am I correct?"

"So what?"

"Do you ever see your brother during your blackouts?"

"Something like that. He's always reaching out to me."

Doctor Staples leans back on her desk. "It sounds to me that your father isn't the problem. It's the regret you're carrying around for the brother you couldn't save. Just like the kid you couldn't save from the shooting or this woman from being kidnapped. The only clear way I see you beating this, is if you let go of that regret and own up to the fact that—in all these cases—there was nothing you could do."

"And how do I do that?"

"Only you know that, Frank. When the time comes where you have to face it, you'll know what to do."

I stand there contemplating the Doc's words. *How am I supposed to know how to beat this thing when I can't get over the fact that I couldn't save Blue?*

The phone rings and Doctor Staples picks it up. "Yes, yes, I understand. I'll let him know. Thank you." She hangs up the phone and looks at me. "The police want to see you, Frank. They're sitting outside in the receptionist area, waiting on you."

"Thanks, Doc. I'll be seeing you next week."

I exit the room and begin walking down the hall towards the receptionist area. A quarter of the way down, I hear the lock to Doctor Staples' office door click. As I turn to look back at the door, I realize what she said right before I left her office. *Why are the police here to see me? And how did they know I was here?* Then, it hits me—the conversation between Doctor Staples and her receptionist was actually a coded message. I can't fault her since she's just doing what's asked of her. But the fact that officers are waiting for me in the receptionist area has me worried.

I'm certain that Kawowski and Lopez are behind this, but then again, it could be Smith ready to pay me back for the broken nose.

As I near the end of the hall, I take a deep breath and enter the receptionist area. The light-skinned woman is now gone and standing in her place, wearing a dark blue policeman's uniform is my Uncle Skeet.

CHAPTER 53

do a double take at Uncle Skeet dressed in his blue patrolman uniform. It reminds me of the times he would come home with my father after a hard day's work and chug down a few beers on the front porch.

"Uncle Skeet, what are you doing here?"

"Shits hit the fan, Frank. You're wanted for attempted murder."

"Attempted murder? What are you talking about?"

"Father Sanchez was shot this morning."

I look at my uncle with eyes wide open. "How? Where?"

"All that is irrelevant right now. We've got to get you out of here before they get here."

"Before who gets here? What are you talking about?"

"Listen and listen hard. Word through the blue line is you're wanted for the attempted murder of Father Cicero Sanchez."

I know my uncle is telling the truth. The 'blue line' is a word of mouth network between cops. If something important needs to be broadcast like an APB on a suspect, it's put out through the Blue Line before any other outlet and within hours every cop in the city knows about it.

I look at Uncle Skeet. "So you heard that Kawowski and Lopez were on their way here and decided to give me the head's up, huh?"

"Something like that."

"How do you know I didn't do it?" I ask.

"Because I'm your uncle, dammit. And you're Joe Calhoun's boy and I know we raised you right."

"Thanks, Unc. Look, I didn't do it, but I'm not about to run from this. They have no evidence I did it."

Uncle Skeet moves over to the window and looks down on the street below. "Preliminary tests show that the slug pulled out of Father Sanchez matches the slugs you fired during Billy Murphy's murder."

"That can't be. Besides, that gun was lost earlier today."

"Well, Kawowski and Lopez just searched your home and found it, so now they're on their way here to arrest you."

My heart drops. If Uncle Skeet is telling the truth, then that means the killers might have followed me to Saint Peter of Alcantara. That's probably how they knew where Rasna Hussein was located and now they're covering their tracks by framing me.

"Dammit! Here they come," Uncle Skeet says moving away from the window. "We've got to go *now!*"

We step out into the pastel green hallway and make our way towards the stairs. When we enter the stairwell, we hear tactical officers forcefully climbing the stairs.

"Shit!" Uncle Skeet says. He closes the door to the stairwell and removes a .45 pistol from his holster and begins beating the butt of the gun against the doorknob until the door is jammed. "Here," he says, handing the gun over to me. "You're going to need this wherever you're going. My car's parked out back near the loading dock."

"Wait, what are you talking about? We have to go together. You're the only one who will believe me."

"Sorry, Frank, but it just isn't going down that way. One of us has to stay behind and keep 'em busy."

Uncle Skeet runs to the elevators and pushes the button. He bends down, rolls up his left pants leg and removes a small revolver from a holster.

"Don't do this, Unc. There's got to be another way."

"Frank, just shut the hell up and follow my lead for once!"

Uncle Skeet stands to one side of the elevator while I stand on the other. We have our guns pointed down as we listen to the elevator ding away floor after floor until the doors finally open. Kawowski and Lopez step off the elevator only to be caught in between the sights of our guns.

"Drop it," Uncle Skeet says, shoving the barrel of his gun into Lopez's temple.

"So you had help after all, huh, Frank?" Kawowski asks, dropping his gun and raising his hands.

"This isn't how I wanted it to be," I reply.

"Yeah, well, you made it this way and we're going to bust your ass for all of it," Lopez says.

"Shut up, Tattoo! Move out of the way," Uncle Skeet commands.

I board the elevator and press the button for the ground floor. I watch my uncle hold off the two detectives as the doors close slowly, knowing that he's just sacrificed it all on the basis of my innocence.

I tuck the .45 into my waistband and hide it with my shirt. When I step off the elevator, I see the receptionist talking to an officer. I pivot and turn in the opposite direction to make my way towards the back of the building. I go through a door for the custodial staff and walk down a long grey hall until I come to the outside loading dock where Uncle Skeet's Mustang GT sits double parked with the keys still in the ignition.

I hop into the driver's seat and pull out of the alley and head west down Harrison Street. As I pass the intersection where Doctor Staples' office is located, I can't help but stare as I see officers putting my uncle into the back of a squad car. It hits me that I have no one to turn to for help. There's only one person I know that may be able to lead me to Rasna Hussein and the killers, but it means I'll have to do him a favor, and possibly forgo the only vow I now believe in: to serve and to protect.

CHAPTER 54

The Pocket Nightclub is located on Madison and Keeler on the city's West side in the space where the old Château Social Club once stood. I stare up at the broken neon sign as the last remnants of the Château hang from the brick building. The façade is made of thick cement-colored bricks from the nineteenth century with stone gargoyles jutting from the roof's edge. When I was a kid, I longed to go to the Château with my father and Uncle Skeet to see the flashing neon lights, hear the partying crowd and taste the foreign liquor which still makes me salivate to this day.

Now, as I stand before the old building, I dread every thought I've ever had of this place. I close my eyes, take a deep breath and say the words I've instinctively come to live by— "only the holy remain"—and push open the doors and step into the club. The space smells like cinnamon and cigarette smoke from years past. The lights are low even though the club won't be open for another eight hours. A few men move about the space, rearranging tables and clearing a large space for the dance floor. The DJ is in her booth testing the sound system when a man dressed in a black tight tee shirt that reads 'SECU-RITY' across the front of it approaches me.

"Who ya looking for?" the man asks.

I size up the bouncer. He's six foot something and probably weighs about 290 pounds with throbbing, I-don't-take-any- shit veins bulging from his forearms. He wears dark sunglasses and has a golden front tooth that shines in the low light.

"I'm looking for Prince Paul," I say, staring through the dark lenses and into the man's eyes.

"Yeah? Who you be?"

"Tell 'em Detective Frank Calhoun is here to see him."

When the bouncer hears the word detective, he misplaces some of his toughness. He smiles, showing his golden tooth. "Don't move. Be right back, *de-tective*."

I watch the man turn and walk towards the back of the club before he splits open a dark curtain revealing pool tables in the adjoining room. I have to hand it to Paul—The Pocket is immaculate with its billiard tables painted across the ceiling. The back of the bar is stocked with expensive vodkas and cognacs and there are lights shaped like pool balls along the face of the shelves, which illuminate the bottles and make the fiery liquor jump with life as though it's a mural of intoxication. The tables are shaped like triangular pool racks held up by thick stands made to resemble pool sticks.

After a few minutes, the bouncer returns to the dark curtain, holding open the flap as he calls out to me. "Right this way." I follow the guard into the back of the club past the pool tables and into another room that is decorated with black leather booths and dark lights.

"This is the VIP section," the bouncer quips. "We call this the Black Ball Room." He sneers with pride as if I'm supposed to be impressed.

When we reach the end of the room, we come face-to-face

with a door made of reinforced steel. The bouncer knocks with three distinctive taps and then slams his palm against the surface of the door. The locks on the other side unbolt and the door swings open revealing a fat black man with a Mohawk.

"This him?" the Mohawk grunts to the bouncer.

"Yeah, this our *de-tective*."

The Mohawk and I stare at one another and then the bouncer says over his shoulder. "Come on, man, I ain't got all day."

I follow him down a narrow hall. When we come to the end of the hall, we climb down a flight of stairs and find yet another reinforced steel door. The guard taps on the door six times and then slaps his palm against the door twice before it's buzzed open.

Inside the office sits Prince Paul behind a black marble desk shaking a magic eight ball. "Frank Calhoun. What down, player?" Paul asks as he gives the ball one more shake.

"I'm here to talk about the key, Paul."

Paul waves his hand and the sunglass-wearing bouncer leaves the room, shutting the door behind him.

"Key? Magic eight ball, do I know anything about a key?" Paul covers the lens of the mystic device and looks up at me. "What do you think it'll say, Frank?"

"I think it'll say that I don't have time for these games."

Paul looks down at the black device and then produces a crooked smile. "The Magic eight ball says that the streets are calling you a wanted man."

"Yeah, well the streets can be wrong."

"I feel you," Paul smiles. "Innocent until proven guilty, right?"

"Look, Paul, I just need to know what you know about the key I'm looking for and then I'm gone."

I open the car's door and hop in the passenger seat. Paul

turns the ignition and the car purrs to life. He taps the controller that hangs from his visor and the metal garage door begins to roll up. He picks up the radio controller off the seat and turns it on. Tupac Shakur's "Me Against the World" comes blasting out of the speakers.

"You never get tired of the classics," he utters, turning the car out of the garage and onto Madison Street.

I start to roll down the tinted windows when Paul stops me and turns on the AC.

"YOU DIDN'T HAVE TO DRAG ME OUT HERE AND TURN UP THE MUSIC JUST TO TALK! I'M NOT WEARING A WIRE! LOOK!"

I lift my shirt to show my bare chest.

Paul turns down the music. "I already know you ain't wired. If I even thought so, I would've laid you down by now." He smiles. "So sit back, relax and listen to my nigga 'Pac until we get to where we're going."

We head west on Madison passing through the shopping Mecca of clothing and shoe spots, cellular phone stores and nail shops that suck millions out of the black community it services. When we come to the intersection of Central Park and Madison, Paul makes a left and heads for the Garfield Park Golden Dome Recreational Center.

"The Dome? That's where we're going?" I ask.

"You got a problem with the Golden Dome?"

"Not at all. Just never took you for a person that visited the Dome."

"You'd be surprised where I go, Frank. When I was a shorty, I used to come and play chess here every Saturday. Now I use what I learned inside the Dome out here on the streets, you know what I'm saying?"

Paul pulls the car into a parking space on the street and we get out. I stare up at the eighteenth century field house with its gold-plated dome. There are ivory colored statuettes of angels and men with superbly crafted white wigs carved into the face of the building. As the last rays of the setting sun hit the top of the Golden Dome, it glows as if the hand of God has touched the building for the very first time.

"You coming?" Paul asks as he crosses the street.

"Right behind you, Bobby Fisher."

Once we climb the concrete stairs and enter the building, Paul leads me down a brown-colored corridor and we enter through two double doors and into a gymnasium.

The sound of weights and dumbbells clanging as they're dropped on mats explode across the room along with the sounds of heavy breathing, boxing gloves making contact with the heavy bag, the whooshing sound of jumping ropes and boxers sparring.

I follow Paul over to the squared ring where a tall, lanky boxer in red briefs extends his long arms and jabs at his opponent's protected headgear. The shorter fighter ducks under the punch and releases a barrage of body shots as he dances from side to side with his black shorts swishing at every movement. The bell rings and Paul calls the fighter in the black shorts over to us. The man ducks in between the ropes and steps down off the ring before removing his headgear and gloves.

"This is my little brother Tavares," Paul says turning to me with a smile like he'd just won the lottery. "He's the favor."

CHAPTER 55

I extend my hand and shake Tavares' hand. The young man is the color of peanut butter with a low cut and a cross earring dangling from his right ear. His nose is thin and sharp. When he smiles he shows a mouth full of perfect teeth, especially for a boxer.

"Tavares, this is Detective Frank Calhoun and he's offered to help you get into the academy," Paul states.

I do a double take and before I can object, Tavares is already shaking my hand faster than a dog can wag its tail.

"Really?" says Tavares, "Do you really think you can help me get into the academy?"

"Well, I ummm..."

"Of course he can," Prince Paul reassures. "Why do you think I brought him over here? I wanted him to see you in action and to see how much you help out your community."

"I'm just trying to give these kids something better than the streets," Tavares replies.

Paul puts his hand on my shoulder. "Let me holler at Detective Calhoun for a sec and then we'll get out of your way, so you can get back to working with the kids."

Paul and I walk off a distance from the ring as the sound of the bell clangs and Tavares goes back to sparring with the red trunks.

"So that was your favor, huh? Well you can forget about it, Paul. I won't disgrace the badge by bringing criminals into it."

"Criminal? My little brother ain't no criminal! He ain't got a record. All he does is go to college and devote the rest of his time to these kids in here. Ever since I can remember, he's talked about being a cop and the only thing I see holding him back from that dream is having a criminal for a brother. But that's where you come in."

"How so?"

"The way I see it, your old man was a police officer and so are you—which means I'm sure you've got a whole buncha connections in the department."

"You might have forgotten that my old man is in jail for killing another cop. His connections are trying to forget he ever existed."

"Yeah, I thought about that. Then I remembered your father's friend, the one who owns that restaurant. Shit, I see how many motherfucking cops be coming out of there everyday. A nigga gotta have a connect."

I smile. Apparently Paul hasn't heard about Uncle Skeet's arrest, which only works in my favor.

"Okay, I'll see what I can do to get your brother into the academy, but your lead about the key better pay off."

"Oh, trust me, it'll pay off." He smiles that crooked grin of his. "In more ways than you know."

CHAPTER 56

The apartment building that Prince Paul pulls the car up too is made of dark brown bricks. It's a three-story multi-complex with arching doorways, the type of place that has broken tiled hallway floors. All the windows are old wooden panes covered with chipped white paint.

"So what's this?" I ask. "Another little brother dreaming of becoming a fireman?"

"No, this is where you'll find the information about the key, funny man."

"You sure?" I look out the dark window at the litter-covered sidewalk and then back at Paul.

"Yeah, I'm sure. Apartment 2B."

"And who am I suppose to ask for?"

"Just tell 'em Prince Paul sent you. Once you're in, I'm sure you can take it from there."

"All right, if that's what you say." I open the car door and step out "You sure it's 2B?"

"For the last time, I'm sure."

I turn from the car just as a little black boy with large eyes runs across my path. I stop in mid-stride watching as the boy chases down his friends in a game of tag. It's rare to see kids running around, playing tag this late in the evening when they're usually inside glued to a television screen with a controller in their hands.

I climb the three-stair stoop and enter the main corridor of the building. Inside is a flight of brown wooden stairs with thick hand-carved banisters from a time past. I ascend the stairs to the second floor, knock on the door of apartment 2B and wait for a response.

"Who is it?" a female voice asks from behind the door. "Prince Paul sent me," I say.

The three deadbolts are unlocked and the door swings open allowing a peach aroma to escape out into the hall. Standing in the doorway is a woman with the complexion of lemon cake, light and yellow. Her eyes are slightly slanted and they seem to hold the power to look into any man's soul. Her lips are small but robust and covered with rose red lipstick.

"Frank Calhoun," she says my name as if it's worse than mud.

I stand at the door flabbergasted. "Tasha?" I question. To any other man looking upon this woman, he'd swear she was the equivalent of the Egyptian goddess Isis. But I simply know her as Tasha Redding, my old high school sweetheart.

"You don't have to look at me like I'm a ghost or something."

"I-I-I didn't know you'd be the person I was coming to see."

"Well, it's not like I was looking forward to seeing you either."

"I didn't mean it like that. I just never would have guessed that you would know someone like Prince Paul."

"Well, the streets is rough. You learn to survive quickly and make friends with those that are surviving."

"Can I come in?"

"I guess so. But only because Paul sent you."

She moves to the side with her hand on her hip and the other hand resting comfortably on the doorknob. She looks me up and down as I enter her apartment and then locks all three deadbolts before leading me down a short hall and into her living room.

"I just can't believe it's you. It's been like—"

"Six years," she says matter-of-factly, rolling her eyes.

"That long?" I look around the room. There's a flat panel television mounted on the wall and a three-piece leather sofa set along with a coffee table and two end tables.

"You mean to tell me you don't remember leaving me for the Marines? I guess you just did your best to forget about me all together, huh?"

"You know it wasn't like that. I was just following the path God laid before me."

"God?" she says with a scoff. "Don't even mention his name in my presence."

"What? That's so unlike you. When we were together, all you use to talk about was the Lord. What happened to you?"

Tasha turns her back to me. "Things change. Why'd Paul send you over here anyway? Or was it God that sent you?"

"I came because I need some information about a key. But I'm starting to think that I just got played. I'll let myself out."

"Wait." She turns her head and looks over her shoulder. "What's the key look like?"

"It's square with the name Erica Rust engraved on the face of it." She studies me curiously and then giggles to herself. "What's so funny?" I ask.

"You, Frank. You're funny." She finally turns to face me with a huge smile on her face and her arms folded over her bosom. "I know quite a bit about Erica Rust, but the question is why do you want to know?"

"What does that mean? I don't have time for games, Tasha."

"And I'm not playing any games, Frank. I've grown up a lot since you've been gone. But before I go telling you what I know, I want to know why you're so interested in that key?"

I exhale. "Fine. I'm interested in that key because I think it might save the life of a woman who's been kidnapped."

Tasha drops the smile from her face. "What? You're not playing with me, are you?"

"No, I'm not. Now I need you to tell me what you know about this key and what it has to do with Erica Rust."

She unfolds her arms. "You've got it all wrong. Erica Rust isn't a person—it's a place. You're looking for American Trust. It's a storage facility on Halstead, leased by the United States Military for its soldiers stationed here in Chicago."

"And how do you know that?"

"Because I use to work there before—"

She drops her head. "Before what, Tasha?"

"Before I became pregnant."

"Pregnant? You don't look it."

"Well, it was a long time ago, Frank. Right around the time you left for Iraq."

"Why didn't you ever tell me?"

"What difference would it have made? You were off following the path that God had laid for you, remember? And I was here. I was here all alone."

"But I could've—"

"Could've what? Prayed for me?"

"I'm sorry, Tasha. I just didn't know."

"Well, there's a lot you don't know about me. But that's the past and I'm done walking down memory lane with you. You got what you came for, so I guess I'll see you in another six years."

I reach out a hand to touch her, but her cold shoulder is too much for me to stand, so I back out of the room and leave the apartment. As I descend the stairs, I cross paths again with the little boy that was playing tag with his friends in front of the building. We smile at one another, passing like two ships in the night, and then the boy turns the corner of the stairs and disappears into the darkness of the hall.

I'm about to exit the building when I decide to stand in the doorway and listen to the boy's footsteps as he climbs the stairs. I want to believe he stops on the second floor, enters apartment 2B and calls out for his mother, but the echo sound of his footsteps bouncing off the hallway walls makes it hard for me to be sure.

CHAPTER 57

When I step out of the apartment building, the scent of rain is deep within the air and Prince Paul's '67 Impala is gone. The small children have all retreated into their apartments for dinner. There are a few people mulling around gossiping, trying to extend their stay outside as long as they can before the rain falls.

I realize that Paul has left me stranded and that Uncle Skeet's car has probably been found and impounded by now. I check the time on my watch. I have eight hours before Rasna Hussein disappears forever.

I start walking up the street and with every step I take away from Tasha's building, I think about her and the possibility of what our lives could have been and what the presence of a child would have meant to my life. I tell myself that I don't have time to mourn for an unborn baby, but deep down in my heart, I know that I will once I bring Father Pantone's killers to justice.

A police cruiser is making its way up the block, so I bend down to make it seem as though I'm tying my shoe. I can't chance one of the officers noticing me. Luckily, the cruiser keeps on its route without a hitch. Once the car is halfway up the block, I rise and sprint in the opposite direction. I wish like hell that I could hail a taxi but there's not a snowball's chance in hell of that actually happening, especially in the hood where a taxi is as rare as the Hope Diamond.

I jog to the L&B livery service station right off of Harrison and Pulaski. Livery services like L&B have been transport- ing Chicago's black citizens for over 75 years. It's a small storefront business that houses a row of chairs and a CB operator, who dispatches drivers across the city. They service neighborhood addresses that the corporate taxi world sees as unfit or dangerous.

"I need a cab," I say to the maple-complexioned female dispatcher housed behind a wire-mesh cage.

The woman looks up from her JET magazine. "What's the address you're going to?"

"American Trust and Storage on Halstead," I say.

The woman picks up the receiver to the two-way CB radio and says into the small black mic. "Tray-four, tray-four. Got a passenger needing to be dropped off at Halstead in Old Jew Town. Do you copy?"

"Copy, Boogie. What's the pickup address?" a voice comes back over the device.

"Home base."

"Copy. Tray-four en route."

"You can have a seat, sir. He'll be here shortly," she says.

I try to take a seat, but my nerves force me to stand and then pace back and forth. I look over at Boogie who seems unbothered by my anxiety, but I can't be too sure. I try to take a seat again, but within mere moments, I stand again.

The crackle of static fills the room as Boogie turns on a small radio. The static leaps in volume with every turn of the radio's dial from one station to the next until Boogie lands the dial on a station that's reporting today's news.

A man's deep voice comes through the speaker. "Police are actively pursuing a fellow officer in connection with the attempted murder of one Father Cicero Sanchez of Saint Peter of Alcantara church in the Wicker Park neighborhood. An official statement was released by the department stating that Detective Frank Calhoun is considered armed and dangerous. He's African-American, five-eight, medium build with short black hair."

"Shit, I know him," Boogie says.

I turn my head away from the woman, rubbing my face with my hand, hoping that it'll help conceal me somehow. I slowly start to shuffle towards the door, hoping that if I pretend to see a long lost friend through the window, I can get out of here before she has a chance to call it in.

"That's every black man I've ever dated and then some," she continues.

I finally exhale a sigh of relief, smile and take a seat. For a second, I thought I was going to have to bolt out of the place. Suddenly, the CB radio comes alive with activity.

"Home base, this is tray-four. I'm sitting outside."

I leap up from my seat and dash for the entrance, fearing that if I stay any longer Boogie may possibly mistake me for one of her long lost lovers.

CHAPTER 58

Old Jew Town used to be a four-block, open street market located on Halstead just south of Roosevelt Road. Back in the day, Jewish shopkeepers would lie out their wares on tables on the sidewalk and watch as the streets filled with shoppers ready to wheel and deal just to save a dollar or two. Now it is nothing more than a memory. The only thing that still stands is the Maxwell Street Polish sausage stand, which fills the air around the area with the scent of grilled caramelized onions. I stand before the celebrated arch entrance of Old Jew Town and stare at what is now being called University City. Surrounding the brick entrance is a wire fence and beyond it is a massive reconstruction of townhomes and condo duplexes built within the confines of a brick wall by the University of Illinois in Chicago. It's a perpetual city within a city, considering the university built the partition to keep out the residents of the Village housing projects, which is located just outside the southern wall of the structure.

"Enemies at the gates, I guess."

I survey the fence that closes off the entrance to the city.

Beyond it, amongst the newly constructed buildings, is the American Trust and Storage Company, the only building older than anyone living within the city's secured walls. I turn and scan the street to make sure no one's watching. I could've used the main entrance on Roosevelt, but the paved road leads straight to the storage company, which means that the killers would have seen me coming.

After I'm sure no one is watching me, I turn back to the fence and begin climbing it before flipping over to the other side. Inside the inner walls, the campus city looks and feels like a ghost town. There are half-finished condos with windowless panes that seem to lead into nothingness along with apartment buildings sprouting up over the entire four- block radius, encompassing everything that made Old Jew Town a Chicago classic.

I trek down a dark street before coming to a corner where a replica of an old English streetlight with a blinking bulb is located. Overhead, the sound of thunder cracks across the sky as rain clouds begin to form. I stand at the corner under the flashing light trying to get my bearings. I know I'm headed south, but I'm not sure if I'm actually moving down the right street that will lead me to American Trust.

I spin to face the west end of the street and that's when I see two black Rottweilers with heads the size of spare tires slowly stalking my way. I back up slowly, looking for the nearest building to duck into, but the dogs have already seen me.

The animals start barking, showing their long jagged teeth and begin to sprint towards me. I turn and run up the street, passing by windowless and doorless structures. I can hear the hounds barking as if they are right on my heels, so I pull the gun from my waist. I don't want to kill these animals, but if push comes to shove, I will.

I duck into a two-story building. The structure smells like

dried cement and fresh white paint. I push close the wooden door and find a two-by-four to jam at an angle between the doorknob and the floor.

The barking from the dogs is getting louder as they approach the building, and before long, they're clawing at the door. I look around the room, taking in the small area. There are two buckets of paint placed in a corner along with a dried-up paintbrush. Other than that, the place is empty. I look back at the barricaded door because something is off. I still hear barking, but it sounds as if there's only two paws clawing at the door.

I slowly turn around from the front door and look down the narrow white hall to the doorless back entrance where the other Rottweiler now stands, practically smiling as he bares his saliva-drenched teeth.

CHAPTER 59

"**S**hit!" I let out, searching the room for an escape. I take a couple steps back, while keeping my sights locked on the dog's eyes.

The Rottweiler barks viciously and it echoes throughout the whole building. Its jaw is trembling with sheer delight as the other Rottweiler outside continues to scratch and claw at the front door, making it known that he also wants a piece of my ass.

I lower the gun. I really don't want to kill this animal, especially since the three or four rounds I'm sure I would have to plug into him will possibly alert the murderers that I'm on to them. I take another cautious step backwards as the Rottweiler at the back door begins to advance. I catch sight of a flight of ill-prepared stairs to my left and ready myself to take the leap.

The front door rattles as the other dog throws its body against it just as the Rottweiler at the back door begins charging down the hall. I spin on my heels and run towards the stairs. The half-finished steps creak under my weight. The Rottweiler in the hall barks even louder as the other at the front entrance throws all of its hundred-and-ninety pounds into the door, moving the two-by-four slightly.

I step on the fourth stair and it gives way, sending my foot into a black hole. The Rottweiler is less than six feet away from me with its jaws open wide and large globs of saliva falling from its teeth. I turn with the gun in hand as the dog leaps at me and smack it across the snout, sending it crashing into the two-by-four below, which knocks it out of place allowing the second Rottweiler to go flying through the front door and into the white hall.

I pull my foot out of the hole and continue climbing the steps. Dashing to my right, I enter a white bedroom with a glassless window frame. I close the aluminum door behind me and twist the lock on the small doorknob. I can hear the Rottweilers climbing the stairs.

I run to the windowless pane in the wall and can see the storage company from where I stand as well as a good portion of University City. I can also see the end of the fence about a block away, which cuts off this portion of the neighborhood from the rest of the development.

BAM! BAM! The Rottweilers barrage the door. I look up from the windowless pane and see a black phone line connected from the house to a wooden pole about fifty feet away. I turn to look back at the aluminum door and find that it's bending inwards from the impact of both dogs throwing their weight against it.

BAM! BAM! BAM! I close my eyes, say a prayer and then stand on the window's ledge while holding on to the inside wall with one hand as I stretch out the other, reaching for the phone line.

BAM! BAM! BAM! BAM! The aluminum door bends inwards even more as the dogs collide with it. I stand on my toes trying to reach the line. My index finger nips at the dark cord.

BAM! BAM! BAM! BAM! BAM! The dogs smash their mallet heads into the door and the wooden frame begins to crack and splinters of wood fall to the floor. I loosen my grip on the wall and lean out the window even further. My index finger brushes against the cord once again.

The dogs run their heads into the door once more, but this time one of them creates a medium size hole in the corner and tries to wrangle his head through the opening. His bark explodes off the walls of the empty room and nearly makes my heart leap into my throat. I grip the edge of the wall with the nail of my fingers as I stretch out my arm even more and three of my fingers brush across the black cable.

While the first dog gnarls at the floor and shoves his head deeper into the room, the other dog throws its body against the door, breaking the wood and knocking it wide open. I look over my shoulder and see the dog leaping towards me. I let go of the wall and jump up towards the cord, grabbing it with one hand, just as the Rottweiler nips at the back of my shoe before falling into the abyss below.

I reach up with my other hand and take hold of the cord, wrapping both my legs around it and shimmying towards the wooden pole. I look back at the house and see the other Rottweiler standing at the window, still barking as I make my escape.

CHAPTER 60

After climbing down the pole, I find myself on a main street filled with what will one day be shops. There are old-fashioned streetlights every twenty feet and large display windows with darkness filling the space as well as painted steel benches and black bike racks shaped to look like actual bicycles.

I can picture what the neighborhood will look like when it's finished. The streets will be crowded with students filling the cafes with books and laptops. Stay-at-home moms with toddlers will meet in the middle of the square for their ritual play-date-and-gossip sessions. It'll be nothing like the Old Jew Town that I once knew.

Twenty-five feet away, I see the chain-link fence from the newly built condo. Just beyond it is the storage facility and somewhere inside are Rasna Hussein and Father Pantone's murderers.

I stop in mid-stride and turn to see four Rottweilers standing a few feet away bearing teeth.

Don't these dogs ever give up?

Then I take off running for the fence and the dogs give chase. I can hear their incessant barking as they draw closer. I pull the gun from my waist and shoot a round into the air hoping the sound will scare them off, but it does no good and they continue their pursuit. The gate is ten feet away. My legs are beginning to burn and I feel as if my heart is going to burst.

I leap for the fence as one of the Rottweilers catches a hold of one of my shoes within its massive jaws. I pull myself up as the dog fights against my will. The other three dogs are closing in and it's only a matter of time before they get a hold of my whole leg. I pistol-whip the dog across the bridge of its nose. He releases his bite and falls to the ground with his paws over his snout.

I climb over the fence just as the last pack of dogs come rushing up to the gate barking and gnawing on the steel links. I sit on the ground with one shoe on and the gun near my side. I turn and look towards the building and remove my cell phone from my pocket, along with the business card that Kawowski gave me.

CHAPTER 61

"Where's Calhoun?" Lopez asks, slamming his palm down on the table inside the interrogation room.

"I told you for the hundredth time I don't know," Skeet replies as he slowly sips his coffee.

Kawowski has been watching the two go at it now for almost four hours with Lopez getting nowhere. For a moment, he thought they might have had him when Lopez brought up the subject of his old partner, Joe Calhoun. But instead of seizing upon the moment, Lopez was lured into a discussion about duty and justice.

Kawowski's cell phone rings and he answers on the third ring. "Kawowski here. How can I help you?"

"It's me."

"Calhoun? Don't make this harder than it has to be."

"I'm not. I'm going to make it really easy, in fact. I'm ready to come in, but you'll have to come get me."

"Where are you?"

"You're a smart man. Trace the call."

Kawowski listens a second longer to the sound of wind blowing into the receiver and then knocks on the two-sided mirror to get Lopez's attention.

Lopez steps out of the interrogation room to a smiling Kawowski. "We've got Calhoun. I'm running a trace on his phone right now."

"Good. I'll be right back."

"Where are you going? We've gotta get outta here."

"Just a second. I want to wipe that smirk off Hellman's face." Kawowski shakes his head and moves down the hall to his desk. Lopez re-enters the interrogation room with a large smile on his face and stares with triumphant black eyes. "Well, well, well, it seems we've caught up to your good old nephew after all. I guess you'll be seeing him a lot sooner than you think."

CHAPTER 62

take off my other shoe and begin walking towards the storage building when I spot the black hearse parked outside of it. I drop the cell phone and pull the gun from my waist. As I draw closer to the vehicle, I lift the pistol and train it on the driver's side window. Even though it's night, I can see clear into the driver's side window. The vehicle looks unoccupied.

I creep along the body of the hearse, stealing glimpses into the interior of the vehicle where a casket is located in the back. I check the cab, but it's empty. I bend down to the side of the vehicle and let out the air in the front left tire, while keeping the gun trained on the warehouse's entrance. I round the car and do the same to the tire on the passenger's side. After both front tires are flat, I creep to the warehouse entrance and pull on the door.

I move into the foyer past a small office where a security guard has been hogtied and placed under the space of his own desk. A line of security monitors show various images of the unoccupied floors. The guard doesn't see me even though I see him squirming and flopping under his desk like a goldfish needing water, so I leave him there. I don't have time to untie him and I can't afford to put him in harm's way. If things go south, then it has to be on me and no one else.

Even in the air-conditioned building, I feel my hair moisten with sweat. I move down a lit corridor, keeping my back to the right wall. The video monitors that I passed by earlier show that the killers are on the third floor. I'll need to play it safe.

I take the stairwell, climbing three at a time. When I finally reach the third floor, I slowly open the door and tiptoe into the large space. The room smells like burned Styrofoam. From the ceiling to the floor and from wall-to-wall, the huge warehouse is covered with steel skeletal shelves that contain crates and boxes of all sizes. On the floor are large blue barrels that sit atop rows upon rows of wooden pallets.

I hear the laughter of two men echo throughout the floor. I have the element of surprise on my side, so this is my best chance to make a move. I crouch down behind the large barrels and use them to conceal myself as I move in closer. When I finally run out of barrels, I decide to keep quiet and listen to the killer's conversation. I have to be sure they're within close proximity to one another, so that I can get the proper jump on them.

"This money is just what we need. We'll be able to take this war straight to their doorsteps," says one of the men whose voice breaks with excitement. "Just think how those ragheads will react when we shove a missile right up their asses."

The two men laugh and I click off the safety on the gun, listening intently to be sure that they're close to one another since I can't actually look over the barrels without giving myself away.

"How much do you think is here?" the same male voice asks. "Enough," says the other man. The whispering tone of his voice sounds vaguely familiar. "Let's get to moving it."

I listen to their footsteps as one of the men takes hold of whatever it is they're about to transport and scrapes it along the floor like a rake against concrete. The item sounds like it's pretty heavy, which leads me to believe that both men will be so busy concentrating on carrying the weighty object, they won't have time to draw their weapons.

It's now or never.

"Wait," the man with the familiar low tone says. "I've got a better idea. I think I'll just move all the crates myself."

There's a cocking of a gun hammer and then a loud thud echoes throughout the floor from the thick crate being dropped against the cement surface. Its creaking handles vibrate against the alloy body as they slowly come to rest.

"What are you talking about? W-w-w-wait, come on, man. It doesn't have to be like this," the partner says with the excitement in his voice now turning to panic and desperation.

From behind the barrels, I pull the gun close to my chest like a rosary as I whisper a prayer to the barrel.

"Look at me, man. Look at me!" demands the once jovial murderer who is now screaming. "We bled together! We're soldiers! I thought we had the same mission!"

"Mission?" the whispering voice chuckles. "My mission ended a long time ago."

"Come on, man. I'm begging you—don't do this. Look, I'm on my knees praying. *I'm praying*. You can't shoot a praying soldier."

The whispering voice chuckles again. "Prayer never got anyone anything from me."

The hammer falls twice as two shots split open the praying man's head.

CHAPTER 63

The boom of the gunshots sends the quietness of the third floor into symphonic chaos. The report bounces off the ceiling and walls as the two shell casings hit the concrete floor.

I jump up from behind the barrels with my gun pointed at the closet man to me. "Police! Don't move! Drop it or I will blow you away!"

The last man standing is wearing a black jump suit with a black mask covering his face. His unmasked partner is laid out on the floor in the same matching black jumpsuit, except his legs are folded under the weight of his body and his arms are extended into a cross. A flap of flesh dangles from the top of his head. His eyes have rolled into the back of his skull, but his boyish features make it easy to see that he's the formerly deceased Sergeant Mitchell Bigsby.

The man in black drops the pistol, but he doesn't raise his hands in the air and I don't expect him to. Between the two of us are ten elongated metal crates, each filled to the top with hundred dollar bills.

"So this is why you killed Father Pantone?" I ask, quickly scanning the room for Rasna Hussein who is tied up and gagged in a corner. The man in black doesn't say a word. "Rasna! It's going to be okay. I'm going to get you out of here." I keep the gun trained on the man in black.

"Frank, do you really want to kill one of your own brothers?" the man in black asks, pulling the mask off his head. My mouth falls open as the man reveals himself to be Andrew Keys, my brother from the Chaplain Corps.

"Drew? Naw, man—there's no way. You didn't kill Father Pantone. You didn't do all this. You-you-you couldn't have."

"The old man left me no choice, Frank. He became all self-righteous, talking about turning all this money over to the DOJ. We worked our asses off to get this money out of Iraq. To get *that bitch* of his into our country, so she could have a better life. You wouldn't believe what a chaplain can get away with when he says he's carrying a crate full of bibles."

"But you took an oath, Drew."

"And we followed that oath to a T, Frank. But you saw the aftermath in Fallujah after they dropped phosphorous all over the city. All those decomposing bodies, all those innocent families killed in the name of war. How could we abide by that oath when our own government couldn't abide by the Geneva Conventions? You were right though—after that day, things changed. We saw the true face of evil. And it was us."

Keys drops his mask and moves over to one of the crates. He reaches down and picks up a bundle of money. "Look at all this money, Frank. There's more than enough to go around. Just let me walk out of here and you're a rich man. You can say you shot Bigsby and this case is closed."

"It's that simple, huh? What about the soldiers who gave their lives in Haditha?"

"They died for a noble cause. Anton understood it was the

only way we were going to make it out of Iraq with her in tow." He points to Rasna. "Somebody had to stay behind to fan the flames."

"And what about her now?" I ask, stealing a peek at Rasna. She's lying prone on the floor as if she's already accepted her fate. Her dark bangs fall just above her eyes.

Keys smiles. "She was the key to the whole puzzle. We needed both keys to access the storage locker. Now that that's done, I'd say she's done her part. I'll take care of her. Officially, she died in Iraq anyway. This money was supposed to give us all new starts. Bigsby believed in an opportunity to finance a secret war against the terrorists, but we both know the cost of such a reality."

I stare at Keys. I can't believe he's ready to kill this woman and move on with his life as if everything he's done up to this point has never occurred.

"I'm sorry, Drew. But I've taken a new oath as an officer of the law, much like the one we took when we became chaplains. And unlike you, I won't break it for my own selfish needs."

Keys tosses a bundle of money into my face and hits me with a right cross. I stumble and let off a shot into the air as we both struggle for control of the gun.

"You're not getting this gun, Drew. It's over! You have to pay for what you did to Father Pantone, Cicero Sanchez and Billy Murphy!"

"I didn't shoot either one of them. You've got your shooter right there. It was Bigsby the whole time. Hell, if it wasn't for me stopping him in that alley in Little India, you'd be dead, too."

"You may not have shot them yourself, but you were the spotter. There's no way Bigsby would have known to shoot Father Pantone unless you singled him out. You forgot that you and Bigsby were in different units, so he and Anton would never have met. That's why you lifted the blinds back at his office. You gave him up and now you have to answer for your crimes."

"Oh yeah? And who's Anton going to answer too, huh?"

"To God."

"Bullshit! Where was God during Fallujah?"

I wrap my leg around Keys' legs and hop backwards, falling to the floor. A round goes off hitting the wall a few feet above Rasna's head. She screams through the bandana that covers her mouth.

Keys pushes the barrel of the gun down and tries to position it under my chin. He's strong and I can feel his muscles bulge against my chest. I push back and my lips quiver with every breath I take. He smiles. His face is changing right before my eyes as if he's now showing me his true identity. I wonder if this was the face that Father Pantone saw before he was shot. Keys pushes the barrel back down, just inches from my chin.

I look up into his eyes and find that my own vision is starting to blur. *No, not now, it can't be happening. I have to save Rasna.* The barrel is now under my chin as Keys tries to interlock his fingers with mine in order to pull the trigger.

I close my eyes, feeling the cool steel brush against my skin. I think about Blue, Father Pantone and Billy Murphy; three lives I couldn't save no matter what I would have done. But Rasna is lying in that corner, waiting for me to take her home and awaken her from this nightmare that Keys and Bigsby have created. I refuse to let her settle for the same fate as the others.

I open my eyes and jam a knee into Keys' ribs. If I'm going to die, I'm going to die knowing I did everything in my power to save her life. Keys throws a right elbow, which I block. I wrap my legs around his body and hammer the heels of my feet into his back. His grip on the gun relents and I eject it out of our hands as it glides across the surface of the skid-marked floor.

Keys hits me with a sharp right cross and rolls off of me to go for the gun, but I grab his foot, sending him falling to the floor. He rises and takes up a boxing stance.

"Just like last time?" he says, slowly dancing from side-to-side.

"Yeah, just like last time," I wipe the blood from my busted lip. "Except now... I'm street fighting."

I rush at Keys, throwing my shoulder into his midsection. He comes down on me, smashing both elbows into my shoulder blades. I fall to one knee and wrap my arms around his waist before lifting him off his feet and body slamming him down on the concrete floor. The impact of his body rumbles throughout the room. I sit on top of him, pinning his arms under my knees and hit him across the face until I draw blood.

"You fucking bastard! If you don't believe in the oath we took as chaplains, if you don't believe in God—then just what the hell do you believe in?" I ask with every punch I land.

Keys smiles, showing a mouth full of blood. "I don't believe in anything but myself."

I roll off of him, recover the pistol and stand over him with the barrel of the gun planted between his eyes.

"If that's all you believe in, then you might as well die," I say.

"F-F-Frank, you-you wouldn't," he replies.

"Why wouldn't I? I'm already on psychiatric leave. I pull this trigger and play my cards right and it comes out as PTSD." I cock the hammer on the gun.

"But the oath—your oath—what about that?" Keys asks with a twang of sarcasm in his voice.

I exhale. At this moment, my oath to serve and protect is all that I believe in. It's become my one reason to live. I look down into Keys' eyes and see my own reflection in them. I look like my father, which in turn makes me think about his warning of the red line between duty and revenge and having the will to keep from crossing it. I look over at Rasna Hussein and see the innocence in her eyes. I think about the life that Father Pantone saved and what it must mean to my own life in regards to his lasting memory. In the end, he was a man of God, of principles, and no matter what he did in regards to his oath, he was a dear friend who cared more for others than he did of his own safety. With Father Pantone in mind, I close my eyes and allow the hammer to fall silently.

CHAPTER 64

Outside the warehouse, Kawowski and Lopez are standing near the hearse. I hand Kawowski the gun and shove Keys in the direction of Lopez.

"Here's Billy Murphy's murderer," I say. "There's also a body up on the third floor. The victim is Sergeant Mitchell Bigsby. He's Father Pantone's murderer. You'll also need to talk to her." I say, looking down at Rasna who's standing by my side. "She'll fill in some of the holes."

Rasna looks up into my eyes then she brushes her soft hand across my face. There are no words between us that can say what we've lost, so we don't try. I turn away and push past the detectives.

"Where do you think you're going?" Lopez asks. "The Department of Professional Standards is going to want to talk to you."

"Tell 'em they can find me at my shrink. I'm going home." As I make my way across the warehouse parking lot, the rain starts to fall. I walk slowly, allowing it to envelop me in an invisible cloak as I think about Fallujah and what Keys said about it changing us. It was on that very day as Marines moved through the dead city that Father Pantone said a prayer for the deceased. And even though I can't remember that prayer in its entirety, I do remember these words: "only the holy remain and the strong survive."

ABOUT THE AUTHOR

Alverne Ball has a M.F.A in Fiction writing from Columbia College Chicago.

Mr. Ball is the recipient of the 2019 Tin House Graphic Novelist Fellowship. He is the 2018 Chi-Teen Lit Festival graphic novel speaker. He is also the recipient of the 2014 and 2015 Glyph Rising Star award for his writing on 133art's OneNation and OneNation: Old Druids. In 2009 Mr. Ball became the recipient of the first-ever Luminarts Graphic Novel Writing Award. He has also received Three Weisman Scholarships from Columbia College Chicago for his other graphic works. Mr. Ball has also created and written an online comic series, *When we were Kings* and *Zulu*, both published by popular entertainment website, Afropunk.com. He is the author of the second freak Calhoun crime thriller, Blue Religion.

His writing has been published in the literary magazine Annalemma, in Columbia College newspaper The Chronicle, online at Brokenfrontier.com, online for the Museum of contemporary Photography in Chicago, online for Comicbookresources.com, and an online graphic story for the literary magazine, Hypertextmag. com. His short stories of suspense have appeared in the Sin anthology by Avendia Press, Criminal Class Review as well as the online magazine, the heatedforest.com.

ALSO BY ALVERNE BALL

Blue Religion.

Detective Frank Calhoun springs back into action after a social worker and a rookie police officer are murdered in Chicago's East Garfield Park.

Flanked by his new partner Fred Lions, while also battling remnants of his father's recent conviction, Frank chases down clues across the city as he begins to assemble pieces of the case. With mounting pressure from his girlfriend Gloria, as well as the Assistant State's Attorney striving to make a career off the case's headlines, Frank must keep his head on straight as he attempts to find the killer and navigate the pitfalls of the blue religion.